The Dreamwalker's Child

STEVE VOAKE

The Dreamwalker's Child

ff
faber and faber

First published in 2005
by Faber and Faber Limited
3 Queen Square London WC1N 3AU

Typeset by Faber and Faber Limited
Printed in England by Mackays of Chatham plc, Chatham, Kent

A CIP record for this book
is available from the British Library

ISBN 0–571–22346–X (HARDBACK)
ISBN 0–571–22752–X (PAPERBACK)

2 4 6 8 10 9 7 5 3 1

For Tory, Tim and Daisy

When the Dreamwalker [illegible]
then shall the East[illegible]
[illegible] from the [illegible] the [illegible]
in a shadow . . . But the [illegible]
rise up against the Dark[illegible]

'When the Dreamwalker's Child walks in Aurobon, then shall the East be in the ascendant; a plague shall descend from the sky and the Earth will fall into shadow . . . but the Dreamwalker's Child shall rise up against the Darkness.'

Book of Incantations

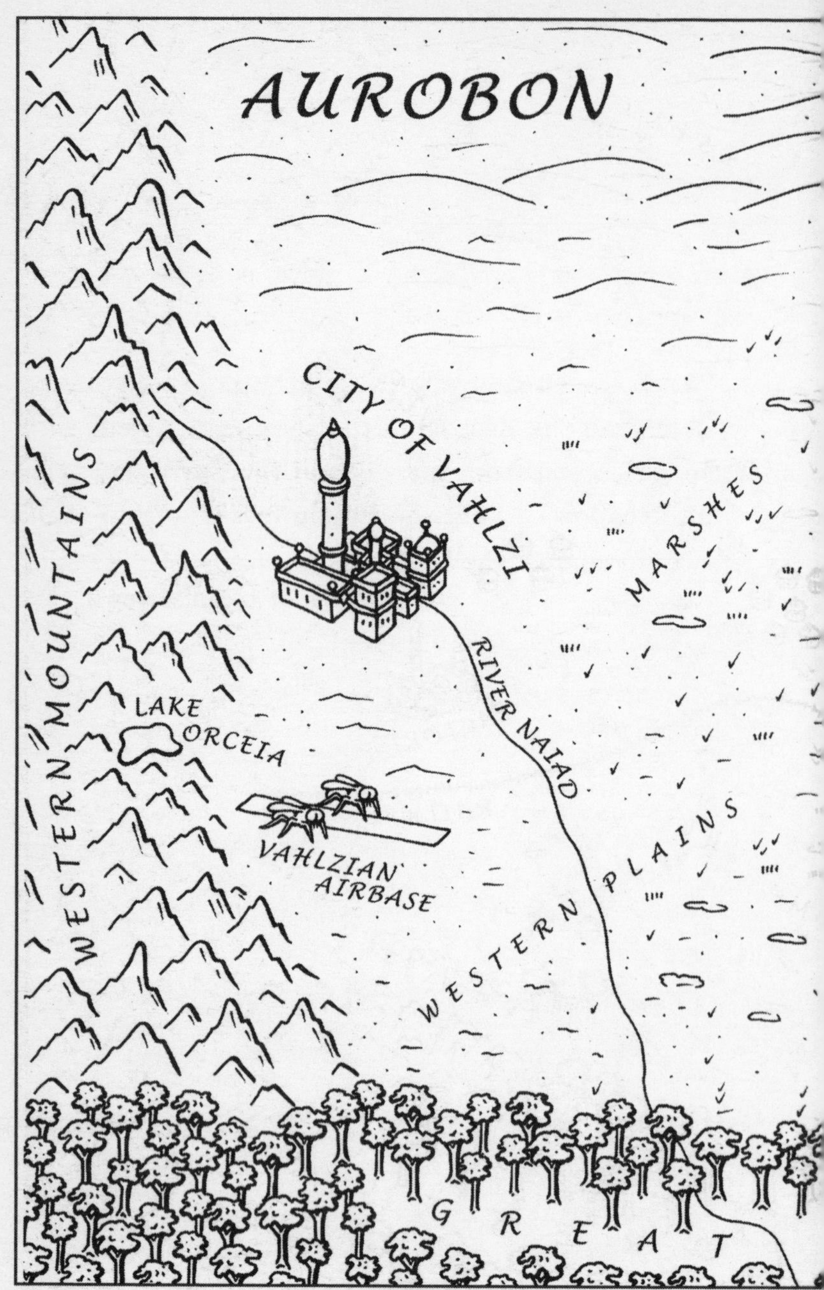
AUROBON
CITY OF VAHLZI
MARSHES
WESTERN MOUNTAINS
RIVER NAIAD
LAKE ORCEIA
VAHLZIAN AIRBASE
WESTERN PLAINS
G R E A T

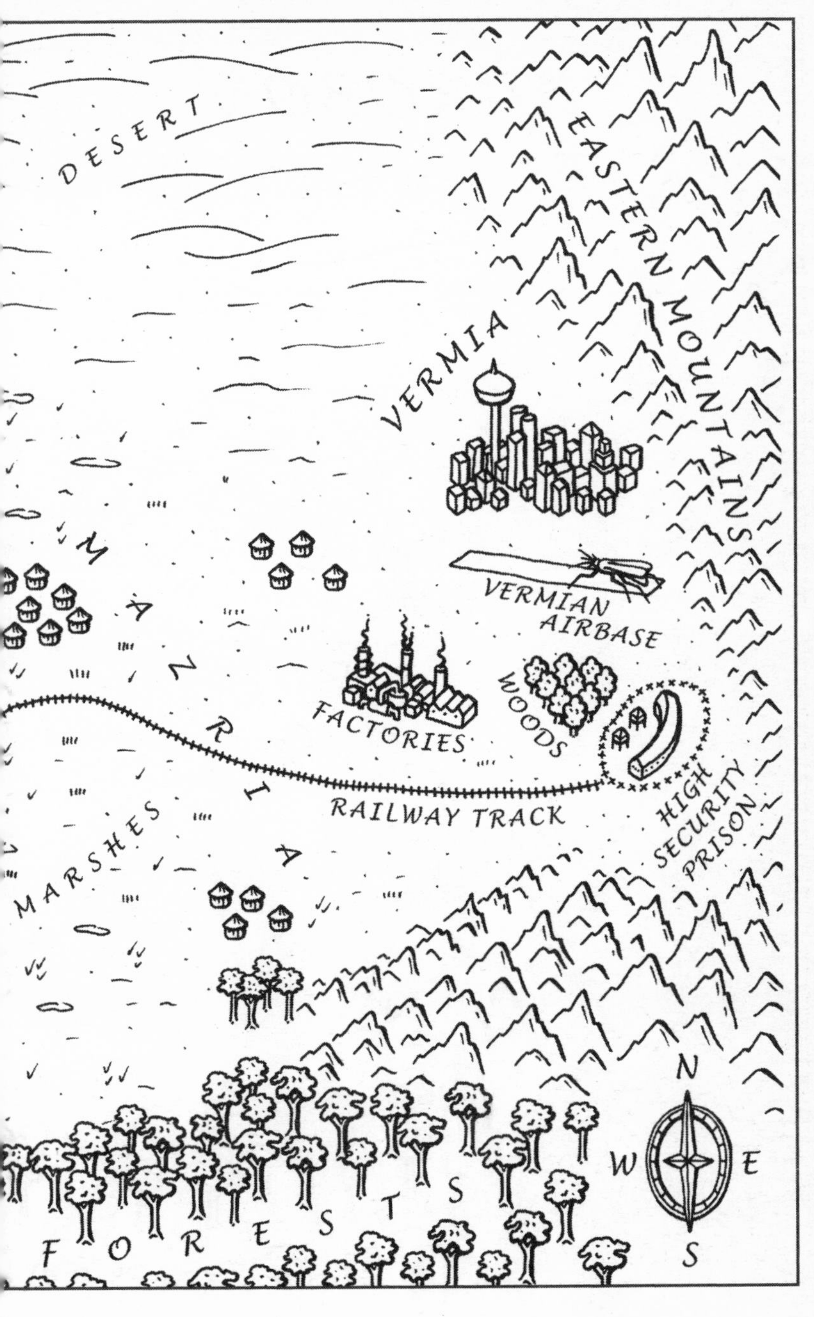
DESERT
EASTERN MOUNTAINS
VERMIA
VERMIAN AIRBASE
FACTORIES
WOODS
MANZRIA
RAILWAY TRACK
HIGH SECURITY PRISON
MARSHES
FORESTS
N
W
E
S

One

When they are first born, most people find the world a fascinating, magical place. It is a place full of colours and sounds and wonderful things that they have never seen before. There are metal boxes that move up and down the street, bags of sweet powder that fill your mouth with explosions of delight, soft barky things that jump up and lick your hand, tall giants with rustling leaves and little feathery objects that fly around in them singing songs.

Everything is new and exciting.

But as time passes, people come to believe that these extraordinary magical things are not really magic at all, but just ordinary things with ordinary, dull names like car, sherbet, dog, tree and bird.

So after a while, they stop noticing them.

They forget how to look.

Which is why the grey speck on the corner of Sam Palmer's bedpost would have gone unnoticed by most people. Most people would be too busy looking at televisions, magazines or each other.

They would never notice something so small and colourless.

Sam, however, was an exception. He had never grown out of his fascination with the world, and what interested him most were the small things that most people never see.

Ever since learning to crawl, Sam had followed woodlice to the cracks in the skirting board, knelt by ants as they cleaned up spilt sugar and watched bumblebees bouncing from foxglove to forget-me-not. Where most children ran away from wasps, Sam ran after them, watching them hunt among the long grass and listening to the faint scrape and scratch of their jaws on the wooden window-frame as they chewed it into a pulp for their papery nests.

But just recently, he had noticed something else.

At first he had thought that it was just his imagination. But the more he looked around him, the more he began to believe that it was true.

The insects were starting to follow him.

It seemed that wherever he went, the wasps went too. Not great swarms of them – just one or two, following him everywhere. Yesterday, walking up the lane on his way home from school, he had seen several of them hovering above his head like small helicopters. It was getting more noticeable, and since moving out here into the country, he had found himself becoming obsessed with insects.

He glanced up at his bedroom walls, covered with the pictures of flies he had carefully copied from illustrations and photographs. Strewn across the floor were the books about insects that he had borrowed from the library and on his desk was an unfinished diagram that he was sketching, showing the mouthparts of a mosquito. He stared at the pictures with a mixture of fascination and disgust.

What was happening to him?

The sun edged its way up over the horizon and in the early morning light Sam sensed the silence and stillness of the air that hangs over fields and woods before an unusually hot summer's day. In the distance, a wood pigeon called softly from the trees at the edge of the meadow that lay behind the house. A gentle breeze stirred the hedgerows and Sam briefly caught the scent of wild honeysuckle before the air was still once more.

He stared out of the window at the dry, parched lawn and thought of the Saturdays he used to have before they moved: riding his bike into town, buying drinks and gum from the shop and then cycling off to meet his friends by the bandstand in the park. They used to play Russian roulette together – shaking up a can of fizzy drink, mixing it up with all the other cans and then taking it in turns to open one up next to their heads. He remembered how Chrissy Johnson had been practically blown off the bandstand and Bobby's sister Kayleigh had laughed so much that she'd had to run home to change.

Good times.

But now they were gone.

Sam sighed and turned back towards his bedside table, where *The Field Guide to European Insects & Spiders* lay open at the 'Bees, Ants & Wasps' section.

He reached out his hand to pick up the book, and at that moment his eyes fell upon the small grey shape on his bedpost. Moving slowly and carefully, he crouched down to take a closer look.

It was a grey, thuggish-looking fly about the size of his thumbnail, with a slight speckling of the abdomen. Its wings were smoky brown and on either side of its broad head were slightly bulging, brightly coloured eyes. Protruding from the front of its head were sharp, blade-like mouthparts shaped like a V.

Sam recognized it immediately as a horsefly.

Keeping a watchful eye on it, he picked up the insect book and flipped through the pages until he found the section entitled 'Horseflies (Family *Tabanidae*)'.

Beneath a small illustration he read: 'Female horseflies need a meal of blood for their eggs to develop. Their bite is painful, and they readily attack people in the absence of livestock. Their preferred habitat is near woodland, streams and marshes.'

'You're in the wrong place,' said Sam.

Picking up an empty tumbler from his desk, he put it over the horsefly, slid a postcard underneath and held the glass up to the window.

He peered at the glittering eyes, watching him through the glass.

'You're a biter all right,' he said, studying the spiky, beak-like mouthparts and the blunt, stubby head, 'but not a very smart one. I'd better let you get back to where you belong.'

He shook the tumbler and the horsefly disappeared off at speed over the hedge at the end of the garden.

Sam watched it fly away into the distance. 'Don't make any more wrong turns!' he said, and closed the window.

But the fly had not taken any wrong turns.

On the contrary, it was a good deal more intelligent than Sam realised.

Two

Somewhere in Aurobon, deep beneath the city of Vermia, General Hekken stood in the middle of a white, brightly lit laboratory and looked at the clear liquid that filled the glass tank in front of him. His long, black leather overcoat and peaked cap contrasted sharply with the sterile glare of his surroundings and his boots creaked as he leant forward to get a better view. Suspended inside the tank was a translucent bag filled with a dark liquid. Within the bag he could make out the movements of many small, yellow objects.

Hekken grimaced. Watching deadly viruses swim around inside the detached stomach of a mosquito was not his idea of a good time. But, he supposed, these things had to be done.

The thin man in the white coat next to him tapped his watch and nodded at the contents of the tank. 'That's the longest they've survived so far,' he said, with a definite hint of pride in his voice. 'Nearly an hour.'

Hekken watched as the strange, yellow organisms floated slowly past on the other side of the glass. Each consisted of a spongy, bulbous growth which tapered down into five thin tentacles waving behind like the fronds of a sea anemone.

'An hour,' repeated Hekken. 'Am I supposed to be impressed by this?'

A worried expression appeared on the face of the other man. 'An hour represents good progress,' he said nervously. 'Survival rates were virtually nil when we first injected them.'

As he spoke, the bag inside the tank ruptured and the darker fluid began to leak out into the surrounding liquid, forming black clouds that swirled and spiralled down towards the bottom of the tank. Hekken noticed that the viruses had stopped moving. He sighed heavily and took off his cap.

'You know how important this is to the Emperor Odoursin?'

'Oh yes,' said the man hurriedly. 'We're close to a breakthrough. We're doing everything we can to make this work.'

'Well,' said Hekken, turning his gaze away from the now lifeless, floating organisms to look at him, 'you're just going to have to do a bit more.'

He paused. 'How is that lovely wife of yours by the way?'

'She's very well, thank you. I –'

'And the children?'

There was fear in the man's eyes now. He nodded and looked away. 'They're – they're fine.'

'Good. That's very good.'

Hekken put his cap back on. 'Well, you make sure you look after them. After all, it would be terrible if something happened to them. I'd never forgive myself.'

The man tried to speak, but his voice was shaking and he could only stutter something unintelligible.

'I know, I know,' said Hekken. 'You're quite right. As long as we all try our hardest, then everything will be just fine. Hmm?'

The man's face was as white as his coat now. 'Yes, General Hekken. We'll have this fixed in no time. I promise.'

Hekken patted his cheek indulgently with a black leather glove. 'That's the spirit,' he said. 'Keep up the good work.'

Surrounded by the shiny green interior of the express lift, Hekken watched the red light flicker up through the floors and wondered what he was going to say to Odoursin.

Things were not looking good. Only yesterday the western state of Vahlzi had accused Vermia of planning to infect humans with a deadly virus. They were right, of course, but the accusation had been strenuously denied by Vermian officials. They were well aware that if the truth came out, Vahlzi would have an excuse to launch an attack against them. And although Vermia's military had been strengthened considerably since the last war, they weren't ready for another one just yet.

There was some good news, however. The Dreamwalker from the prophecy had been sighted again last night and for the first time they had succeeded in tracking her back to Earth. If they moved quickly, they might just be able to turn things to their advantage.

But Hekken knew it wasn't going to be easy.

The lift whined softly to a halt and the doors slid open to reveal a huge, circular room with a large, round table in the centre. A clinical white light shone from a steel disc overhead, but otherwise the room was in shadow. Outside, dark storm clouds rumbled and a howling wind threw torrents of rain against the windows of the tower.

Eleven members of the Council sat around the table, each staring intently at the tall, hooded figure in the centre. They turned at the sound of Hekken's boots clacking across the hard stone floor and, as he approached, the figure slowly lifted its head. Cruel, red eyes stared out from a face that was hideously twisted, blanched and distorted like a piece of melted wax.

Hekken stood to attention and forced himself to hold Odoursin's steely gaze.

'General Hekken,' said Odoursin in a low, menacing voice, 'do you bring us good news?'

'Yes, Your Excellency,' Hekken replied, clicking his heels together and bowing slightly. 'I am pleased to report that, generally speaking, the programme is progressing well. We have finally succeeded in isolating a deadly virus from a rare pitcher plant that grows on Earth, in the heart of the Amazon rainforest. It is a virus of such potency that, once released, it cannot be stopped. The problem of its delivery, however, still remains.'

'Indeed,' said Odoursin. 'Please explain.'

Hekken cleared his throat. Suddenly, all the hours he had spent listening to tedious explanations from dull scientists seemed worthwhile. He was glad he had done his homework.

'Experiments have shown that the human blood system provides the virus with the perfect breeding environment. The virus invades human cells by injecting its own DNA through its tail into them and making copies of itself. By doing so it rapidly increases in number and quickly overwhelms even the strongest immune system. Death follows in a matter of days.'

Odoursin's eyes lit up. 'Go on.'

'But the problem has always been with its delivery. How are we to ensure maximum infection of humans in the most efficient manner?'

'I hope you are going to enlighten us, General Hekken.'

'The only viable way of spreading the virus quickly is by using mosquitoes,' Hekken continued. 'However, we discovered that when the virus is injected into the gut of a female mosquito, it releases an enzyme which dissolves the lining. The gut bursts, killing both the mosquito and the virus.'

A rather podgy, overweight man with small, sunken eyes struggled to his feet. Hekken recognized him as Martock and his pulse quickened.

'Forgive me, General Hekken, but if this is good news then I live in fear of the occasion when you bring bad news to the Council.'

There were murmurs of agreement and Hekken held up his hands to ward off further criticism. He noticed that Martock was enjoying his discomfort and forced himself to remain calm.

'Let me assure the Council that even as we speak there are teams of our best people working on the problem. They are carrying out trials using a new chemical that combines with the lining of the mosquito's gut and protects it. If it works, it will enable the mosquito to carry the virus to humans on Earth.'

There was a pause as everyone worked through the implications of Hekken's words. Odoursin's eyes narrowed into suspicious slits. '*If* it works, you say?'

'It will work,' Hekken reassured him. He thought of the nervous man in the white coat and his little family. 'They're very keen to make it work down there,' he added. 'Very keen indeed. It's simply a matter of time.'

Odoursin nodded, then turned to Martock.

'I think there is something else you should know, Your Excellency.'

Odoursin blinked, moistened his dry, papery lips and stared at Martock.

Martock glanced briefly across at Hekken before continuing. 'Last night,' he announced, 'we tracked down the Dreamwalker.'

Odoursin's voice quivered with barely suppressed rage.

He turned to Hekken. 'Were you aware of this, General?'

Hekken gave Martock a look which indicated his anger at being upstaged. That was *his* piece of news. Martock smiled back: a smug, self-satisfied smile.

'I was about to inform the Council when I was interrupted.'

Odoursin glared furiously at Hekken. 'Why was I not told of this earlier? I made it clear that I wanted to be informed immediately she was located.'

'Her appearances were only intermittent at first,' Hekken explained hurriedly, trying to ignore the sweat that was now running down his back. 'It's been very difficult to pinpoint her exact position. But yesterday we successfully followed her back to Earth. And we made a discovery which I know will be of great interest to Your Excellency.'

'What did you discover?' asked Odoursin, his voice a chilling whisper.

'She has a son,' replied Hekken.

There was silence in the room as the implications of this news began to dawn on each and every member of the Council. One by one they turned to look at Odoursin, uncertain of how he would react. But his expression gave nothing away. He simply nodded slowly, as if this was something he had been expecting for a long, long time.

'Well then,' he said at last, 'you had better bring him to me.'

Three

As he replaced a book on the shelf, Sam noticed the little pink teddy bear he had won for his mum at the arcade last summer. He'd wanted to cheer her up. He had been looking forward to seeing her smile when he gave it to her, but when she returned from her walk she had seemed so distant and sad that he'd just pushed it quietly into her beach bag. He had hoped that she would find it and that it would make her happy again. But the next morning she had put it on his shelf, thinking it belonged to him. And although he wanted to tell her, *No, I won it for you*, he never found a way.

So there it sat, a small monument to things left unsaid.

He was worried about her. She always seemed tired these days. Since becoming pregnant she'd suffered from bad dreams and Sam often heard her crying out in the middle of the night. He would lie awake in the dark and hear his father's low, muted voice trying to comfort her.

They were so busy setting up the gardening business, doing up the house and preparing for the arrival of the new baby that Sam sometimes felt as though he was in the way.

And the insects . . . the insects were really getting to him now. They were starting to occupy all his thoughts.

A wasp settled on the outside of the window and began to crawl across it. Sam banged on the glass with the back of his hand. 'Leave me alone!' he shouted angrily, and the wasp flew away.

Sam shut his eyes. He felt troubled in a way that he had never experienced before. It was suddenly as though his whole life had been put on hold – as if he was just sitting around, waiting for something to happen. With every day that passed his mood darkened and his sense of foreboding deepened. He passed a hand wearily over his eyes and then glanced at the mosquito drawing on his desk. He would finish it today and then do some more research. There was still so much to find out, so much more to know . . .

'Sam!'

It was his dad, calling to him from the kitchen.

'Sam – come down here a minute!'

Hidden in the shade of the hedgerows, tiny grey shapes began to rise like spectres from the earth, twisting unseen between the blades of grass that grew by the side of the road.

Somewhere in the distance a dog barked, unnerved by the strange sounds that whispered in the dust.

The grey shapes came together now and began to merge and flow as one body through the tangled undergrowth – quickly, urgently – like a hungry animal moving in for the kill.

Sam's mum sat at the kitchen table in faded blue dungarees and his dad stood behind her, sipping a mug of coffee and looking serious. He gestured towards the chair opposite.

'Sit down for a minute, Sam.'

Sam sat down, staring intently at a small section of the table. He began polishing it with the tip of his finger.

'Your mother and I are worried about you, Sam.'

The finger-polishing became more intense.

'I'm fine. Honestly.'

'But you're not though, love, are you?' His dad drained his coffee and sat in the empty chair next to Sam. 'I mean, look at you. You're always shut away in your room drawing pictures of bugs. And when I spoke to your teacher the other day, she told me you spend all of your break times in the library, looking at insect books.'

Sam shrugged. 'So?'

'Look, I know it's not been easy for you,' said his mum. She reached out and touched his arm. 'I know you miss your friends. But things will be OK. Just give it time, that's all.'

Sam pushed his chair back and stood up. 'I'm fine,' he said. 'Really, I am.'

Sam untangled his bike from the rest of the junk in the garage and thought about what his parents had said.

It was possible that they had a point about the whole insect thing. He had to admit, it was getting a bit weird.

He needed some time to think.

Maybe he would just take a ride down to the river for a while and sit quietly in the shade of the willows. Perhaps he would see the kingfishers dart among the trees, watch the sparkle of their blue feathers and hear the splash as they folded their wings and plunged into the silent world beneath the surface.

And perhaps – in the cool green silence of the woods – he would forget all about wasps and mosquitoes, and about being alone.

Stepping from the dust of the garage into the morning sunshine, he heard a low, insistent humming sound in the distance.

It came from the fields beyond the hedge.

As he turned to look, the humming became almost deafening and then a furious yellow and black cloud of wasps suddenly plunged over the hedge and fanned out as if frantically searching for something. He instinctively ducked and fell to the floor, waving his hands in blind panic as the wasps swarmed wildly around him, but as quickly as they had arrived they were gone again, spreading out above the house before fading like smoke into the blue sky.

Breathing heavily, Sam got shakily to his feet and watched in amazement as the buzzing maelstrom of insects dispersed. Four wasps continued to hover several metres above his head, but Sam was too intent on the main group to notice them.

For some reason he felt strangely exhilarated, as though he had scratched the surface of the world and caught a brief glimpse of something beneath it.

He would follow the insects; find out what was going on.

Without another thought he climbed onto his bike and pedalled off down the drive in the direction of the disappearing swarm. Behind him, his mother called his name, but her voice was lost on the breeze.

The well-oiled chain slipped smoothly over the cogs and the wind made Sam's eyes water as he began to pick up speed. Milk-white cow parsley foamed in the hedgerows beneath the blue skies of summer.

Changing up a gear, his speed increased still further and the wind whipped through his hair. It was almost as though he was flying.

But then suddenly a tearing, stabbing sensation in his neck made him cry out in shock and bewilderment. As his hand flew up to investigate there was a screech of rubber on tarmac, followed by a sound so loud and furious that it seemed as if the very sky had exploded around him. Pain twisted and burst into a million violent stars. Then the fields and sky whirled and sucked him down into the shadows with a deep and terrible roar.

Back at the house, Sam's father heard the sickening crunch of metal and glass. Dropping his coffee cup, he ran desperately towards the road, while behind him his wife's screams split the air. High above the fields the crows flew noisily from the treetops, croaking and flapping into an empty sky.

Four

Much later, after the long and empty silence that followed, something stirred. There was a beating of wings and a sparkle of blue; a feeling of flying instead of falling, and a sudden sweet, warm breath on Sam's face. He felt as though he was being carried and laid gently to rest in a soft bed where sleep would come once more. But then there was a crack like thunder and with a sickening lurch he was falling again, falling down into the cold and inky blackness that drew him in and enveloped him.

He awoke to the sound of the wind and the smell of stagnant water. It was night-time, but the landscape was dimly lit by a strange, blue-green light which filtered through the clouds. He could see that he was surrounded by flat marshlands which stretched all the way to the horizon. Pools of leaden water lay in grey pockets and green vapours rose like ghosts from the damp bogs all around, curling up to meet the yellowish mist that hung in heavy clouds above giant reeds. Far away in the distance he could make out the shapes of towers, columns and blocks rising starkly against the skyline. Ribbons of silver lightning ripped through the sky, illuminating the clouds that gathered above the strange city.

Sam shivered and stared into the gloom. *Where am I?* he thought fearfully. *What is going on?*

The storm strengthened as it swept across the marshes and the bitter wind quickly developed into a howling gale. Sam suddenly found himself caught in a torrential downpour which flung droplets of stinging rain into his face and soaked his mud-spattered clothes.

Huddled there in the freezing mud he knew that he must find shelter quickly. His teeth chattering, he staggered to his feet and began to stumble and splash across the boggy ground towards the lights of the distant city. Maybe there would be someone there who could tell him where he was. Someone who would help him find his way home.

Half an hour later, he slipped and fell exhausted into a muddy pool. The city seemed no closer than when he had started out.

Spitting out a mouthful of foul-tasting water, he raised his head wearily and stared out across the bleak and desolate landscape. It was then that he noticed a single light in the distance, away to his left. It seemed to be getting nearer all the time. Sam gradually became aware of a faint rumbling sound and the ground beneath him began to shake. It was only when he had scrambled to his feet and was running towards the fast approaching light that he realised it was a train.

Crouching behind a clump of reeds only a few metres from the track, Sam watched as the long silver train pulled smoothly to a halt. The windows were lit from within by a dull orange glow but there were no obvious signs of life on board.

Shivering with cold, he decided to make his way to the front of the train. He would see if he could find the driver, explain that he was lost and try to get a lift into the city. As he was about to step out from behind the reeds, however, a series of strange thumping sounds from inside the train made him pause. Seconds later, the doors hissed open and to his horror twenty or thirty dark, dog-like shapes leapt from the train and began running across the marshes, snorting and growling as they went.

Sam immediately felt his muscles tense with fright. Every instinct told him that his life was now in danger. He knew that these strange creatures were searching for something and that, whatever their plans, staying out on the marshes with them was not an option. And so, fuelled by his fear, he took a deep breath, ran from the cover of the reeds and threw himself desperately onto the train. Moments later the doors hissed shut and the train slid away into the darkness.

As it began to gather speed, Sam breathed a sigh of relief and began cautiously to look around. Orange lights ran the length of the ceiling and merged together at the far end of a tubular steel carriage. Here there was an oval hatch which connected to another carriage and through it he could see many others stretching away into the distance. The right-hand side was divided up into a series of compartments and on the left of the corridor was a long window. Sam struggled to his feet and leant his forehead against the cool glass. Through it he could see constellations of stars scattered randomly across the night sky in patterns he had never seen before.

Wherever he was, it was a long way from home.

'What is going on?' he whispered, his voice hesitant like a tiny moth fluttering into the gloom. 'Where am I?'

A coldness entered the pit of his stomach, flipping and turning like a dark-green serpent. He suddenly began to feel very scared indeed. 'Enough,' he whispered. 'I want to go home.'

Shivering, he turned his face away from the window. As he did so, something moved in the shadows further up the train. Sam jumped and his heart began pounding rapidly.

'Who's there?' he called out nervously, his voice wavering in the silence.

There was a pause, and then the very faint sound of laughter from the shadows. It was cruel, cold laughter: the sound of someone enjoying his fear.

'Look, I know you're there,' Sam called hesitantly. 'I

just need some help, that's all. I'm lost and I need to get home.'

There was no reply. Sam began to walk slowly up the corridor towards the shadows from where the laughter had come.

'Anyone?' he called. 'I just want to know where I am, that's all.'

Every dark and dusty corner seemed to watch him now. He walked past the sliding metal doors of unlit compartments. They were all open, but his eyes focused on the third one along. It was from here that he thought he had heard the laughter.

Sam sensed eyes watching him as he made his way fearfully up the long, dark carriage. A shuffling sound behind him made him turn with a start, but there was nothing except the swaying orange lights and the long shadows beneath.

Reaching the compartment, Sam peered inside and saw, to his utter relief, that it was empty. He leant against the door-frame and let out a sigh. It was just his imagination. The creatures had gone and the train was empty.

He stepped inside and saw strips of dark, ebony-like wood slotted together to form benches on either side of the compartment. He sat down and leant his head back against the wall. Maybe this was all some horrible dream. Maybe he would just have to go along with it until he woke up.

Feeling somewhat reassured, Sam looked up at the luggage rack opposite and saw that someone had left something behind. He got up to take a closer look and realised it was a black cloak that had been bundled up and stuffed onto the rack. Thinking that it would help to make him a bit warmer, Sam reached out his hand to pull it down.

Suddenly, everything seemed to happen at once.

The moment he touched it, a loud howling filled the compartment and the cloak flew open to reveal a sight which sent Sam reeling backwards in terror. Crouched up on the luggage rack was what at first glance appeared to be a ferocious dog, its fleshy lips drawn back in a snarl as it bared its sharp yellow teeth. Saliva dripped from its mouth and pooled onto the floor below. But as he looked, Sam saw to his horror that the neck and head were human-shaped, the smooth forehead and eyes suggesting a boy of about twelve or thirteen. Below the eyes, however, the nose and chin had elongated and mutated into the jaws of a vicious, snarling dog. The rest of its body was covered with coarse black hair, matted with layers of dirt and grease.

The creature thrust its snout forward and sniffed at the air, never taking its eyes away from Sam for one moment.

'I smell you,' it said.

It licked its lips, raised its claw-like hands and growled. Sam just had time to register the broken talons and mangy fur sprouting from cracked, leathery skin before it launched itself at him with a vicious screech.

Instinctively, Sam stepped sideways and the creature slammed into the wall. With a bellow of rage it sprang backwards onto the floor, shook its head and turned to face Sam again. It laughed, an evil laugh, and began snapping its jaws together.

'I bite you now,' it said. Then it began to edge its way across the compartment towards him. 'Bite you. Bite you!'

It made a sudden lunge for his leg but Sam managed to pull away and its teeth cracked together with such force that a string of spittle flew from the corner of its mouth. As it growled angrily, Sam saw his chance and kicked the creature as hard as he could under the chin.

'Bite *that*!' he shouted.

There was a yelp as Sam slammed the compartment door shut behind him and ran up the corridor as fast as his legs would carry him.

The door slid open again and he heard the sound of claws scrabbling over metal as the creature raced after him, panting heavily. Then, to his horror, Sam saw the shapes of more snarling dog-creatures emerging from compartments further up the train. They turned to face him and began to gather together across the width of the corridor, cutting off his only escape route.

Sam stopped, realising that he was trapped. He glanced over his shoulder to see his pursuer running at full pelt, grunting as its short, stubby legs pumped up and down. The other creatures now began to approach at speed from the opposite direction, snorting and shrieking their way down the corridor like a pack of blood-crazed hyenas.

I'm going to die, thought Sam. He felt more frightened than he had ever felt in his life. *They're going to rip me apart.*

Sick with fear, he pulled frantically at the door of the compartment next to him, but it wouldn't open. Seeing his attackers closing in, he took a step backwards and with a strength born out of sheer terror, punched his fist hard through the window of the compartment door. The skin on his knuckles shredded as the glass shattered, but he felt nothing. Reaching through blood-streaked glass, he snatched at the handle on the inside and turned, but it wouldn't move. Crying out in fear and frustration, he turned just as the first dog launched itself at him with a howl and sank its teeth into his shoulder.

The pain was indescribable. Sam's piercing scream momentarily stopped the other animals in their tracks. They paused and crouched lower as Sam staggered backwards under the weight of his attacker. Then they began to approach again, snarling softly with their yellow eyes unblinking and their ears flat against the sides of their heads.

The first dog unclamped its teeth and dropped to the ground as Sam fell against the compartment door, clutching at the agonising wound on his shoulder. The dog grinned and stared at him, licking its bloodstained lips.

'Mmmm!' it breathed in a low, husky voice. 'Oh, mmmm!'

The other dogs began to encircle him now, a low growling in their throats. One of them began to sniff and lick at his ankle, but a warning bark from Sam's attacker made it retreat again.

The first dog looked at Sam. 'Boy scared?' it asked.

Sam pressed back against the carriage door and gritted his teeth. 'Get away from me!' he hissed.

The dog-child stared at him for a moment, then drew back its lips in a grotesque smile. 'We bite you now,' it said. It nodded and ground its teeth together. 'We hurt you lots.'

Sam watched in horror as the creature moved towards him again, its eyes glazed over with the madness of bloodlust. He knew that there was no one here to help him now. No one to save him but himself. And so, as the snarling animal launched itself at him with a howl of fury, he ducked neatly sideways and it flew past his shoulder, smashing headfirst into the broken window.

There was a loud squeal and then all hell broke loose. The animal fell shrieking backwards and to Sam's amazement the other creatures leapt upon it with demented howls, tearing at its flesh with their razor-sharp teeth. They seemed to sense the injured animal's sudden weakness and the smell of blood sparked them off into a feeding frenzy. For a brief moment, Sam was forgotten. Sensing his opportunity, he turned and ran for his life.

His breath came in desperate gasps as he tried to put some distance between himself and his attackers. His whole body ached but he knew he had to keep going; he wouldn't have the strength to fight them off if he were cornered a second time.

He looked around for any possible hiding places and then a terrible realisation began to dawn on him as he saw what he should have known all along. The train, although incredibly long, was not of infinite length. Ahead of him was a solid steel wall.

There was nowhere else to run.

Reaching the end of the carriage, he fell gasping against the cold metal wall and slid down into a sitting position, facing back the way he had come. He felt utterly wretched. The dark shapes were gathering again, advancing towards him. But this time they were in no hurry: they knew they had him trapped.

Suddenly there was a jolt and the train began to slow down.

Sam quickly leapt to his feet and peered out into the darkness. With a squeal of brakes the train emerged from a tunnel into a vast underground station. Waiting on the platform was a group of men dressed in black uniforms. They looked official, like police or soldiers.

Turning quickly, Sam saw that the creatures were getting closer and he realised his only hope was to try to attract the group's attention. The train shuddered to a halt as he hammered desperately against the glass with his fists.

'Help me!' he shouted. 'Somebody help me! Please!'

One of the men looked up and pointed in his direction. Instantly the whole group came sprinting across the platform towards his carriage. Sam glanced back up the corridor and saw the snarling mass bearing down upon him.

'Hurry up!' he screamed. 'They're going to kill me!'

The man who had first noticed him pulled something from his pocket and pointed it at the side of the train. With a soft hiss, a panel slid open in front of Sam and he leapt onto the platform just as the creatures clattered to a halt where he had been standing. He fell to the ground with a cry and waited for the attack. But it never came.

Raising his head from the dusty platform, he saw that the revolting dog-creatures were huddled together at the entrance to the carriage, staring and snarling at him.

Sam shivered and the pain throbbed in his shoulder wound. He was cold, frightened and exhausted and he was caked from head to toe in mud. When would this nightmare be over?

'Stand up, you piece of filth,' said the man. 'Let me look at you.' He was tall, and powerfully built, and spoke with a cold, authoritative manner. On his head he wore a shiny black peaked cap and Sam could see dark, close-cropped hair beneath the rim.

Sam got slowly to his feet and looked up at him.

The man reached out and grabbed his face, pulling Sam towards him in an iron grip. Sam's cheeks were crushed inwards and he smelt the sweat and leather of the black glove.

'I don't think it's him,' he said at last. 'But treat him as a high-priority suspect until we can be sure.'

One of the other soldiers twisted Sam's arms up behind his back and pushed him roughly across the platform towards a flight of stairs.

'Get off me!' Sam shouted as he was dragged up the steps. 'There's been a terrible mistake!'

He tried to struggle free, but the hands that held him were too strong. His cries echoed around the station, rising up through the cold, still air to the high vaulted roof above and gradually becoming fainter as he was dragged away.

The man watched them go and then turned to the creatures waiting in the doorway of the train.

'Go and find out what's happening on the marshes. Report back to me as soon as you know anything. Oh, and one more thing.' He raised a warning finger. 'There will be no second chances. Understand?'

He signalled towards the front of the train and the creatures whimpered and nodded, moving back into the shadows of the carriage. The doors hissed shut and the train began to move slowly out of the station into the darkness of the tunnel.

The man adjusted his cap, turned on his heel and strode purposefully towards the stairs.

The station was empty now.

A cold wind began to blow from the mouth of the tunnel, ruffling the torn edges of a poster which had been pasted to a board on the wall. At the top of the poster, the word 'WANTED' was printed in capital letters.

Beneath it was a photograph of Sam.

Five

Several hundred miles away, in an airbase not far from the great city of Vahlzi, Commander Firebrand stood beneath the main control tower and watched an aircraft climb high into the violet blue of an early morning sky. He watched until it became a speck above the distant horizon and then faded to nothing.

He took a cigar from his top pocket and lit it, the end glowing deep red as the first rays of sunlight began to show above the mountains.

Firebrand's brilliant leadership of the air squadrons during the war had successfully driven Odoursin's armies out of Vahlzi. The President had rewarded Firebrand by giving him overall command of Vahlzian forces and things had remained relatively peaceful in the years since then. But Firebrand knew that although the war between Vahlzi and Vermia had officially ended a decade ago, the uneasy truce between the two states couldn't last for very much longer.

All the evidence pointed to the fact that Vermia was developing some terrible new weapon to use against the people of Earth. The President of Vahlzi had informed Firebrand at a recent briefing that as soon as there was enough proof, he would give his permission to launch a pre-emptive strike against Vermia. But until that time, Firebrand would have to make sure that any missions against Vermian forces were carried out in secret.

There was, however, another more pressing issue.

It seemed almost certain now that Vermian forces had somehow managed to kidnap the boy and bring him back into this world. If the intelligence was correct and Hekken's mob really had got hold of him, then Firebrand would have to move fast. And to his mind there was no one better than Skipper for such a dangerous assignment.

There had been a lot of talk about her age and lack of experience, but she had already shown that she had the skill of pilots twice her age. More than that: she had a gift, something that no amount of training could provide.

She was a natural flier.

He thought back to the spring afternoon three years ago when she had first arrived at the airbase.

He had been up in the control tower co-ordinating a sortie of twelve aircraft over the marshes and had just cleared the last group to land when he happened to look out through the window.

Standing outside the fence that surrounded the compound he saw a small, blonde-haired girl. She was staring up at him through the gaps in the wire, not waving or moving.

Just standing there, all alone, with the breeze in her hair and a hundred miles of wasteland behind her.

Firebrand had watched her for a minute or two and then made a call to security.

'We have a visitor,' he said to the duty officer, hearing him tap hesitantly on the open door before entering the room. He gestured towards the window. 'Down there.'

The duty officer looked down at the tiny figure and nodded. 'Yes, sir, I know. She arrived late last night. Said she wanted to see you.'

Firebrand raised an eyebrow. 'To see me?'

'Yes, sir. She said that she wanted to speak to whoever was in charge.'

'Hmm. And what did you tell her?'

'I told her that this was a top-security base and that she wasn't going to be seeing anyone, sir.'

'I see. And what did she say to that?'

The duty officer began to look distinctly uncomfortable. 'Well, sir, she said . . . she said in that case she would just wait right there until such time as you saw fit to see her, sir.'

'Did she indeed?'

Firebrand turned back to the window once more and the duty officer allowed himself a surreptitious glance at his superior's face. As usual, the square jaw was set firm and the serious brown eyes gave little clue as to the thoughts that lay behind them, indicating only the strength and determination that had brought their owner to such a position of power. Anyone less familiar with the Commander's fearsome reputation might have been forgiven at that moment for thinking that they saw the faintest hint of a smile cross his lips.

But of course they would have been mistaken, and the duty officer knew better than to think such a thing.

'Do we know where she's from?'

'Hard to say, sir. Looking at her clothes, you'd have to guess she's from one of the tree tribes in the eastern forests, but the colouring's all wrong.'

Firebrand looked down at the small girl, who remained standing quite still, staring up through the fence at the control tower. She wore the thick, roughly woven natural fibres of green and brown that were common to the forest people. But the pale skin and blonde hair marked her out as someone from the lowlands, an area which had been laid to waste by Odoursin's retreating army a decade before. Even at this distance, he was struck by the blueness of her eyes.

'You'd better send her up,' he said.

'But, sir,' the duty officer protested, 'she could be a security threat.'

Firebrand looked disdainfully back at him. 'Sergeant,' he said, 'I hope you aren't suggesting that I am unable to defend myself against a small girl.'

She'd stood there with her hands on her hips, staring him straight in the eye and acting for all the world as though she owned the place.

'You need me,' she told him in a small, clear voice. 'You don't know it yet, but I can help you. Just train me, give me a chance. Whatever it takes, I'll do it. I'm going to be the best pilot you ever had.'

Ridiculous though it was, there was something about her that touched him in ways that he couldn't define. It was like catching sight of something through the rain, a glimpse of sunlight on a faraway mountain top.

When he had asked why she had come, why she wanted this so badly, her answer had been equally surprising. 'Because,' she replied simply, 'I've got nothing to lose.'

And now, only a few years later, that same strength of spirit had left him no choice but to reluctantly agree to this dangerous mission. As she'd pointed out, they both knew she was the best, and if anyone could pull this thing off then it was her. He couldn't argue with that.

But what Firebrand hadn't realised, what he hadn't seen right up until the very second that he watched her aircraft disappear over the horizon, was that you never really know how much something means to you until you have to let it go.

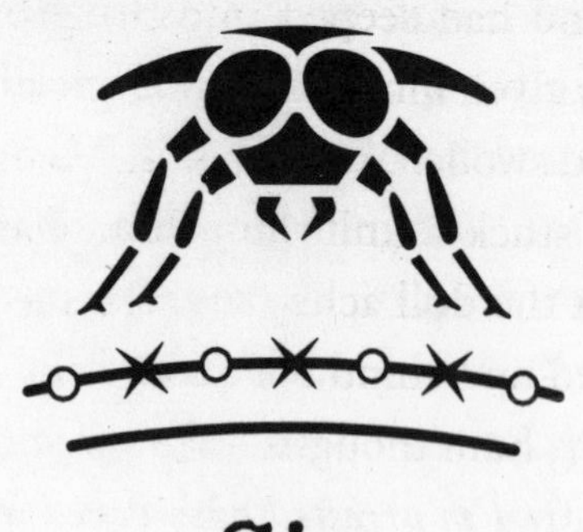

Six

The cell was dark, dingy and damp. The only light filtered through a small window set into the wall about six feet up. Three iron bars blocked the opening and through the gaps between them Sam could see that the morning sky was dull and overcast.

He flicked a small stone at the rusty steel door and was rewarded with a metallic clang as the stone struck and bounced off.

'He shoots, he scores,' Sam said quietly into the darkness. Picking up a stale crust that had been thrown into his cell, he pulled off a patch of fluffy green mould and then hungrily swallowed the rest of the bread before draining the last drops of water from a chipped, enamel mug.

The wall felt cold and damp against his back and he stood up, stretched and began to pace around the small, square cell. Trying to sleep on the freezing stone floor had left him tired and sore all over. Blood from his shoulder wound had seeped into the grey prison uniform they had given him and the muscle around the bite was purple and swollen. It felt raw and tender, as though someone had stuck a knife into him. Sam rubbed his wrists and felt the dull ache that remained after having them wrenched up behind his back.

This is crazy, Sam thought. *One minute I'm riding my bike and the next I'm arrested and locked in a prison cell.* He was exhausted, lost and confused. If this was a nightmare, then it was one heck of a long one.

He put his face against the brickwork and felt its rough surface, cold against his cheek. Scratching at the wall with his toenail, he watched tiny pieces of masonry crumble onto the wet floor. It was then that he saw the tiny ball of crumpled paper lying next to a small hole in the base of the wall. Frowning, he picked it up and opened it out. Written on the paper in tiny writing were the words:

Do not tell them who you are.

'What is going on?' he said in a baffled voice, his breath forming small clouds of mist in the cool, damp air. 'What is happening to me?'

He screwed up the piece of paper and flicked it away into the corner. Walking over to the door, he felt the wet, slimy floor beneath his feet where green algae had started to grow on the surface of the damp stone. He put his hands on his hips and peered up at the small window. It was set high into the opposite wall, which made it impossible to see anything except a small patch of sky. Perhaps if he could get up there he would be able to work out where he was. Or perhaps – even better – he would wake up to find himself in his own room again.

'Come on,' he said. 'You can do this.'

He pushed himself off from the door and ran the short distance to the far wall, leaping at the last moment to plant one foot halfway up and gain the extra height he needed. As he reached the highest point of his leap, he made a desperate grab for one of the bars and wrapped his fingers around it. The pain in his shoulder made him cry out in agony, but as he felt the cold iron against his palm he quickly grabbed onto another bar with his free hand and pulled himself up so that his head was level with the window.

'Yes!' he shouted triumphantly. He hooked his arms around the bars and looked out, half hoping to find himself waking up and staring at the ceiling of his own bedroom.

But instead the sight that met his eyes made him gasp in astonishment.

He was several hundred feet above the ground, seemingly on the top floor of a huge, bleak building that curved in a semicircle around a vast stone courtyard. Far below, tiny figures scurried back and forth, all dressed in the same black uniforms he had seen at the station.

The grey, imposing walls rose high into the cool morning air and Sam could see hundreds of small windows cut into the thick, ancient stone. He appeared to be in some sort of prison. Again his mind spun with confusion. What was he doing here? And where was *here* exactly? The man at the station had spoken English and yet . . . everything felt different somehow. As for those creatures on the train . . . Sam shuddered. He needed to find some answers. But how?

Down to his left was a steel gate set into a security fence. Several empty trucks were parked in a siding near a group of wooden huts and outside the huts were long trestle tables piled high with items of clothing and personal possessions. He recognised it as the place where he had been forced to stand the previous night with other new arrivals as they were processed and stripped of their belongings. He could hear dogs barking somewhere behind the huts and what sounded like a woman crying. There was a loud scream, followed by a brief silence. Then there were more shouts and the dogs began barking again. Sam's stomach tensed with fear and he gripped the bars more tightly as he looked around.

Two security fences had been erected around the prison complex, each three or four metres high and strung with horizontal and vertical barbed wire. The fences were a couple of metres apart and the area in between them was covered with thick coils of razor wire. A few metres back from the inner fence – inside the prison compound – was a double strand of barbed wire with warning notices fixed at intervals along it. Tall wooden watch towers manned by security guards stood in the corners of the main compound and there were regular patrols around the perimeter.

On the other side of the fence Sam could see a muddy track leading into a dense wood of evergreens. Beyond these trees he could make out a complex of buildings surrounded by what appeared to be rows and rows of aircraft, but they were too far away to be seen clearly.

To the left of the wood was some kind of industrial settlement. Steel chimneys pumping out thick black smoke jostled with huge rectangular blocks of concrete. These were interspersed with more complex structures of intricately latticed metal with spaghetti-like pipework running around the outside.

Away in the distance to the right he could make out the tall, closely grouped structures and buildings of the city that he had first observed from the marshes. Rising above the city was a construction quite unlike any of the others. It was a colossal cylindrical tower, stretching so high into the clouds that the top of it was concealed from view. It was metallic green in colour and so highly polished that – although the day was overcast – it glittered and shone like a precious emerald.

The ache in Sam's shoulder had become too painful now. He let go of the bars and dropped to the floor Looking around at the cold, dark walls of his cell, the hopelessness of his situation began to sink in.

This wasn't a nightmare that he was about to wake up from.

This was reality.

He wanted his parents so badly – longed to see them, to touch them and know that the life he had once had was real. But he could no longer be sure. His parents were gone, and so was everything else that he had known and loved. All that remained were these four walls and an unknown future.

It was more than he could bear. Fear and panic rose within him and, rushing across to the steel door, he began to kick at it furiously, his shouts of frustration echoing through the dusty silence of the prison corridors.

'Let me out!' he cried. 'I'm innocent! I haven't done anything!'

A door slammed. Heavy boots stamped over stone steps, the footsteps growing louder until they stopped suddenly outside his door.

Sam listened nervously, wondering what would happen next.

A bunch of keys jangled as the lock was turned and then, with a loud crash, the door was kicked open by a black leather boot.

Sam leapt backwards to avoid being struck by it and looked up to see a tall, blond-haired man in a black leather coat standing in the doorway. Behind him stood two other men, burly and unsmiling in their dark uniforms.

'Is this him? The one from the train?'

'Yes, General Hekken,' answered one of the men. 'He was brought in last night.'

The man referred to as Hekken removed his cap and

began to tap it impatiently against the leather palm of his glove. He wore an exasperated expression which suggested that he really didn't have time for all this. But there was something else there too: a ruthlessness, a barely concealed threat of violence which suddenly made Sam feel very afraid.

'So,' he said, 'the boy from the marshes.' He continued to beat the cap gently against his hand. 'Tell me. What were you doing on my train?'

Sam watched as Hekken looked around in the manner of a prospective buyer interested in purchasing a new apartment. He felt ice creep into the pit of his stomach. 'I was lost,' he said. 'I needed to get out of the storm.'

Hekken paused to flick some dust off his sleeve. 'I see,' he said. He smiled. 'It's Sam, isn't it?'

Sam stared at Hekken and saw something beyond the smile, something dangerous which told him that this man could not be trusted. As he lowered his gaze and looked away into the corner of his cell, he noticed the tiny piece of paper lying in the shadows.

He swallowed hard. 'I don't know what you're talking about,' he said.

Hekken smiled again, but his eyes were cold; dead as a fish on a slab.

The punch, when it came, was so hard that it sent Sam sprawling against the wall and left him clutching his stomach in agony. Hekken grabbed him by the front of his prison uniform and pulled him to his feet again.

'Don't lie to me,' he hissed, his voice full of venom. 'I

own you, do you hear me? You belong to me now. Understand?'

He threw Sam back into the corner with such force that all the wind was knocked out of him and he collapsed in a heap on the wet floor.

'I'll give you a few hours to think about it,' he said, turning back to look at Sam from the doorway. 'If you can't come up with something better, then I'm afraid I will have to arrange another meeting with your friends from the train.' He shook his head sadly. 'They mean well, of course, but between you and me . . .' Here he paused, then whispered in a conspiratorial voice, 'They can be awfully unpleasant. Just something for you to think about, that's all. I look forward to discussing it with you later.'

The door slammed shut.

Sam heard the key turn in the lock and footsteps disappearing down the corridor.

Then there was silence; nothing but the sound of his own breathing and the desperate beating of his heart.

Sam sat in the corner where he had fallen and drew his knees up to his chin. Then he covered his head with his arms and wept.

It was after the last of his sobs had subsided that he heard the sound.

At first he thought that he was mistaken, that it was merely his own breath or his imagination playing tricks on him.

But no – there it was again.

What was it? It seemed to be coming from the small hole at the base of the wall.

He crawled carefully from the shadows and put his ear next to it, listening intently.

He waited and held his breath.

And there it was.

The faint but unmistakable sound of someone calling his name.

Seven

'Sam,' the voice whispered. 'Sam, can you hear me?'

Sam could hardly believe it. It was a young girl's voice; she sounded about his age.

'Yes, I can hear you,' he whispered excitedly back into the hole. 'Where are you?'

'I'm in the cell next to yours,' the voice replied. 'I've been waiting for you, Sam.'

Sam thought about this for a moment. What did she mean, she'd been waiting for him? How could anyone have possibly known he was coming?

'I think you must have got me mixed up with someone else,' he told her. 'My name's Sam Palmer, and there's been a terrible mistake. I shouldn't really be here.'

'Oh, I know who you are,' said the girl. 'And that's why I'm here. I've come to help you.'

Sam frowned. None of this was making any sense.

'But what am I doing here?' he asked.

'Long story,' she replied. 'Long and complicated. But don't worry – I'll explain later.'

'Who are you?'

'I'm Skipper,' she answered. 'Glad you got my note. How are things in there? Are you all right?'

'Oh yeah,' said Sam, rubbing his injured shoulder. 'Everyone's so friendly.'

'Ah, yes. I heard your little meeting with the staff. They do so enjoy their work.'

Sam winced at the memory. 'Who are those people anyway?'

'That was Hekken and his henchmen. They work for Odoursin, the Emperor of Vermia. Hekken's bad news, Sam. I'd stay out of his way if I were you.'

Sam gave a sarcastic laugh. 'That could be a bit tricky, don't you think? I mean, I don't know what your cell's like, but mine's a bit short on hiding places. And it doesn't sound as though I'm going anywhere any time soon.'

'Oh, I wouldn't be too sure about that,' said Skipper.

There was a pause while Sam considered this strange reply. Who was this girl with her quiet confidence? There was something about her that made him feel hopeful again, but he would have to tread carefully. It could be a trick.

'What are you doing here anyway?' he asked, remembering what she'd said about coming to help him. 'Did they take you away too?'

'Not exactly. Let's just say I got caught.'

'Doing what?'

'Oh – it's a bit involved. But listen, we haven't got much time. The important thing is, they mustn't find out who you really are. When they come for you – which they will – they'll do all kinds of things to try and make you admit it, but you mustn't tell them.'

Sam was puzzled. 'But they already know who I am,' he said. 'That man – Hekken. He called me Sam just now. You must have heard him.'

'I know, but the thing is they're not sure. They *think* that you're Sam, they really want you to be Sam, but something's happened to make them think they've made a mistake. It's up to you to convince them that they have.'

'I don't understand. What do you mean something's happened?'

There was another pause.

'I'm not sure, but I think one of the Olumnus must have given you a helping hand on your way down here. Changed the way you look for a while.'

'The *Olumnus*?' Sam was becoming more confused by the second. 'Who are they?'

'Look, I can't tell you too much right now, but if you can convince these people that you're not who they think you are, they'll lose interest and drop their guard. And that's when we make our escape.'

Sam glanced at the stone walls surrounding him.

'Well, that's simple then, isn't it?'

'Yes,' said Skipper, 'I suppose it is.'

'Look,' said Sam, 'I don't want to sound negative here or anything, but the way I see it, we're locked into stone cells a couple of hundred feet up and the place is swarming with guards, one of whom is threatening to turn me over to a bunch of wild dogs. Put yourself in my shoes. Escape doesn't sound too realistic, does it?'

'I know this is hard, Sam, but just think for a minute. If someone had told you a few days ago that you'd be snatched away from home and thrown into a prison cell, would it have sounded realistic?'

'No, I suppose not, but –'

'Nothing's ever certain, Sam. There are no guarantees about anything. Which is actually quite good news for us, as it happens.'

'What do you mean?'

'Think about it,' replied Skipper. 'If nothing is certain, then anything is possible. I agree that escape sounds unlikely. But the fact of you being here at all is even more unlikely. And yet here you are. So all things considered, the chances of escaping are, in fact, quite good.'

Sam heard Skipper chuckling happily to herself on the other side of the wall and in spite of everything his spirits began to lift.

'But where am I?' he asked.

'In deep trouble,' replied Skipper. 'Smack bang in the middle of it, to be precise. But don't worry. I'm here to fix that.'

'Tell me something,' said Sam, changing tack. 'How do I know that I can trust you?'

'You don't,' Skipper answered. 'But then if you *knew* you could trust me, it wouldn't be trust, would it?'

'But you could be working for them,' said Sam. The fear he had felt earlier was creeping back again. He was beginning to think about what Hekken had said, how he would turn him over to those vicious creatures from the train. 'Why should I believe you?'

There was a long silence. At last, Skipper spoke. 'Because you don't have a choice,' she said simply.

At that moment there was the sound of boots on the stairway again, and the clanging of keys opening doors along the passageway.

'What's happening?' asked Sam in alarm.

'They're taking us down to work in the tanks,' said Skipper hurriedly. 'They'll probably come for you later, when the rest of us have gone. Look, just tell them someone attacked you and stole your clothes, OK? Tell them you got on the train to shelter from the storm. That should buy us a bit more time. Be strong, Sam. It'll be all right. Believe me.'

Sam held his breath as he heard Skipper's door being unlocked.

'Come on. Out!' a guard shouted into Skipper's cell, and he heard the sound of light footsteps padding across the stone floor.

'Patience is a virtue, you know.'

Skipper's voice was small, clear and confident: a light in the darkness. But then came the sound of a stinging slap and a little cry.

'You wanna watch that mouth of yours, kid. Now move out!'

Sam's stomach flipped at the sound of this rough treatment and, running to the door, he heard Skipper's voice call softly as she went past, 'Don't worry about me – just look at the sky!'

There was a grunt and a kick, then more shouting and the sound of a hundred footsteps fading away down the long, echoing stairway.

Sam was alone.

Look at the sky. What had she meant?

He scrambled to his feet, leant back against the steel door and then ran at the wall, jumping towards the window as he had done before and hauling himself up by the bars.

He looked up at the sky, but there were only dark clouds casting deep shadows across the landscape. Down below he could see the prisoners being led in a long line across the courtyard towards the gates. Some were viciously punched and kicked for not moving quickly enough.

Sam realised that there was no one to look after him, no rules to protect him in this terrible place. He began to feel very frightened indeed. What would happen next?

He let go of the bars and dropped to the floor. Suddenly he felt very cold, hungry and tired. Shivering, he curled himself up in the corner and within a few minutes he had fallen into an exhausted and fitful sleep.

Later, when he awoke, the cell was much darker and Sam realised that it must be night-time. He had been asleep for a long time. Although the room was in shadow, a bluish glow shone through the window, which Sam presumed was the light from the moon.

He remembered what Skipper had said to him before she was taken away.

Look at the sky.

Sam ran to the door, pushed himself off from it and leapt up at the window. Wrapping his arms around the bars, he rested his chin on the window ledge and looked out towards the far horizon.

Through a break in the clouds Sam could see that the sky was a deep violet and bright stars sparkled across the heavens. It was a breathtaking, beautiful night.

But what made Sam's heart leap – what shook him, scared him and filled him with exquisite feelings of danger and excitement – was his first glimpse of the source of the light that had filtered through his window.

Hanging low in the sky just above the horizon were two moons, one red and one green. A third moon, pale blue in colour, was just beginning to rise above the tree-tops. Sam's mouth dropped open in amazement and wonder. It was the strangest, most wonderful sight he had ever seen.

A different world.

He remembered the other thing that Skipper had said to him: Anything is possible.

He rested his forehead against the cold metal bars and

breathed in the cool night air. Then he heard the sound of footsteps echoing down the corridor, and his stomach turned over.

They were coming for him.

Eight

Sally Palmer drew back the curtains and winced as bright sunshine flooded the room. Outside, the sky was blue and the birds were singing. It really was the most beautiful summer's day.

She shut her eyes tightly and felt hot tears spring up under her eyelashes. There had to be some mistake. How could it possibly be such a lovely day? Why wasn't the sky dark? Why wasn't it raining? Why weren't thunder clouds pounding the pavements in anger and sorrow at the terrible tragedy that had occurred?

She sat on the bed and put her face in her hands. It had been two days now. Two days since Sam's accident. But in spite of the fact that her world had changed completely, the world outside remained just the same. The sun still shone brightly from a clear blue sky. People still laughed and enjoyed themselves. They still watched television, ate ice creams and went for walks in the park.

Of course they did. How could they know?

They couldn't see the dark storms that raged inside her. They couldn't feel the chill of the bleak, desolate ocean that surrounded her or the currents that tried to drag her under. She was drowning in her own sadness and nobody knew it. There was nothing left to reach out for, no lifeline that would carry her to the shore.

Her husband, Jack, tried to comfort her, but he was suffering as much as she was. What words of comfort are to be found when your only child has been taken from you?

Your only child. Sally wiped her eyes and laid a hand softly on the swelling beneath her nightdress.

No, not her only child.

She stared out through the window at the fields of ripening corn and thought about how she had wanted this second child so badly. Something stirred in her memory and she began to remember last summer. That business on the beach . . .

It had been Jack's idea to spend a day at the seaside, and Sam was having a wonderful time in spite of the rain. But Sally had suddenly been overcome by a wave of sadness and, feeling the need to be alone for a while, she had left Jack and Sam at the penny arcade and wandered slowly back along the pier to the stone steps which led down onto the beach.

Walking along the stony shore, she had listened to the pebbles rattle beneath the shallow rim of the ocean and wondered if the emptiness inside her would ever be filled.

A sudden voice carried on the wind had made her turn towards the sea wall. She saw a man dressed in a shabby suit standing all alone, with his arms outstretched and a mane of long, dark hair blowing around his face. Next to him was a large board upon which a sheet of paper had been taped and it fluttered wildly against its fixings. Spelled out on the sheet in red felt pen were the words 'Behold he cometh: for the time is at hand', but the rain had made the ink run and it trickled down the paper in bloody streams.

'The truth is Alpha and Omega,' he shouted into the wind, 'the beginning and the end, which is, and which was, and which is to come . . .'

Sally had put her head down as she hurried past, hoping that the man wouldn't notice her, but she heard the crunch of boots across the stones and then he was standing in front of her.

'Are you saved, sister?'

Sally had stared into those wild eyes filled with madness and wanted only to run away as fast as she could, back to the pier and the lights of the arcade.

But she didn't run. She just stood and looked down at her small, scuffed shoes, listening to the crash and thunder of the waves behind her. And then, as she raised her head and looked into the man's eyes once more, she saw in a moment how all the madness had suddenly disappeared, evaporating like a wraith into the stormy air. He stood there blinking, staring at her as though seeing her for the very first time.

'I know what you are looking for,' he said, and took her hand between his. Her eyes were drawn momentarily to the blue sparkle of a tiny sapphire set into his earlobe, an unexpected fleck of colour in a grey and ordinary world. She stared at it and remembered all the years of trying for another baby, of seeing endless specialists and waiting in draughty hospital corridors. Suddenly she could bear it no longer; her lower lip quivered and the tears streamed down her face.

The man continued to hold her hand but made no other effort to comfort her.

'You know,' he said quietly as the wind howled between them, 'sometimes the things we want most are the hardest of all to get.'

'Yes,' said Sally softly, 'I know it.' Her face was wet and crumpled.

'But perhaps,' the man went on, 'when we want a thing so badly, that thing will try and find us too.'

Sally wiped her eyes with the back of her sleeve. 'Who are you?' she whispered.

The man ignored her question and squeezed her hand. 'Look in your dreams,' he said, 'and I think you may find what you are searching for.'

Walking quickly back along the windswept pier, Sally had thought about the man's words, turning them over in her mind and trying to make some sense of them. Stopping and leaning over the balustrade, she had looked down at the beach again, hoping to catch sight of the stranger who had so unexpectedly touched her heart.

But there was no one; only the endless pebbles and an empty sea wall stretching away into the distance.

The beach was deserted.

Some days Sally had wondered if she was really losing it.

But soon after that, the dreams had started.

Now, as she stood at the bedroom window and watched a pair of swallows twist effortlessly through the blue, cloudless sky, Sally made a solemn promise. 'I will find you,' she whispered as the tears ran down her face. 'Wherever you are, I will find you and bring you home.'

Nine

Sam sat in the back of the car, wedged between two massive prison guards. Both had shaved heads and were wheezing loudly from the effort of bundling him into the back seat. With each wheeze, he was treated to a face full of stale, garlic-ridden breath so disgusting that he thought he might be sick.

He was handcuffed to the fatter one of the two, who seemed to have been stuffed into a uniform that was several sizes too small for him. The material was stretched tightly across his enormous stomach and the five buttons appeared to be under such strain that Sam thought it must be only a matter of time before they went pinging off in all directions.

The man suddenly turned to him. 'What are you looking at?' he grunted.

Sam stared down at his bare feet dangling over the edge of the seat and tried not to breathe in. 'Nothing,' he said. 'I wasn't looking at anything.'

Which wasn't strictly true, but 'Your big fat gut' seemed unwise in the circumstances.

The man nudged him roughly with his elbow. 'Just don't try nothing.'

Sam made no reply. He raised his eyes slightly, enough to see between the front seats and through the windscreen. It was raining heavily, the wipers clunking backwards and forwards over great splurges of water that splattered against the glass as if thrown from a bucket.

The driver, a thin, weasel-faced man who sniffed constantly as he steered them through the dark city streets, removed a white, hairless hand from the wheel in order to wipe his nose on the back of his sleeve.

'You boys mind if I turn the radio on?'

One of the guards grunted and there was a brief crackle and whine from the speakers as he twisted the tuning knob through the frequencies before finding the station he was after.

'. . . and the Central Office for Economy and Administration released encouraging figures today showing that industrial production has more than doubled over the past year. A spokesman from the department said that this was largely due to the success of the relocation centres and corrective labour camps. The increased rate of preventive arrests has led to the rapid removal and rehabilitation of enemies of the state, who are now able to spend their lives usefully working for the good of the Empire.'

'And we all know what *that* means,' sneered the driver. 'Serves 'em right, too. Parasites, the lot of them. But then, you'd know all about that, wouldn't you, kid?'

Sam looked down at his feet and said nothing.

'Yeah, well. You'll find your tongue soon enough where you're going.'

'. . . and the weather forecast for tonight and tomorrow: a heavy band of rain will sweep in from the east overnight . . .'

The driver switched the radio off and Sam saw the man's hard little eyes studying him in the mirror.

He looked away and watched the rain-soaked streets slide past into the night. The car sped on through four lanes of traffic and the bright, gaudy windows of shops, offices and restaurants were blurred and reflected in the dark, shining pavements. A queue of people waited beneath a blue neon sign which read: 'NOW SHOWING: *HEROES OF VERMIA*'; next door an orange kiosk advertised 'HOT MEAT SANDWICHES FOR SALE'. As they accelerated into the mouth of a brightly lit tunnel, Sam saw several figures in black uniforms drag a man from his car and bundle him into the back of a windowless van, which drove off with its siren blaring and a green light flashing on its roof.

'Scum,' said the driver, adjusting his rear-view mirror for a better look.

He waited until the van had overtaken them and then, to a chorus of angry horns, he swung the car left across three lanes of traffic and Sam heard the hiss of its tyres over wet tarmac. He peered out at the lighted buildings stretching up into the blackness and saw an arrowed sign above the road which read: 'VERMIA CENTRAL OFFICE: PERMIT HOLDERS ONLY'. The car slowed to a halt at a thin metal barrier and the driver wound down his window. The guard in the security booth peered at Sam through the hatchway for a few moments and then turned his attention back to the driver.

'Clearance documents?'

The driver reached into his top pocket and handed the security guard a crumpled piece of paper. The guard smoothed it out on his desk, nodded and spoke a few words into a microphone. Then he handed the piece of paper back through the window and said, 'OK. They're expecting you. You're to drop him off in Zone One.'

'Zone One?' The driver looked worried. 'You sure?'

At that moment there was the roar and clatter of heavy machinery and Sam turned to see two armoured vehicles approaching. One pulled up behind the car and the other flanked them on the left-hand side. Soldiers wearing steel helmets and goggles stared at them from the top of the vehicles and the turret guns swung around to point at the car.

'Like I said – Zone One.' The security guard nodded in Sam's direction. 'Seems as if you're carrying a pretty important package.'

Sam was dragged from the car towards a tall cylindrical structure that soared high above them into the night sky.

He looked up in awe at the sheer size and scale of the building. It shone metallic green in the light of the powerful arc lamps and Sam recognised it at once as the tower he had seen from the window of his cell.

A shiny metal door slid open and Sam felt his handcuffs being unlocked. Then he was shoved inside with such force that he fell to the floor. He heard the men laugh but the sound was cut off abruptly as the doors shut behind him again and he was on his own once more.

'Hey, blubber boys!' he shouted back defiantly. 'Get some exercise!' But inside his stomach churned at the thought of what horrors might lie ahead of him.

The room hummed. There was an electrical-sounding whine and then he felt his stomach drop; he had the sensation of moving upwards at great speed and guessed he must be in a lift. He stood up, closed his eyes and shook his head to try to clear it. Droplets of water scattered around him like rain.

When he opened his eyes again, he found himself staring into the pale, drawn face of an unkempt, dark-haired boy who looked as though he hadn't had a decent meal in months. As the boy stared back at him with frightened brown eyes, Sam remembered something Skipper had said to him back at the prison about the Olumnus changing the way he looked. It suddenly dawned on him that he was looking at his own reflection.

Or rather, the reflection of someone he had never seen before in his life.

When the lift doors slid back, Sam found himself in a stark, circular room constructed mainly of glass and steel. The floor was green marble, shot through with patterns of white that twisted like currents in a deep ocean. Walls of lightly smoked glass curved round on all sides and through them Sam could just make out the dark shapes of more storm clouds stacking up in the distance. He decided that he must now be at the very top of the tower.

In the centre of the room a group of men was gathered around a steel table, its polished surface reflecting the harsh glare of a disc-shaped light hanging from the ceiling above.

Sam recognised Hekken standing to one side of the table, but found himself unable to take his eyes off the man seated behind it.

He was wearing a long coat of dark-green leather and his skin was blanched white, stretched taut and paper-thin across the sharp, angular bones of his face. But the face itself was twisted and disfigured, like a wax model that has melted in the heat of the sun. Eyes filled with hate glowed like hot coals, burning their way deep into Sam's mind.

Sam bravely tried to stare him out, but it was impossible and he quickly dropped his gaze.

'Is this him?' the man said quietly, continuing to stare in Sam's direction.

'We think it could be,' said Hekken uncertainly. He sounded surprisingly nervous.

Almost imperceptibly, the blue lips tightened. 'What do you mean, it could be? Is it or isn't it?'

Hekken continued to look distinctly uneasy. 'There was a problem with the transfer. The receiving party had to cover a wider target area than expected and the boy was lost during the crossover from Earth to Aurobon. But we do know for a fact that he must have landed somewhere in the marshes. And we found this one on the train, wearing the target's clothing.'

Hekken cleared his throat nervously before continuing. 'Problem is, he doesn't fit the description. We've carried out a DNA analysis and agents are trying to retrieve samples from the suspect's bedroom. Hopefully we can get a match that way. But it's proving difficult to get access: Vahlzian forces have locked the whole area down tight.'

The man's white face twitched with barely suppressed anger. But when he spoke again, his tone seemed calm, almost friendly. 'I expect you're wondering who I am,' he said, turning to Sam. 'Please allow me to introduce myself. My name is Odoursin and I've been looking forward to meeting you, Sam. Looking forward to it very much.'

He paused as if half expecting some sort of reaction, but Sam remained silent.

'I really must apologise,' he went on, pushing back his chair and standing up for the first time since Sam had entered the room. 'You must be very confused and frightened by all of this.'

He was even taller than he had first appeared, towering

over Sam as he approached. The unexpected sympathy and friendliness of his approach took Sam by surprise and he felt his bottom lip begin to quiver. But he bit into it and remained silent, listening to the low rumble of the gathering storm outside.

'I'm afraid there are some people who have made some serious mistakes,' he continued. 'For this, of course, they will be severely punished.'

He looked at Hekken, who stared hard at the floor.

'Obviously, however, my biggest concern at the moment is to ensure that you are returned as quickly as possible to your family. Would you like me to arrange that, Sam?'

Sam squeezed his eyes tightly shut and fought the impulse to cry out and beg to be taken home. But remembering Skipper's advice about not revealing his identity, he said nothing.

Slowly, Odoursin moved towards him. 'Sam,' he said. 'Sam, what's the matter? Don't you want to go home? I know your mother and father are very worried about you.'

It was the hardest thing that Sam had ever had to do.

He took a deep breath and looked straight into Odoursin's eyes. 'I think you've got me mixed up with someone else,' he said. 'My name isn't Sam. And I haven't got a mother and father. I'm an orphan.'

At that moment he saw Odoursin's expression change, saw beyond the fire in his eyes to a place of terrible, desolate emptiness, and knew for certain that Skipper had been right.

'There was a storm blowing across the marshes,' Sam went on, desperately trying to remember the story Skipper had told him, 'and I was looking for some shelter. Suddenly, someone attacked me from behind and knocked me out. When I came round again they had stolen my clothes. They left their own clothes behind and it was so cold that I had to put them on. Then when the train stopped and I found the doors unlocked, I climbed in to get out of the storm.'

Odoursin was now staring at him intently. 'And did you – by any chance – manage to see this person who attacked you?' he asked slowly.

'Well,' said Sam, 'it all happened very quickly. But yes – yes I did catch a glimpse of his face.'

Odoursin began to walk slowly and deliberately across the room towards him. 'Think carefully,' he said. 'What did he look like?'

Sam swallowed hard. He thought of the photograph albums on the shelf at home, of the face that used to smile back at him from the mirror in the mornings before school. 'He had brown hair that sort of stuck up,' he said. 'But the thing I remember most about him, the thing that really struck me about him . . .'

'Go on,' breathed Odoursin.

'. . . was his green eyes. He had these really bright green eyes.'

'Is this true?' Odoursin hissed. He was now only inches away from him.

Sam nodded. 'That's what I saw,' he said. 'But when I

came round again, he was gone.'

Odoursin towered over him and as Sam looked up he felt those cruel eyes burning directly into his own. They seemed to light all the dark places inside of him, illuminating a thousand fears and horrors that crawled and slid from every shadow.

'He's lying,' said Hekken.

'It would seem so,' said Odoursin. 'Perhaps it is time for a little persuasion.'

Sam felt his hands shaking with fear, fluttering at his sides like two dying birds, but he squeezed them into tight fists and stared defiantly back into his tormentor's face.

'I told you,' he cried angrily, 'you've got the wrong person!'

A heavy blow to the back of his head sent him sprawling onto the floor and fireworks of pain exploded behind his eyes.

'Your choice,' said Odoursin. 'We can do this the hard way.'

Sam was hauled roughly to his feet and thrown into a heavy wooden chair. Ropes were tied tightly around his wrists and ankles, securing him to the arms and legs of the chair. As Sam struggled, he heard the sound of a door opening and the rattle of a chain, followed by the tapping of claws over stone. Jerking his head around, Sam saw to his horror that a guard had brought in one of the dog-like creatures from the train. Its fur was lank and bloodstained and its yellow eyes bulged as it strained against the choke chain. It stared hungrily at him, saliva dripping from its mouth.

'Hello, boy,' it said.

The guard loosened his grip on the chain slightly and there was a clunk as the dog took up the slack and moved closer to Sam, sniffing greedily at the air.

'Boy smell good,' it growled, nodding slowly and grinding its teeth together. 'I bite him now, I bite him . . .'

Sam fought desperately to escape from the chair, but the ropes that bound him were too tight.

The dog bared its teeth, tensed its muscles and snarled.

As Sam cried out in terror, the door opened again and footsteps echoed across the marble floor. Odoursin quickly held up a hand and the guard pulled the marsh dog back in mid-flight. With a surprised yelp, it fell heavily to the ground and its claws slipped and scrabbled around on the smooth surface. Finally it managed to right itself and turned back to face Sam again, growling menacingly at him.

Odoursin turned to look at the new arrival.

'What brings you here?' he asked.

'Forgive the interruption, Your Excellency, but I have news of the boy.'

'Indeed.' A pause. 'I hope for your sake it is good.'

His heart pounding in his chest, Sam turned his head and saw a young soldier in the now familiar black uniform.

'According to our latest reports, his Earth body is still functioning, but only just.'

'You mean he's still up there?' The anger in Odoursin's voice was obvious now.

'Oh no, Your Excellency. The operation went like clockwork and the team definitely got him. I was there when they took him down.' Sam sensed a degree of pride in the young soldier's voice as he spoke. 'It's only the shell that's still up there.' He smiled, half expecting to be congratulated on a job well done.

'Oh, really?' said Odoursin. Sam suddenly felt cold fingers in his hair and the next moment his head was yanked backwards so that he was staring straight up at the soldier.

'Is *this* who you are talking about?'

The soldier looked at Sam. 'No,' he said. 'No, that's definitely not him. We've rounded up about twenty suspects from the marshlands who fit the boy's description. We're just processing them now and I'm expecting a positive ID within hours.'

Odoursin let go of Sam's hair and his head fell forward again.

'I must apologise, Your Excellency,' said Hekken hurriedly. 'I think perhaps the fact that this boy was caught wearing the suspect's clothes has led to something of an overreaction by our security forces. I will make sure that they are severely reprimanded.'

Odoursin glared at Hekken and he fell silent.

'Tell me,' said Odoursin, turning back to the soldier

with slow menace, 'what happens if you don't get a positive ID?'

The young soldier was obviously flustered now. Success was rapidly turning into failure right in front of him.

'I remain confident that we will find the boy, Your Excellency. We definitely pulled him through a fabric gap and he arrived somewhere out on the marshes during the night,' he said. 'If our soldiers haven't found him already then it's only a matter of time before they do. There are marsh dogs all over the area. He can't escape.'

'But if what you say about his Earth body is true, then there's still a chance he may find his way back,' said Odoursin, a cold fury in his voice.

The others remained silent.

'You know the prophecy. We *have* to find him and keep him in Aurobon. And we have to find him before they do.'

There was a moment's pause while everyone looked at each other as if unsure what to do next.

It was Hekken who broke the silence. 'Well, what are you waiting for?' he shouted at the groups of uniformed guards around the room. 'Get on to it now!' And suddenly the place burst into life as men began running towards the lift.

'What shall I do with this one?' asked Hekken, gesturing at Sam with a gloved finger. 'It's obviously not him. Do you want me to kill him?'

'Not yet,' replied Odoursin, who seemed suddenly to have lost all interest in Sam. 'Put him on the work programme with the others for now. And if the tests show up negative,' he added, 'let the dogs have him.'

Hekken was unusually thoughtful as he rode the express elevator down to the ground floor.

He knew that, according to the prophecy, bringing the Dreamwalker's Child to Aurobon would tip the balance of power in favour of the East. He had no argument with that. Vahlzi's western forces were powerful and Vermia needed all the help it could get.

But he also knew that if Vermia was to be successful in its plans for Earth, then the Dreamwalker's Child would have to be killed once it arrived in Aurobon. It was a bit like using a maggot to clean the infection from a wound: when the job was done, you got rid of it.

Unfortunately, however, Odoursin didn't see it like that. He failed to see that if you allowed a maggot to turn into a fly, it would spread infection everywhere.

Odoursin wanted to keep the Dreamwalker's Child alive in Aurobon. He believed that the Dreamwalker's Child would increase his power and enable him to rid Earth of its human plague.

The Dreamwalker's Child shall
rise up against the Darkness.

Odoursin thought that the people of Earth were the Darkness. It allowed him to believe that all his terrible deeds were somehow justified by the words of the prophecy.

But Hekken was under no such illusion. He was well aware of the shadowy paths that they had all chosen in their quest for ultimate power. He knew that the darkness in the prophecy referred not to humans but to Vermia itself.

And therein lay the problem. The prophecy was working against them and time was running out. He would have to find a way of making Odoursin see the truth.

If they were to win, then the Dreamwalker's Child would have to die.

Ten

High in the mountains above the city of Vahlzi, the Olumnus people – or what was left of them – still lived quietly in their mountain caves. They followed the ancient teachings of Salus, who they believed – even now – walked between the worlds of Aurobon and Earth, guiding those who sought to restore them to their proper state of harmony.

While the Mazrian tribes worked the land, the Arbous people colonised the forests and the Nomads roamed the great deserts of the north, the Olumnus alone had worked secretly to fulfil their ancient purpose of maintaining the balance of life on Earth.

Moving unseen through gaps in the fabric between the worlds, they repaired damaged crops, guided underground springs to the surface of lands ravaged by drought, fought clandestine battles to keep pests in check and helped even the tiniest of creatures adapt to a changing world. The Olumnus so loved the Earth that they devoted their lives to it.

But then Earth's people became industrialised. As their

cities grew, the Olumnus had found it increasingly difficult to keep pace with the huge changes that followed. The battle to preserve the balance of nature became much harder.

It was at this point that a group of younger Olumnus began to copy the technology that they saw on Earth, rapidly developing their own in an effort to keep up with the changes.

The Olumnus Elders became afraid for the future stability of their own world. They worried that Earth's mistakes would be repeated, bringing greed, pollution and war to Aurobon. They accused the younger ones of going against the teachings of Salus and ordered that all new technology should be destroyed.

But the young Olumnus refused and were banished from the mountains for ever.

And so they had come as settlers to the western plains and built the great city of Vahlzi.

Eleven

Vahlzi took its name from the desert flower which – for a few brief hours after the rains came – covered the surrounding plains in a riotous explosion of blooms, ranging in hue from the deepest red to the palest of yellows.

The name was appropriate, for over the years the city had grown into a huge and delicious confusion of sound and colour; its narrow cobbled back streets twisting erratically beneath the feet of traders as they piled their stalls high with dried fruit, spices, salted fish and wine-skins filled with dark, sweet-smelling liquids.

In contrast, the streets widened towards the city centre, sweeping past modern, white-walled courtyards towards the main street, where bridges of intricately carved stone arched their way across the River Naiad. Along the banks of the river, pebbled walkways meandered past neatly kept flowerbeds and sprinklers hissed and shimmered over bright emerald lawns.

It was here, on the main road that led back towards the old part of town, that Commander Firebrand paid the cab driver and stepped quickly out onto the warm pavement. Night was falling and already the streets were alive with people in search of a good time. A young couple barged past him, arguing loudly above the music blaring from a nearby club, while further down the street a group of men staggered drunkenly into the path of a hooting taxi, hammering their fists onto its bonnet as they passed. A thin, bony-faced woman in her early twenties called out to him from a shop doorway where she crouched next to a mangy, undernourished dog.

'Hey, mister. Spare us enough for a hot meal?'

Throwing a handful of loose change into the woman's hat, Firebrand waved away her thanks and turned a corner into an adjoining street. From here he negotiated a series of narrow, dimly lit alleys, walking quickly past steaming kitchens and fire escapes hung with washing until he emerged at last on the edge of a small square. In the middle of the square was an overgrown park with a few trees and a little pond surrounded by iron railings and a gate.

Pushing the gate open, Firebrand heard the hinges creak and felt the rust flake beneath his fingers. Moving through the dark-green shadows, he listened to the sounds of the city floating through the night air and noticed that they were fainter now, like a radio playing softly in another room. He kept on walking until he stood before a large block of stone that marked the centre of the park.

The stone was black, cube-shaped and twice Firebrand's height. Ancient signs and letters covered its surface, embedded with the tiniest fragments of crystal that glittered with light despite the relative darkness of their surroundings.

The Foundation Stone, he thought.

Firebrand stared at the strange letters carved into the stone so many years before, stared at the dead language that was forgotten by all but a few, and began to read what his father had once taught him to know from memory:

> **Herein lies the first stone of the new age. Our city shall rise from the dust and the true of heart shall forever preserve the purpose of the Olumnus. But all must know this: that knowledge is power, but power without wisdom is the path of destruction; and the greatest of all wisdom is love.**

Firebrand remembered his father telling him of the legend that somewhere at the Foundation Stone's core lay the Earthstone, a magical stone of great beauty and power. It was said to be a gift from Salus himself, a reminder to the Vahlzian people that the fortunes of Earth were forever linked with their own.

'Your faith must be like the Foundation Stone,' Firebrand's father had said. 'Strong enough to shield your heart from the many storms that will try to destroy it. If your faith should crumble, then your heart will be lost.'

Despite his ancestors' split with the Olumnus over the use of technology, Firebrand still believed in the old ways, still tried to follow the teachings of the Olumnus.

Like them, he wanted to restore order, balance and harmony in both worlds.

It was the proper way of things.

He stood up, walked across to the stone and placed his hands upon it. It was cold and solid beneath his touch and he felt a keen sense of its permanence; of the days and the years whirling past its calm and silent centre. He thought of his ancestors bringing the stone to this place all those years ago. They had believed in a better future back then. What would they think now?

Before the war, Firebrand and Odoursin had been friends. Using their knowledge of new technology, they had successfully developed the Insect Programme and led many joint missions to Earth. But after the death of his brother in the air crash, Odoursin had lost all faith in the old ways. He quickly lost interest in protecting the Earth and became determined to overthrow the Vahlzian government and seize power for himself. His army of followers had struck without warning one night, and although the Vahlzian army had succeeded in driving them out, the battle had left thousands dead.

Now, while the people of Vahlzi tried to maintain the old values, Odoursin continued to build up his forces in Vermia. Firebrand had always known that Odoursin was ambitious and hungry for power. But he had still believed that Odoursin was on the side of good, right up until that terrible night when he had betrayed them all, tipped over the brink into madness by the loss of his brother.

Intelligence sources showed he was now developing a new and deadly weapon that he wouldn't hesitate to use against the people of Earth. And that, of course, would only be the beginning.

Power without wisdom is the path of destruction . . .

Firebrand stared at the Foundation Stone, illuminated by the coloured light from the three moons that hung above the treetops. He had come here this evening with a mind full of doubts, his faith shaken by setbacks and betrayal. But as he touched the ancient stone and remembered his father's words, he felt his faith returning. Whatever happened, he had to believe that the origins of the prophecy lay rooted in the goodness of the past; that these difficult times were simply stepping stones out of the darkness.

Removing his hands from the stone, Firebrand thrust them into the pockets of his overcoat and looked up into the night sky. There had been no word for three days. The signs were not good. But then of course, he reminded himself, Skipper was highly trained in covert operations of this nature and no one had expected a quick result. He had to push his concerns to one side and believe that she could get the boy out. Failure in this particular mission was not something he would allow himself to think about.

This time the stakes were too high.

Twelve

Sam awoke to the sound of shouts, keys rattling in locks and the metal clang of cell doors being flung open. It was still dark and he guessed it must be early morning. Rubbing his eyes, he pushed himself up into a sitting position. He could only have been asleep for a few hours and his right side ached from lying on the cold stone.

A key turned in the lock and his cell door swung open. A guard stood silhouetted in the doorway with a long black baton in one hand. He pointed it at Sam.

'Get up!' he shouted.

Sam put a hand on the wall and levered himself to his feet. 'Where am I going?' he asked.

'Just move out, prisoner,' barked the guard, in a tone that suggested it would be unwise to ask any further questions.

As Sam stepped out of the cell, the guard turned him roughly so that he was facing down the corridor. A line of prisoners stood motionless outside their cells, all dressed in the same grey material and staring straight ahead.

From behind him came the sound of a little cough, the kind that someone makes when they want to be noticed.

Sam turned and saw another line of prisoners stretching the other way. But his eyes were drawn to the small figure standing in front of the cell next to his own.

It was a girl with short, tousled blonde hair the colour of dirty straw. Although only a few inches smaller than Sam, she looked tiny compared to the other prisoners, an impression that was heightened by the fact that her prison uniform was at least three sizes too big. Despite having managed to roll up the legs and sleeves, she still looked as if she was trying to fight her way out of a large tent.

But what struck Sam most about her were her sparkling blue eyes. They shimmered with light, like the surface of the ocean on a summer's morning, and, for the first time since arriving in this terrible place, he felt the loneliness begin to drain out of him.

The girl brought her hand up in front of her chest and gave him the tiniest of waves. 'Hello, Sam.' She smiled warmly at him.

'Hello, Skipper,' Sam replied. He was about to smile back when a sharp blow in his stomach doubled him over and left him gasping for air.

'Eyes front, prisoner!' yelled the guard, jabbing him again with the heavy baton. He grabbed Sam by the front of his uniform and slammed him up against the wall. Sam cried out in pain and fright.

'You'd better be a real fast learner, son,' the guard whispered nastily as Sam struggled to get his breath back. 'Cos if you ain't, me and my stick are gonna teach you real quick. Understand?'

'Yes,' said Sam, his voice shaking. 'I understand.'

He struggled to stand up straight again and tried not to show his fear. His body was bruised and he ached all over.

'Now fall in, prisoner!' shouted the man.

As Sam limped over to join the others, he caught sight of a cross-eyed Skipper pointing at the guard's back and scratching under her arms like a chimpanzee.

In spite of the pain, he managed a weak smile and took his place in the line.

The column of prisoners halted at the tall iron gates on the far side of the courtyard, waiting for them to be unlocked. Although it was still dark, the stars were beginning to fade as morning approached, and the moons lay hidden in cloud.

Over to his left, Sam could see a group of new arrivals standing on the unloading ramp, caught in the cold glare of the metal lamps that shone from the top of the wooden huts. A group of men had been separated from the others and made to stand to attention, facing the wall. They were chained to iron rings and a guard was trying to hold back his dog as it barked fiercely at them, straining at its leash. Sam noticed that the guard was smiling. He shouted something to one of the other soldiers, who laughed loudly, his smoky breath forming like a small ghost in the bitter morning air. Sam shivered and turned away.

The gates creaked open and the prisoners moved forward once more. Sam saw how thin and undernourished they all looked, shuffling along in filthy grey uniforms, their sad hollow eyes staring out at a life that had become merely an exercise in staying alive. He remembered what he had heard on the radio about enemies of the state being re-educated. *Some education*, he thought bitterly.

After following a muddy path through the woods for about a mile, they emerged in an open expanse of land where hundreds of trees had been recently felled. The ground was dotted with roughly hewn tree stumps and piles of freshly cut timber were stacked up on either side of a long straight road that stretched away into the distance. Running alongside the road was a high fence topped with razor wire, curled over in an arc to deter intruders and prevent escape. Sam breathed in deeply and caught the scent of sawdust and pine needles on the icy wind.

Beyond the fence he could make out groups of buildings dotted across the compound and what appeared to be vast squadrons of aircraft laid out as far as the eye could see. Powerful searchlights played back and forth across the area, their white beams occasionally sweeping along the line of prisoners and forcing Sam to screw up his eyes against their harsh light. In the middle of the whole set-up was a tall building with large windows around the top which Sam presumed was the control tower. He felt sure that it was an airfield of some sort, but where were the runways?

The road branched off into the compound, which comprised of row upon row of military barracks, vast aircraft hangars and a complex of workshops and factories with chimneys belching black smoke into the darkness. The gates swung open and a barrier across the road rose with a mechanical whine. In the distance Sam could hear the hum of electrical generators and the muffled sound of heavy machinery whirring and thumping through the stillness of the morning.

As they continued their way across the compound Sam noticed that Skipper had moved up the line and was now walking beside him.

'What do you think?' she said. 'Pretty impressive, huh?'

'What are you doing, Skipper?' Sam whispered anxiously. 'Get back in line. They'll kill you if they see you!'

'Relax,' said Skipper. 'There's only two of them now and they're just thinking about the end of their shift. Look.' She nodded towards the front of the line.

Sam looked around nervously to see who else might be watching, but discovered to his relief that the guards who had escorted them from the prison had gone. Only two remained: one at the head of the column and another one bringing up the rear.

'What is this place anyway?' asked Sam. 'It looks like an airport or something, but there aren't any runways.'

'What would they need runways for?' said Skipper.

'Well, how else are the aircraft going to take off?' said Sam. 'Maybe they just store them here or something.'

'Oh, they take off all right,' said Skipper. 'Believe me. I've got the scars to prove it.'

Sam was puzzled. 'What do you mean?' he asked.

The prisoners at the front of the line were disappearing around the corner of a large building and, as they approached it, Skipper said simply, 'Take a look for yourself.'

They turned the corner and Sam let out a cry of shock, put one hand up to his mouth and used the other to steady himself against the wall.

A few metres away, the huge green eyes of an enormous horsefly bulged from its monstrous head, suffused in the half-light with a dull metallic sheen. It was the size of a jet fighter and it crouched above them on six gigantic legs, each covered in coarse black hairs the thickness of industrial power cables. Two sharp, scissor-like blades protruded from its mouth and folded back behind its thorax was a pair of translucent, smoke-coloured wings with black veins running through them. They moved slightly in the breeze and the sound was like canvas flapping in the wind.

Sam felt a small hand in his and the next thing he knew he was being pulled away from the wall by Skipper, whose strength was obviously much greater than her small frame suggested. She looked at him apologetically.

'Sorry, Sam,' she said. 'I should have warned you. Not a pretty sight, are they?'

She brushed some dust from his arm and then pushed him forward as others began to overtake.

'Better keep moving. We don't want old Stick Boy teaching you any more lessons, do we?'

Sam stumbled forward and fell into step with the others, unable to keep his eyes from the incredible sight that surrounded him. He realised now that the lines of aircraft he had seen earlier were in fact massed ranks of huge insects. In spite of his initial terror at encountering these monsters at such close range, his natural curiosity was already beginning to take over.

The nearest insects were all horseflies of the type he had seen in his bedroom. When was it? The day before yesterday? Longer?

It already seemed half a lifetime ago.

They were lined up in rows of maybe twenty or thirty, and the rows stretched away in columns that reached far into the distance.

Up ahead he could see several fields covered with more insects, but these appeared thinner, lighter and more graceful. Their legs were skinny and their slender abdomens pointed upwards at an angle to their heads. A long tube tapering to a sharp point stuck out from the front of each one and Sam immediately recognised them as mosquitoes.

'Look over there,' said Skipper proudly, pointing towards the control tower.

Sam followed her gaze to a point a few hundred metres short of the tower. An area had been cordoned off with coloured tape beyond which Sam could make out what appeared to be the black and yellow wreckage of an enormous wasp. Its thorax was partially caved in and one of the wings was missing.

'Bit of a shame really,' Skipper went on. 'I only had it serviced last week.'

'What do you mean?' asked Sam. Once again, he had no idea what Skipper was talking about.

'Sorry, Sam. I keep forgetting you're new to all this.' She looked ruefully across to where the smashed insect lay. 'That was my wasp. I crashed it into the compound in the hope they'd lock me up in solitary. We've known for a while that they save the top floor of this prison for special cases while they figure out what to do with them. So we worked out that's where you'd be too.' She smiled. 'Clever, eh?'

Sam was even more confused by this revelation, but before he could ask any more questions the group stopped by the entrance to a large, whitewashed building with a tangle of shiny steel pipes sprouting from its walls. There were no windows, but Sam could see clouds of steam rising steadily from vents somewhere high up in the roof. A metal door opened to reveal long strips of thick, transparent plastic hanging down across the entrance.

The guard at the front of the line spoke into a small grille and a few seconds later a man dressed in a green rubber suit pushed his way out through the plastic. He had two cylindrical tanks on his back connected to a black hose with a silver nozzle on the end of it, which he held in his right hand.

The guard pulled the first prisoner forward and the man in the rubber suit began spraying him all over with a white powder. Apparently used to this routine, the prisoner held open the neck of his boiler suit to allow himself to be sprayed inside as well as out.

'What are they doing now?' whispered Sam.

'Don't worry,' Skipper reassured him. 'It's just disinfectant. They don't want anything to happen to their precious babies, you see.'

The line shuffled forward as the first prisoner entered the building and the next stepped forward to be sprayed.

'Babies?' said Sam. 'What babies?'

'Inside are the larvae tanks,' explained Skipper quietly. 'This is where they breed the mosquito larvae so that they can make those things.' She nodded towards the fields of mosquitoes in front of them. 'Lovely, aren't they?'

'Seriously?' said Sam. It sounded incredible, but then so did everything else in this strange, frightening place.

'Cross my heart and hope to fly,' said Skipper with a grin.

'I used to collect mosquito larvae,' said Sam, thinking of the tiny wriggling creatures that he used to scoop out of ponds and water butts with a jam jar. 'I saw one hatch once. It stepped out onto the surface of the water like a little ice skater.' He stared at the ground, remembering.

'It was a lot smaller than the ones they've got here though,' he added.

Skipper smiled. 'It's all relative,' she said.

'What about those?' asked Sam, looking back at the horseflies that towered above the airfield.

'The horsefly larvae are bred out in the marshes, but they bring the adults to the airbase. That way they can organise all their secret missions from here.'

Sam peered through the gloom at the gruesome features of the nearest fly.

'Are they dead?' asked Sam.

'No,' said Skipper. 'They're not dead. At least, not in the way you mean.'

'Well, they don't seem to be moving very much,' Sam replied. 'In fact,' he added, 'they're not moving at all.'

'That's because at the moment they're missing a vital component,' explained Skipper. 'Normally, mosquitoes are driven by their instinct to bite, drink blood and lay eggs. Horseflies are the same. They don't really think about it – they just do it. But the insects you see here are different. In the factory their natural development is interrupted during the final stage of their life cycle so that instinct can be replaced by something else.'

Sam looked at her quizzically but remained silent, listening intently.

'Instead of instinct,' Skipper continued, 'they use something that can think for itself.'

In the distance Sam could hear the sound of several vehicles approaching at speed. He shook his head. 'I don't know what you're talking about,' he said.

At that moment a group of trucks roared onto the field and skidded to a halt in front of where the horseflies were standing. Seven or eight men leapt from the back of each truck and began running towards the flies, strapping on helmets and masks as they ran.

Skipper looked at Sam and nodded in the direction of the new arrivals. 'I'm talking about pilots,' she said.

Sam watched as they extended long ladders beside the huge flies and scrambled up to stand on the upper body of the insects. Several flashes of brilliant blue light followed and then the pilots disappeared from view.

Almost immediately there was a low humming sound and Sam saw that the wings of several horseflies were starting to move.

'Get down!' shouted Skipper.

The next moment Sam was blown off his feet by the powerful downdraught from the enormous wings and the sound of humming rose to a deafening whine. He covered his face with his hands and heard the dust and debris whipping over his head as the ground shook beneath him. Seconds later it was over, and when Sam looked up again the flies were tiny specks in the distant sky.

All around him, prisoners were picking themselves up and dusting themselves down. Sam noticed again the haunted look in their eyes and realised it was the look of hopelessness and despair. He realised that he had never heard any of them speak a single word.

A hand grabbed his arm and pulled him to his feet. He found himself staring at the man in the rubber suit, who was pointing the disinfectant nozzle straight at him.

'I don't think you need to –' Sam began, but his words were quickly lost in a cloud of white powder which left him coughing and gasping for breath.

Rubbing his eyes, he staggered towards the doorway and looked back. He just had time to notice that the sky was growing lighter before he was pushed roughly through the plastic sheets and away from the morning sun that was beginning to rise above the far horizon.

Thirteen

In her dreams, they were closing in on her.

Sally could hear the shouts and screams from the burning village and the harsh voices of soldiers calling to one another across the marshes.

Ahead of her lay the trees: tall silhouettes of pines stretching up into the night sky. If she could make it across the last few feet of open ground then she could escape.

Taking a deep breath, she stood up and ran for the tree line.

Somewhere behind her, guns began to fire and the ground erupted, sending chunks of earth flying up against her legs, but she kept on running until at last she stumbled onto the dark floor of the forest. Bullets smacked and whined through the branches above her head but soon she had left them behind and could hear them no more.

She pushed her way deeper into the forest, moving slowly and quietly through the thick, fragrant branches, stopping at every sound in the undergrowth. She waited, as still and silent as the trees that surrounded her, and breathed in the cold scent of pine before moving on.

Presently she came upon a small clearing where the trees grew less densely and the canopy of branches opened to reveal a sky littered with stars.

Ahead of her, crouching in the darkness, she could make out the figure of a young woman. Glancing over her shoulder to see that no one was watching, the woman placed something behind the thick trunk of a large pine tree and partially covered it with bracken so that it would be hidden from view.

Sally heard voices. The soldiers were only minutes away now.

The young woman knelt by the tree and stretched out her hand. 'Goodbye, my love,' she whispered. Then she stood up and Sally found herself looking straight into her sad blue eyes.

'Please,' said the woman, 'look after her for me.'

Then, as the sound of heavy boots came crashing through the undergrowth, the woman ran away.

Sally saw dark shapes moving through the trees and the fear caught in her own throat; she ran quickly in the opposite direction, faster and faster, wanting only to get away from the terror and sadness that surrounded her in this place.

At last, exhausted, she felt her legs give way and she fell down onto the dark woodland floor.

The wind blew high in the treetops and the sound of a gunshot rang out across the forest.

Sally screamed, and then her husband's arms were around her and she was staring at the curtains as the first light came into the bedroom.

It was morning.

As Jack held her close and told her, 'Shhhh it was only a dream,' she shut her eyes and listened to the beating of her heart and the sound of rain, soft against the window.

Fourteen

'So, General.' Odoursin stared at Hekken across the table, his eyes alert and unblinking. 'What news?'

Hekken bowed slightly and gripped the two brown envelopes more tightly behind his back.

'I am afraid, Your Excellency, that none of the children brought in from the marshes has been positively identified.'

Odoursin's stare hardened. 'I presume you have not come here to waste my time, General Hekken?'

Hekken thrust his chin forward and made sure that he was standing to attention. This was a dangerous game he was playing. He would have to proceed with caution if he was to achieve the result he intended.

'I hope not, Your Excellency. You see, my original hunch about the boy from the train was correct. He was lying. I have just received word that the tests have proved positive. His DNA is a perfect match with samples gathered from the boy's bedroom on Earth.' He allowed himself a brief dramatic pause before adding: 'We have found the Dreamwalker's Child.'

Hekken glanced at Odoursin and saw that his withered lips had twisted themselves into something approaching a smile.

'This is most pleasing, General Hekken. For this, you shall be rewarded.'

Hekken took a deep breath and took a step forward. It was now or never.

'Thank you, Your Excellency. There is, however, one more thing that I think you should see.'

He produced one of the envelopes from behind his back and placed it carefully on the desk in front of Odoursin. Odoursin frowned.

'What is this?'

'It is classified information that has only just come to light, Your Excellency. We managed to obtain it yesterday from sources inside Vahlzi.'

Odoursin opened the envelope and pulled out a large black and white photograph. It was blurred and had obviously been enlarged several times from a poor-quality original. It showed a young woman standing alone in a kitchen.

'This photograph was taken over a decade ago by a search-and-rescue team,' said Hekken.

Odoursin stared at the photograph for a few moments and then looked up at him. 'What exactly is your point, General?'

'Please understand, Your Excellency, that I have no wish

to reawaken unpleasant memories,' said Hekken. 'But the Council felt you should be made aware of this important development. The photograph that you are looking at now was taken many years ago, at the scene of your air crash. You see, this is the woman who killed your brother.'

Odoursin's eyes flashed angrily, but he remained calm. 'If this is true,' he said bitterly, 'then she is of no concern to us now. She will simply die with all the others.' He stared past Hekken at the layers of grey cloud that stretched away across the city. 'If, as you say, the Dreamwalker's Child is in Aurobon then the prophecy will soon be fulfilled. We will rid the Earth of its human Darkness once and for all.'

Hekken waited until Odoursin had finished and then quietly placed the second envelope on the desk in front of him.

'Forgive me,' he said, 'but I think you should look at this too.'

Odoursin opened the envelope and pulled out another photograph. It was in colour and showed an auburn-haired woman dressed in blue dungarees, standing in the middle of a vegetable patch. She was in her early to mid-thirties and she was leaning on a garden spade.

'We've had both photographs analysed by several different labs and they've all reached the same conclusion,' said Hekken. 'We are confident that they are both photographs of the same woman.'

Odoursin glared at Hekken. 'I really do not see the relevance of this, General Hekken,' he said angrily. 'Why should the fact that this woman is still alive be of the slightest interest to me now?'

'Because,' said Hekken, 'she is the Dreamwalker.'

Half an hour later, General Hekken sank back into the comfortable leather seat of his staff car and smiled. He watched contentedly as the driver pulled smoothly away behind the motorcycle outriders that flanked Odoursin's armour-plated car and realised that things couldn't really have turned out better.

It was well known that Odoursin's hatred of humanity stemmed from his hatred of the woman who had killed his brother. Now, by convincing him that she was the Dreamwalker, Hekken had finally managed to destroy Odoursin's belief in the Dreamwalker's Child. The boy was not an ally: he was a dangerous threat to Vermia's plans and therefore he would have to die.

Hekken smiled again. He had to hand it to those Intelligence boys. He'd only given them twenty-four hours to come up with something, but that black and white photograph was a stroke of genius. For a moment, they'd even got him believing it.

As the convoy took a left onto the road towards the air-base, Hekken realised how much he was looking forward to seeing all of Odoursin's hate and bitterness unleashed on the Dreamwalker's Child.

There was only one thing driving Odoursin now and that was revenge.

By the time he'd finished with the boy, there would be nothing left of him.

Fifteen

Stepping through the door, Sam felt the warm, steamy air all around him and caught the heavy scent of decay. It reminded him of the smell of the water in a flower vase which has been left to stagnate, of apples and plums rotting at the bottom of the fruit bowl, of the dead cat he had once found in the churchyard under the shadow of a yew tree.

Guards appeared and shouted orders at the prisoners as they gathered inside the door. Sam felt his stomach lurch. More shouting came from outside and then suddenly Skipper came flying through the doorway at high speed. She lost her footing and Sam thought she would fall head first onto the concrete floor, but to his amazement she tucked her head down onto her chest, flicked her feet up behind her and executed a perfect somersault in mid-air. She landed gracefully on the balls of her feet and stretched her arms up in a Y shape, like an Olympic gymnast finishing a gold-medal performance before a panel of judges.

'Tah-dah!' she said, smiling. 'Don't you just *love* Monday mornings?'

In spite of everything, Sam found himself smiling too. He watched as she brushed the white powder from her hair, heard her mutter something about 'terrible dandruff' and remembered what she had said about the wreckage on the airfield.

'That was my wasp . . .'

Surely she couldn't mean that she had flown it? A child, the pilot of a *wasp*? It was ridiculous, of course. But as he looked at her standing there, so small and confident with her hands on her hips and those deep-blue eyes taking everything in, he was sure of one thing. He had never met anyone quite like her in his life.

'You and you!'

It was Stick Boy, as Skipper had called him. He was using his stick to point at them.

'Get over to tank thirty-seven. You're on feeding detail.'

He turned his attention to a group of men standing behind them.

'You four – egg maintenance. And there'd better not be any accidents this time. You know the penalty. Remember what happened to prisoner 453.'

The men shuffled off and Sam silently bet that whoever prisoner 453 was, he didn't get 'Employee of the Month' award.

'Are you two still here? Get moving!'

The guard raised his stick as if to strike them, and Skipper quickly pushed Sam towards a spiral staircase leading down to the main part of the building below ground level.

At the bottom of the steps, Sam stopped and let out a low whistle. 'Wow,' he said. 'Check it *out*!'

'Mmm,' said Skipper, deadpan. 'Delightful, isn't it? No expense spared.'

They were on the floor of a large factory. Running around the walls were a series of metal gantries on several levels which was patrolled by fearsome-looking guards. Every now and then one of them would stop and shout orders to a prisoner working below, or alert one of the guards patrolling the floor to a problem that had been spotted from above.

Overhead, huge pyramid-shaped lights glared down upon fifty or more tanks of water, each one the size of a small swimming pool. The sides of the tanks were a couple of metres high and made of a silver-coloured metal. Steam drifted upwards in ghostly wisps as the heat from the factory caused some of the surface water to evaporate, and high above a cloud of water vapour spread itself out over the lights like a grey spectre. Condensation ran down the walls and trickled into drains set into the floor.

'Come on,' said Skipper.

They made their way across the floor between several tanks with rafts of glistening, jelly-like spheres floating on the surface of the water. Each sphere was about the size of a football and contained a white, comma-shaped dot which every now and then would twitch and squirm.

'Those are the eggs,' Skipper told him. 'They'll be ready for transfer to the nursery tanks in a couple of days.'

'What are the nursery tanks?'

'That's where we're going,' replied Skipper, steering him around a prisoner who was withdrawing a long probe from one of the tanks. 'It's where the young mosquito larvae are fed on nutrient-rich food for a few days. That gets them to the stage where they are ready to pupate. After that –'

'Let me guess,' said Sam. 'They take them to the pupation tanks?'

'Very good, Sam,' said Skipper. 'Are you sure you're not in the mosquito-breeding business?'

They stopped next to a large pile of white, granular powder with the consistency of sand. The pile was twice as high as Sam and several metres wide. Two large spades were stuck into it.

Skipper slapped the side of a tank underneath a square plaque with the number 37 printed on it.

'This is us. Tank thirty-seven.'

A guard with a shaven, egg-shaped head leant over the railings of the gantry above the tank and glared down at them.

'Get to work down there!' he shouted. 'This ain't a holiday camp!'

'Here,' said Skipper, handing Sam a spade. 'Get shovelling, quick.'

She picked up the other one, dug into the pile and in one smooth movement threw a spadeful of the stuff into the tank. There was a *ffflump* as it hit the water and the next moment the surface erupted, bubbling and boiling as the larvae went into a feeding frenzy, their tails thrashing against the tank and sending waves splashing over the sides.

Sam, who had been standing right next to the tank, was drenched in warm water as it slopped onto his head. He shook himself and plunged his own spade into the pile of what he now realised was larvae food, throwing it quickly over the side into the churning waters.

The two of them carried on in silence for a few minutes. The combination of hard manual work, heat and humidity meant that Sam's face was soon running with perspiration. He was breathing heavily too, and when he saw after a while that the guard had walked along the gantry in the opposite direction, he stopped, leant on his spade and wiped his brow with a damp sleeve.

'How long do we have to do this for?' he asked.

Skipper stopped work for a moment and looked at him. 'All day and every day,' she said. 'These things eat like pigs, and when they're finished they just move a new batch up. It's never-ending.'

'Couldn't they get machines to do it?' asked Sam. 'I mean, it would be easy enough, wouldn't it?'

'Oh yeah, they could do it, no problem,' said Skipper. 'They've got the technology all right. But they don't need to. This way, they not only get free labour but get to punish all those who don't happen to think the same way as they do. Enemies of the state, that's what we are. And they're making us pay for it.'

Sam had never considered himself to be an enemy of the state, but he was intrigued nonetheless. 'So who are all these people? What did they do?'

'Most of them just got in the way,' replied Skipper. 'After the war, when Odoursin was defeated by the Vahlzian armies, he retreated back through Mazria and took his anger out on the towns and villages which were in his way. Some people escaped, lots more died, but those left were rounded up and put to work.'

'So where are we now?' asked Sam.

'Just outside Vermia. Before the war Vermia was called Kilvus, the capital city of Mazria, but Odoursin captured and renamed it. He used the surviving inhabitants to modernise and rebuild it. Other prisoners from the surrounding villages were put to work in his factories. He wants to get rid of them all eventually. That's why he keeps bringing more in.'

'That's terrible,' said Sam. 'How long ago did all this happen?'

'Well, the war ended about ten years ago. So I suppose that's how long some of them have been here.' Skipper shook her head unhappily. 'It's a bad business.'

Sam looked around at all the workers toiling away across the factory floor.

'Why are most of them men?' he asked. 'What about all the women and children from the villages?'

Skipper looked sad and paused as though she was

remembering something. 'Well, some of them were children when they first came here,' she said. 'Odoursin picked the strong ones to come and work in his factories along with the men. But as you saw at the prison, conditions are harsh, food is scarce and it gets bitterly cold in winter. Unfortunately, many didn't even survive the first year.'

Sam could hardly believe his ears. This place was much, much worse than he had imagined. 'What about the women?'

'Some were left to fend for themselves after their villages had been destroyed. Many were killed. But generally Odoursin believes women are so useless they can't possibly pose any threat to his plans.'

For a brief moment Sam noticed a hardness in Skipper's eyes, a flicker of hatred that rose from somewhere deep inside of her. Then she smiled and it was gone.

'You can probably guess how much I look forward to proving him wrong on that one.'

Sam stared at the small girl standing next to him, trying to figure her out.

'How long have you been here?' he asked.

'Not long – only since I crashed and burned. It was pretty hairy stuff, I can tell you.'

Skipper stuck out the thumb and little finger on her hand like tiny wings and demonstrated a steep dive. She acted looking horrified, said a little 'Oh no' and added the noise of an explosion at the end for dramatic effect.

Sam looked at her with admiration. 'So you really can fly those things?'

Skipper grinned. 'Been flying them for about two years now. And,' she added ruefully, 'crashing them for about as long.'

Sam thought for a moment. 'You said you came to try and find me. How did you know I was here?'

'Intelligence,' said Skipper. 'They've been watching you for some time. But your change of appearance was never mentioned in the planning – I think it's taken everyone by surprise, including Odoursin's mob, luckily. It seems someone else is looking out for you too, Sam. Probably the Olumnus – they're the only ones with the ability to change the way you look. Whoever it is, they saved you from Odoursin for a while.'

'Skipper,' said Sam, 'why is it that whenever you try and explain something to me I end up even more confused?'

As he spoke, his head began to feel incredibly itchy. He put a hand up to scratch it and saw that Skipper was staring at him with a worried expression on her face.

'Oh no,' she said. 'I think I spoke too soon. Whatever they did, it's wearing off.'

Sam brought his hand down and saw that some hair had come away from his head. The itching suddenly became much stronger and as he scratched himself again, great clumps of black hair fell from his scalp onto the floor. Simultaneously his skin started to twitch and his face began to move and stretch involuntarily. Sam put his hands up to his face and felt the muscles doing a crazy dance.

'What's happening to me?' he cried.

The twitching intensified until it felt like a thousand small animals running about under his skin. Sam fell against the side of the tank and curled up into a ball, his whole body trembling and jerking spasmodically until finally the convulsions subsided and he lay panting on the wet floor.

He felt a hand on his shoulder. Skipper knelt beside him and gently pulled him up into a sitting position.

'What happened?' he whispered.

'Look,' said Skipper. She turned him so that he was facing the metal wall of the tank.

Sam looked at his reflection. The brown eyes and black hair were gone. Instead, a familiar pair of surprised green eyes stared back at him from beneath a thatch of brown hair and he recognised the face as his own once more.

'Welcome back, Sam,' said Skipper. 'Now we really are in trouble.'

She helped him to his feet. He felt dizzy. Taking a deep breath, he looked up and noticed a group of people moving quickly towards them along the gantry from the far end of the building. Hekken led the group and a little way behind him, shielded by four or five guards, was a tall man wearing a long green leather coat. Sam shuddered at the memory of his previous encounter with Odoursin.

He guessed why they were here. Either their DNA testing had surprised them by proving positive or they must have discovered that his story about the boy on the marshes was false. Either way, now that his appearance had changed, there could be no question about his true identity.

Skipper saw the worried look on Sam's face and turned to see the approaching group. Moving like quicksilver, she seized Sam by the front of his uniform and threw him hard into the pile of larvae feed.

'What the hell are you doing?' he protested.

'Quickly, dig yourself in,' she hissed. 'If they see you now we've had it!'

She seized a spade and began shovelling the white feed over him. Sam dug feverishly with his hands in a desperate effort to bury himself in the stuff, hands scrabbling frantically like a dog in the sand. The larvae feed had a fishy, eggy smell and it clogged his mouth and nostrils as he tunnelled down into it.

His whole body was covered now. The weight of the feed pressed down on him and he twisted round onto his back in order to breath. Skipper threw several more spadefuls over him and then used her hands to cover his face until only his eyes and nose were left uncovered.

'Don't move,' she said. 'I'll handle this.'

Sam watched as she picked up the spade again and started pitching feed into the tank. The weight of the feed piled up on him and the fact that his mouth was completely covered made it almost impossible to breathe, but the thought of being discovered was enough to keep him motionless.

He heard a shout from the gantry.

Skipper kept right on shovelling.

Sam heard the sound of boots clanging down metal stairways. Moments later, Hekken and his henchmen arrived. Stick Boy was with them.

'Ah,' said Hekken, 'if it isn't the little pilot girl. Things must be bad if they had to send you to do their dirty work for them.'

Skipper thrust her spade into the pile as if to carry on, but Stick Boy moved forward and held his baton across her chest, barring her way.

'My, my, and such a keen worker too,' Hekken continued. 'I wonder, did you find what you were looking for?'

Skipper remained silent.

'What's the matter? Cat got your tongue?' He moved towards her. 'The thing is, you see, His Excellency has lost something that belongs to him, and he's very upset about it. So upset, in fact, that he's come all the way down here himself to help us find it.'

Hekken looked up at the gantry, where Odoursin stood watching. Then he took another step forward, so that his face was inches away from Skipper's.

'Tell me,' he said, 'where's your little friend?'

'I don't know what you're talking about,' said Skipper.

'Oh, I think you do,' said Hekken. He drew a long silver knife and stroked the flat of the blade against Skipper's cheek. 'Shall I help you remember?'

'Oh, you mean the boy I was working with?' Skipper said.

Hekken looked across at Stick Boy and raised his eyebrows.

Stick Boy nodded.

'Yes,' said Hekken. 'Well done. I see your memory is miraculously returning. Now, suppose you tell us where he is.'

'He went off about five minutes ago,' said Skipper. 'Said he was fed up with working here and he was going back to the marshes. I don't think he'll get far with all those guards around though, do you?'

Hekken's eyes flashed angrily. 'Seal the building,' he ordered. 'Then bring in the hunters.' He turned on his heel and walked back towards the steps.

As Stick Boy and a couple of the guards ran off in the direction of the entrance, Sam looked out from his hiding place and saw, just for a moment, a look of real fear on Skipper's face. With a sinking feeling he realised that, however bad things had been up until now, they were about to get worse.

Sixteen

The sound of the siren was deafening as it climbed from a low, moaning bass note to a sustained, high-pitched howl. For perhaps thirty seconds or so the noise split the air and then, as suddenly as it had started, it stopped. An eerie silence followed. No one moved and no one spoke.

Then came the crackle of a public-address system being switched on, and the building filled with the quiet, menacing whispers of a voice that Sam knew only too well.

'Hello, Sam,' said Odoursin. 'I know you're here. I can feel it . . .'

Beneath the pile of larvae feed, Sam started to tremble.

'. . . and we both know that you lied to me. That's right, Sam. You lied, told me things that weren't true. And now you think that you can hide from me too. You have much to learn.'

Sam was shaking now. He felt sick with fear. Why had he listened to Skipper? If he'd told Odoursin who he was in the first place then none of this would have happened. Now they would find him and there was no escape. He lay still, frozen with terror, as the voice continued.

'You have a choice, Sam. You can give yourself up now and we can start again. That would be the sensible thing to do. Or, alternatively, you can carry on hiding and we will come and find you. Either way, this foolish charade will soon be at an end. But you must understand that if we have to come and look for you, your safety cannot be guaranteed. Our methods will not be pleasant. So what is it to be? You have ten seconds to decide.'

Sam just wanted it to be over and done with. If he gave himself up now, he would still have a chance, wouldn't he? He might still be allowed to go home. But then he remembered all the things Skipper had told him about Odoursin, and he knew in his heart that what she had said was true. They would find him anyway, and bad things would happen, of that he had no doubt. But he wouldn't make it easy for them.

He bit his lip and stayed exactly where he was.

'I see that you are obstinate and foolish as well as a liar,' said the voice over the loudspeakers. 'Very well then. Expect no mercy. From darkness you came and to darkness you shall return.'

There was a pause. Sam felt his heart thump in his chest and heard the blood roar in his ears.

Then came the voice of Odoursin once more, hard and insistent: 'Seek him out,' it hissed. 'Seek – him – out!'

There was the rumble of doors sliding open, followed by loud shouts and cries of alarm. Sam could hear people running and he watched despairingly as Skipper fell sobbing to her knees in front of Hekken as he strode back towards her.

'Please,' she cried, 'please don't let them hurt him. He hasn't done anything wrong!'

She grabbed hold of Hekken's jacket, seemingly half out of her mind with terror, but Hekken simply kicked her sprawling backwards against the tank.

'Save your prayers for yourself, little girl,' he said. 'You're going to need them.'

He turned away and walked back towards the gantry.

Sam turned his attention back to where Skipper had fallen and was amazed to see that she was already up on her feet again. The tears had miraculously disappeared and she was running towards him with a look of steely determination on her face. She promptly began digging with her hands, talking hurriedly to him as she did so.

'OK, Sam, listen to me. Listen carefully. In a minute you're going to see some things that might scare you a bit.'

She looked quickly away to her right, as if checking something beyond Sam's line of vision, and then turned back and began digging even more furiously.

'But whatever happens, whatever you see, try not to panic. And whatever you do, don't freeze up on me, because when I say go you're going to have to run like you never ran before in your life. Do you understand?'

Sam nodded. His arms were free now and he helped dig himself out.

'OK,' said Skipper as Sam pulled his legs free, 'here they come. Remember – stick close to me!'

As he emerged from the feed pile, Sam heard a commotion over to his left and turned to look at the source of the noise. What he saw stopped him in his tracks and he heard himself cry out in terror.

A huge, six-legged creature with reddish skin was bearing down on them at great speed, scuttling between the tanks and swaying its head from side to side as it searched for its prey. Poison dripped from its pincer-like jaws, hissing and steaming as it hit the floor. Above its head two antennae twitched, sniffing out the chemical signals that would lead it to its quarry.

Straight away, Sam recognised it as a red ant; he had studied them many times in his garden. He knew that they had a painful bite and an excellent sense of smell, but he had never before had any reason to fear them.

But then, the ones in his garden were just a few millimetres long and generally paid him no attention. This one was the size of a bus and it wanted to kill him.

It was a crucial difference.

A worker at a nearby tank dropped his spade and tried to make a break for it. The ant swivelled its head at the sound of the spade hitting the concrete floor and with lightning speed seized hold of him and yanked him up into the air. He flailed his arms around and cried out for help, but it was of no use; the ant crunched its powerful jaws together and tossed his broken, lifeless body to the floor. Then it began to move towards them again.

'Run!' shouted Skipper.

The ant's shadow fell across the feed pile and Skipper hared off between the breeding tanks with Sam sprinting after her. He felt the wind from the ant's head as it lunged at him and heard the hiss of poison as its jaws cracked down onto the hard floor where he had been standing only seconds before.

Ahead of him, Skipper reached the end of tank thirty-seven and took the corner at full pelt, holding the edge with her left hand as she skidded around it. Sam flew around after her, tripped over a spade and crashed into Skipper's back, sending them both tumbling to the floor. He looked up and saw that another ant was advancing rapidly towards them.

'What now?' shouted Sam. He glanced over his shoulder to see the head of the first ant emerging between the tanks. 'We're trapped!'

He turned back to see Skipper interlacing her fingers and turning her hands palm upwards. She held them out to Sam like a kind of stirrup.

'Skipper, what are you doing?' he cried. 'They're going to kill us!'

'No, they're not,' she answered, her voice surprisingly calm in the circumstances. 'Put your foot in here.'

'But –'

'Just do it, Sam!' Her voice was more urgent now.

The ants were nearly upon them. He could hear the clacking of their legs on stone and the snap, snap, snap of their jaws.

He stepped forward and placed his right foot into Skipper's upturned hands.

'Hold on to my shoulders,' she instructed.

Sam quickly did as he was told and felt her lift him off the ground. He could see out across the murky waters of the nearest tank now, see the dark shapes of the mosquito larvae hanging upside down, the breathing tubes in their tails breaking the surface like snorkels.

He just had time to turn his head and register the fact that he was staring directly into the hideous, slavering jaws of a monstrous ant before Skipper jerked her hands upwards and threw him, arms flailing, over the side of the tank.

He hit the surface with a loud smack, sending a plume of water high into the steamy air. Waves cascaded over the sides and as he sank down into the warm, soupy water he opened his eyes and saw larvae the size of dolphins wriggling away to the shadowy depths beneath. Above him, a trail of bubbles marked his own unexpected descent.

His lungs empty and crying out for oxygen, Sam gave a desperate kick and swam up to the surface. Coughing and spluttering as he emerged, he trod water and frantically looked around for a means of escape.

Below him, dark shapes moved through the murky waters. Gradually the mosquito larvae began returning to the surface, probing the air with their tails once more. Sam felt a strange current swirling beneath his feet. Trying not to panic, he attempted to lift his feet clear of whatever was down there.

Without warning, something clamped itself hard onto his leg and pulled him violently beneath the surface. Opening his eyes in the gloomy waters he saw to his horror that one of the larvae had fastened its mouth to his calf and was trying to drag him down to the bottom of the tank. The large maggoty white head twitched and jerked blindly from side to side as it tugged him lower and lower, its pale, sightless eyes unable to distinguish anything but light and shadow.

Exhausted and starved of oxygen, Sam felt like giving in. It was all too hard, too much effort trying to stay alive when everyone wanted you dead. The light was fading and the darkness closing in. Soon it would be over. He could sleep for ever.

But as his eyes closed and he started to drift away, Sam thought of Skipper. Hadn't she risked her life to save him? She could have run and saved herself, but she had stayed to help him instead. He couldn't let it all be for nothing. He had to survive, if only for her sake. She needed him.

He shook his head and, with a supreme effort, opened his eyes.

The light above him was fading fast. The creature was dragging him down towards the darkness at the bottom of the tank and Sam knew that he would have to act quickly. Summoning all his strength, he drew back his free leg and kicked at one of the larvae's unseeing eyes. The resistance of the water slowed his movements and when his foot struck the creature's eye it bounced off again. It was like kicking a child's inflatable toy.

Undeterred, he kicked out again and again until finally the creature recoiled and released its grip. Thrusting his arms above his head, Sam cupped his hands and swam hard until he broke through the surface into the harsh glare of the factory lights. Treading water for a few seconds to get his breath back, Sam saw the shadows begin to move beneath him and he quickly struck out for the side of the tank.

Pulling himself up so that his stomach was resting on the edge, he was relieved to find that there were no ants patrolling the section of floor below, although several pairs of antennae were visible between the tanks nearby. Skipper, however, was nowhere to be seen.

He had to try to find her.

He jumped over the side and ducked down, staying low and running along the alleyways that criss-crossed between the tanks. Reaching the end of one of them, he peered cautiously around the side to check that the coast was clear before darting across to the cover of the next. He knew it was only a matter of time before he was either spotted from above or hunted down by the vicious ants, but this time he wouldn't give up until he had found Skipper. He owed her that much.

His heart racing, he finally reached the end wall of the factory and found himself beneath a gantry that ran along its entire length. Above he could see the shiny black boots of the guards pacing back and forth, but he knew that unless they looked directly beneath their feet they were unlikely to spot him.

For the moment at least, he was safe.

Scanning the deserted factory floor, he realised that it must have been cleared to make it easier to track him down. There was still no sign of Skipper. All he could see were the huge ants weaving their way methodically between the tanks, antennae twitching, searching him out.

He leant heavily against the wall, exhausted. His eyes stung from the feed in the water and he rubbed them in an effort to ease the pain. As he did so he heard a clatter, followed by a loud clang. It came from the direction of the nearest tank.

Dropping his hands from his eyes, he saw to his dismay that an ant was standing only a few metres away from him.

Sam flattened himself against the wall and held his breath.

The ant stopped and moved its head slowly from side to side as though sniffing the air. Its antennae twitched, searching for clues.

Oh, please, he prayed. *Please don't find me . . .*

The ant turned and took a few steps in the opposite direction, then stopped again.

That's it – go on, keep going! urged Sam silently.

The ant seemed to hesitate for a moment, as if uncertain how to proceed.

Then it turned and stared directly at him.

Sam looked desperately around for an escape route, but there was none. The huge, monstrous ant scuttled straight towards him and, as the terrible jaws lunged forward, Sam sank to his knees and moaned in terror, waiting for it all to be over.

There was a loud thud, followed by silence. He waited for the pain, for the agonising slice of the jaws, but they never came.

Gingerly, Sam opened his eyes and was faced with the unexpected sight of the ant standing with its front legs bent and its head, which was the size of a small family car, resting on the ground in front of him. A small pool of yellow poison steamed on the floor next to its powerful jaws and its antennae continued to twitch unabated. It was staring straight at him and was obviously still very much alive.

As Sam watched, a patch of skin on the top of its head appeared to become much thinner. It wobbled and shimmered like tarmac in the heat, then suddenly dissolved away to nothing, leaving a neat, circular hole.

To his utter amazement, a small girl popped her head out of the top and winked at him.

'Hello, Sam,' said Skipper. 'Did you wonder where I'd got to?'

Seventeen

'Don't step in that stuff,' Skipper advised as Sam skirted around the steaming yellow poison pooled beneath the ant's jaws. 'It's acid. It'll burn your feet.'

Sam stepped over it and put one foot on a section of pincer that looked poison-free. He put his hands against the cold skin of the creature's head to steady himself. It felt taut and smooth with a slight grain, like old leather.

'Here,' said Skipper, leaning down and stretching her hand out. 'Grab hold.'

Sam took her hand and used his feet to scramble up the side of the head as Skipper pulled from above. After several slips, he made it to the top and sat with his feet dangling over the edge. His grey uniform steamed and he wrung out part of his sleeve. There was a hiss as droplets of water hit the poison below.

'I think we'd better get moving,' said Skipper.

She jumped back through the opening and then stuck her head out again.

'Come on in,' she said.

Sam climbed down through the hole in the ant's head and found himself sliding into a leather seat with arm- and headrests. It was very comfortable.

Laid out in front of him was an instrument panel with numerous backlit dials which glowed red in the darkness. He noticed one marked 'GLUCOSE LEVELS' and another with 'FORWARD-SPEED INDICATOR' written next to it. A third showed a three-dimensional diagram of the ant and had 'DAMAGE INDICATOR' printed underneath. A small red light was flashing on the underside of the diagram.

Further along was a small, square screen displaying the words 'CHEMICAL ODOUR MATCH' with some sort of green block graph above it and '93% MATCH' showing at the top. Next to it was another screen with a line down the middle. It had the words 'SUBJECT IDENTIFICATION' written beneath it.

Sam was surprised to see that on one side of the line was a picture of him standing against the factory wall with his mouth open in terror, obviously taken only minutes earlier. More shocking still, however, was the image next to it. It showed him standing in his bedroom next to the window, wearing his stripy pyjamas. At the top of the screen were the words '100% MATCH'.

Skipper tapped her finger on the screen displaying the image of Sam in his pyjamas. 'Nice outfit,' she said. '*Very* nice.'

She stood up, took a silver torch-like object from her

pocket and pointed it at the hole above them. The end pulsed with a brilliant blue light and the hole disappeared, as if painted out with an invisible brush, leaving no sign that it had ever been there.

'Wow,' said Sam. 'How did you do that?'

'With this,' said Skipper, waving the little torch. 'It's a compact generator with an enhanced CRB. I whipped it from Hekken's pocket when I was being all soppy and pretending to cry. He'll go nuts when he finds out I've nicked it – they cost a fortune.' Seeing the confused look on Sam's face, she said, 'Sorry. A CRB is a cellular-restructuring beam. You can use it to rearrange the cell structure of biological organisms without actually damaging them. It's like jumbling up the pieces of a puzzle and then putting them back together again. It was originally used in medicine for surgery and that kind of thing. But now it's used in all the insect programmes. It means you can have a door where and when you want it without causing any long-term damage to the organism.'

She leant forward and began flicking switches. A large, curved screen lit up in front of them and Sam could see an image of the factory wall where he had been standing a few minutes earlier. He watched as she pulled a pencil-sized stick towards her and he felt the head of the ant begin to rise.

'I should fasten your seat belt if I were you,' said Skipper. 'I think we could be in for a bit of a rough ride.'

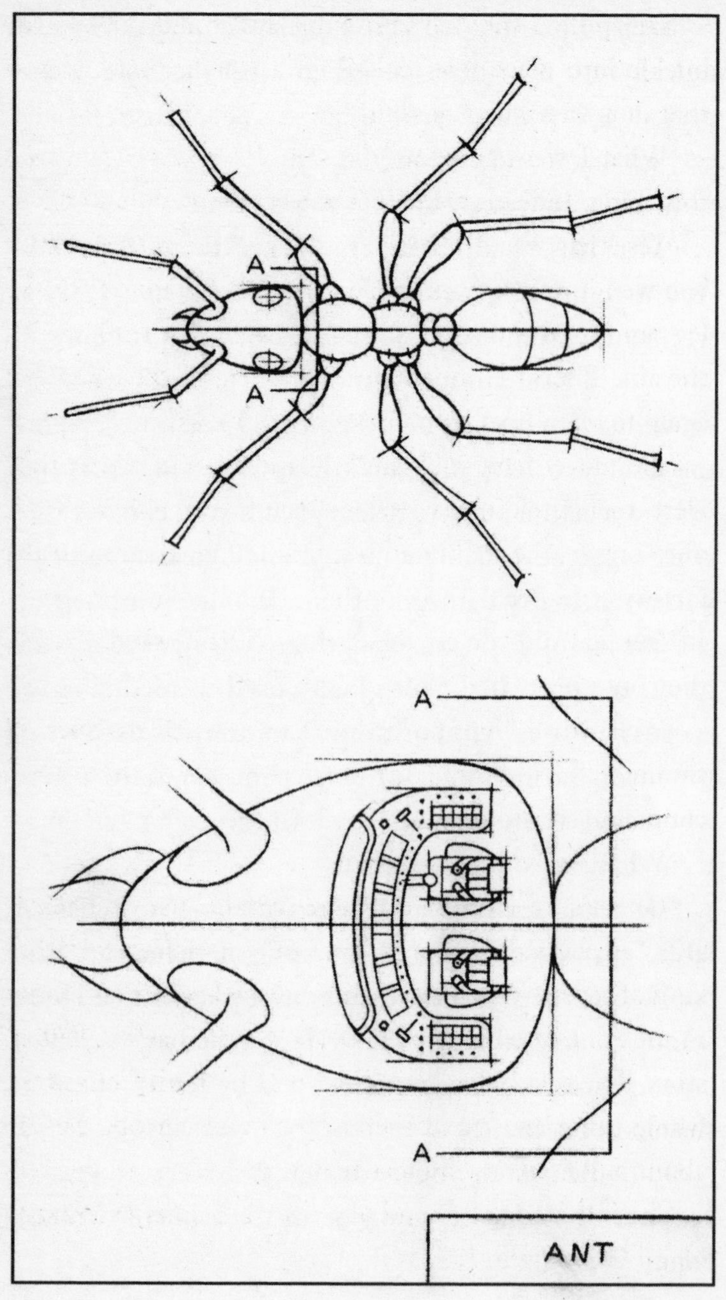
A
A
A
A
ANT

Sam pulled the belt across his chest and clicked the buckle into place. He looked up at the screen and saw that they were turning round.

'What I want to know,' he said, 'is how you got into this thing. I mean, weren't there already people in it?'

'Yes, that was a bit tricky,' Skipper admitted. 'After you went into the tank I managed to climb up one of the legs and used the CRB to make a small hole underneath the ant. Then I climbed onto the ant's head and used it again to open up a hatch into the cockpit.'

She moved the stick slightly and Sam saw that they were turning left past the end tank and moving back onto one of the main paths which led up a ramp to the factory entrance.

'But how did you get the crew out?' Sam asked. 'Didn't they put up a fight?'

'Well, no – not at first anyway,' said Skipper. 'I shouted, "Drill bomb!" and they were out of there like a couple of greyhounds.'

'What's a drill bomb?' asked Sam.

'Oh, it's an explosive device that we use to destroy ants,' explained Skipper. 'They're cone-shaped with a kind of screw at the pointy end. All it takes is for a soldier to stick one into the ant's underbelly and that's it. End of story. The bomb drills up into the body cavity, blows the whole thing apart and there's not much anyone can do about it. Ant crews are terrified of them.'

She imitated the sound of a drill. 'Zzzzzzzzzzzzzzzip, blam! Goodnight, Mr Ant!'

Sam frowned. 'But you didn't have a drill bomb.'

'Well, I know that,' said Skipper, 'and you know that. But the important thing is, they didn't. And the hole I'd made underneath the ant showed up on the damage indicator inside the cockpit, with exactly the sort of damage you'd get if someone had just put a drill bomb there.'

'Ingenious,' said Sam, impressed. He wondered where she had learned all this stuff.

'Of course, once they climbed out and saw me, they smelt a rat,' Skipper continued. 'But by then I had the element of surprise.'

She leant across the instrument panel and eased a small handle forward. Sam saw the display on the speed indicator lengthen and felt himself being pushed back in his seat as they accelerated.

'So what happened?'

Skipper chuckled. 'They went swimming,' she said. 'I hear the water's lovely at this time of year.'

Sam looked up at the screen. There were several ants in front of them now and he could see others moving down the alleyways to their left. Skipper flicked a switch and the screen cut to a rear view showing more ants following behind.

'Looks as though we're all headed in the same direction,' said Sam as the picture returned to its original view of the way ahead.

'Mmm.' Skipper sounded worried. 'Let's see if we can find out what's going on.'

She pressed a button above her head and speakers on either side of the cockpit crackled into life. There was the sound of a man's voice speaking, although it was distorted and hard to hear. Skipper moved one of several slider controls and the static disappeared. The voice could now be heard clearly: '*Confirm that Subject A cannot be found and is believed to have left the immediate area. All units to conduct immediate external search of compound. Search now extended to second Subject B, suspected of assisting Subject A. Image now loading for identification . . .*'

Skipper pressed a green button on the instrument panel and the image of Sam in the small display window was replaced by one of Skipper next to a larvae tank with her hands in the air. Part of Sam's foot was just visible at the edge of the frame.

'Good action shot,' said Sam, 'You look a bit serious though.'

Skipper sniggered. 'Shh! I want to hear what else they're saying.'

'. . . *imperative that they are found immediately. The escape of subjects would constitute breach of security at the highest level and any preservation orders that were previously in existence have now been terminated.*'

Sam glanced across at Skipper and saw that her smile had vanished.

'What was all that about?' he asked. 'Preservation orders have now been terminated. What does that mean exactly?'

'It means,' said Skipper, her expression thoughtful in

the red glow from the instruments, 'that if they catch us, they'll kill us.'

Sam felt the fear returning and the colour drained from his face.

Skipper noticed and put a hand on his arm. 'Don't worry,' she said. 'They've got to catch us first.'

They approached a steep ramp leading up to a huge pair of double doors which were being opened to let the ants out into the main compound.

Outside, a grey blanket of cloud hung in the sky above the fields and a curtain of mist and rain was sweeping across the damp airfield. A cold wind wrinkled the surface of the puddles that lay dotted across the tarmac.

Sam counted. They were fourth in a line of ants now, waiting their turn in the queue. He looked to his left and watched scores of mosquito larvae wriggle away from the surface as the ant's shadow moved across the water of their tank.

They shuffled forwards as the first ant moved through the double doors. Two more and they'd be out.

The second ant moved forwards a few steps and then paused.

'Come on,' said Skipper quietly. 'Come on.'

Suddenly several soldiers appeared and began pointing excitedly at the line of ants. Sam noticed that they all carried shiny guns with short, stubby barrels.

An armoured car reversed up next to the ant in the doorway and stopped. A panel in the top slid open and a ladder began to extend upwards from it. Two more men now joined the group by the doors. They appeared to be extremely wet and agitated.

'Uh oh,' said Skipper. 'This is not looking good.'

The ladder stopped at the ant's head and two soldiers climbed up. The first used a CRB to create an opening in the head just as Skipper had done, while the second trained his gun on the hole as it appeared. A crewman emerged from the opening and after a brief discussion he disappeared back inside again. The soldiers climbed down the ladder and the ant moved out through the doors.

Sam watched the ant in front of them walk forwards up the ramp and stop next to the ladder. The soldiers climbed onto its head and began opening it up.

'They're going to check them all,' said Sam anxiously. 'They're going to check them all and we're next.'

Skipper stuck out her bottom lip and nodded, her blue eyes hard and determined. 'I think we're going to have to make a run for it,' she said. 'Are you ready?'

Sam tightened his seat belt. 'Yeah,' he said. 'Go for it.'

Skipper took a deep breath, switched the screen to rear view and pushed the stick back as far as it would go.

Sam was thrown forward against his belt as the ant powered backwards and the image of a larvae tank filled the screen. There was a loud crash as they hit the side of it, followed by a thunderous roar as the thin metal buckled inwards and thousands of gallons of water poured out onto the factory floor. Sam was slammed back into his seat and as they skidded forward Skipper's fingers danced expertly across the levers and switches. Sam saw the screen return to a front view just as they crashed into the ant in front of them, which crumpled to the ground. A soldier who had been standing on it fell with a thump against the screen, slid off and disappeared into the torrent of water which swept down into the drains, leaving the huge white larvae flapping and twitching on the floor like stranded fish on a beach.

Skipper rammed the lever forward and they accelerated up the ramp, through the double doors and away across the compound. There was the sound of gunfire and a line of bullets ripped through the cockpit just behind Sam's head, missing him by inches and punching four neat exit holes in the roof.

'Hell's teeth!' shouted Skipper, and pushed the stick to the left. They swerved violently sideways and she switched the screen to rear view again. Sam could see that a group of ants was closing in on them.

A second red light began flashing on the damage-indicator display, accompanied by a loud, intermittent buzzer. 'What's that?' shouted Sam, pointing at the red light on the lower abdomen, next to the first.

In one smooth, fluid sequence of movements, Skipper unbuckled Sam's belt, pulled the CRB from her pocket, opened a large circular hole in the floor and pushed him through it. Before he even realised what was happening, Sam was falling through the air and bouncing and tumbling across the wet grass, finally slithering to a halt beneath the dark, looming shape of a large horsefly.

He sat up in time to see Skipper hit the ground and roll over as the ant thundered on towards the perimeter fence with the others close behind it. He saw her run towards him and then there was a blinding white flash followed by the thump of a large explosion. Sam watched in horror as Skipper was blown off her feet, while behind her a sheet of red and orange flame ripped through the ant and tore it apart, hurling white-hot fragments high into the air and gouging a deep, smoking crater into the earth. Then a powerful pressure wave from the explosion hit Sam full in the face, scorching through his hair and blowing him backwards. Something fell down heavily next to him and, turning his face sideways, he saw that it was Skipper. She was on fire.

Struggling to his knees, Sam threw himself on top of her in a desperate attempt to smother the blaze, rolling her over and over in the wet grass until the last of the flames was extinguished.

He heard the shouts of soldiers in the distance and the dull thud of debris falling from the sky. Droplets of rain glistened on blades of grass and, as he gulped the cool morning air deep into his lungs, the smell of damp earth filled his nostrils.

Skipper lay on her back next to him. Her eyes were closed and she wasn't moving.

'Skipper,' breathed Sam. 'Skipper, are you OK?'

There was no reply.

Sam's heart was pounding.

'Skipper,' he repeated more urgently. 'Skipper, please say something.'

He knelt over her and looked down at her face. She looked as though she was asleep. *No,* thought Sam. *She can't be. Please don't let her be . . .*

He frantically loosened the clothing around her neck and put his head on her chest. If he could just hear a heartbeat, even the faintest one . . .

Three unexpected little taps on his head made him sit up and he was taken aback to see Skipper's face, wide-eyed and grinning, beneath him.

'Now that,' she said, 'is what I call an *explosion*. Fantastic!'

Sam sat back on his haunches and, as Skipper raised herself up on one elbow, he cuffed her lightly around the head with a mixture of relief and exasperation.

'I thought you'd gone and died on me!' he said.

Skipper sat up and rubbed her head. 'Nah! Takes more than a drill bomb to finish me off.' Little bits of black ash floated out of her hair. 'Heck of a bang though, wasn't it? Sorry to push you out like that – but you really don't want to be sitting on top of one of those when they go off.'

Sam took a deep breath and put his hand on her arm. 'Thanks, Skipper,' he said. 'That's twice you've saved my life today.'

Skipper looked over his shoulder to where the ants were gathering around the flaming wreckage. Sam followed her gaze and saw that they were already beginning to fan out towards them.

'Well, I don't want to worry you,' she said slowly, 'but I think I'm going to have to make that a hat trick.'

As Skipper helped him into the cockpit, Sam saw that the interior of the horsefly was infinitely more complex than the inside of the ant had been. There were at least twice the number of dials, buttons and screens and the whole cockpit was bathed in a dim green light. As he strapped himself in he noticed that the scramble up the horsefly's leg had brought his arms out in a livid red rash. He made a face and rubbed them against the front of his uniform.

'Nasty,' said Skipper. She flipped on the external monitors and the whole cockpit brightened as the screens flickered into life to show a 360-degree view of the airfield.

'Yep, they've spotted us. Don't give up, do they?'

The ants had come together and were rapidly approaching their position en masse.

'I don't understand why they want us so badly,' said Sam. 'What did we ever do to them?'

'Well, let's see,' replied Skipper, her hands moving rapidly across the instrument panel in preparation for take-off. 'We've wrecked a larvae tank, stolen an expensive CRB, blown up a hi-tech search-and-destroy ant, hijacked a top-of-the-range horsefly, crashed it . . .'

'What do you mean, crashed it?' Sam interrupted. 'We haven't even taken off yet.'

Skipper grinned wryly as she flipped a couple of switches above her head. 'Well, you know me – I'm a creature of habit. Trouble is, I've got a tendency to laugh at the wrong moment, and my front teeth pop the airbag.'

'You *are* joking,' said Sam uncertainly, watching the approaching ants on the external monitor. He'd learned not to take anything for granted where Skipper was concerned.

'Relax,' she said. 'I could fly one of these things with my eyes shut.'

Sam looked worried. 'Please don't.'

'OK. Eyes open it is.' Skipper pushed a glowing red button and Sam heard the low hum of the wings starting up. 'Right, if we go now, they won't get up in time to catch us.'

'But all that damage we did,' Sam went on, 'that's not why they're after us. That happened *because* they were after us. They want us for something else.'

'Correction,' said Skipper. 'They want *you* for something else. Not me. They're not interested in me, except for the fact that I'm stopping them getting to you. It's you they want. Now – if you'll just let me concentrate . . .'

'But why?' he whispered. 'Why me?'

'Good question,' said Skipper as the horsefly lifted up into the air and little puffs of anti-aircraft fire began to explode in the sky around them. 'I think maybe it's time you met the Commander.'

Eighteen

They had been travelling for several hours now and there were no signs of Vermian aircraft pursuing them. For the first hour or so, Skipper had flown the horsefly at such speed through narrow mountain passes that at first Sam had felt certain they would crash, but after a while he had begun to realise that Skipper was simply an exceptional flier. Even if they had been followed, Sam doubted that any Vermian pilot would have been able to get anywhere near her.

Now he peered out through the screen and saw that they were flying over a steep river valley. Below them a thick pine forest covered the valley floor, gradually thinning out on the higher slopes where dry bushes and the occasional broad-leaved tree seemed to grow straight out of the hard, barren rocks. It was late afternoon and the sun was weakening above the horizon, deep shades of orange and yellow spilling out into the surrounding sky like paint on wet paper.

'Beautiful, isn't it?' said Skipper.

Sam nodded. 'I thought it would be a while before I saw open spaces again,' he said.

Skipper pushed the control lever forward and they began to descend. Sam caught sight of a silver stream twisting through the forest, its surface glittering as the fading sunlight shone through the trees and was reflected in its bright waters.

'I know what you mean,' said Skipper. 'Sometimes when things are bad you start to wonder if the good things in your life were ever really true. You start to think that maybe the world was always full of people who wanted to hurt you.'

Sam turned to look at her. 'But you always look so happy. Like nothing can touch you.'

Skipper shrugged. 'You've got to keep on keeping on. I always say to myself, "Skipper, something will turn up." And you know what? It usually does. Generally when you're least expecting it. Thinking about that helps you through the bad stuff.'

'Yeah, I s'pose so,' said Sam.

He watched Skipper lean across the control panel and noticed for the first time that her arms were covered in bruises. He realised then how she must have suffered; how they must have tried to break her, to crush her spirit.

But as he looked into her deep blue eyes and saw how the fire inside her still burned as brightly as ever, he knew that – whatever happened – there was no one else he would rather have by his side.

The afternoon shadows were lengthening as Skipper flew the horsefly out of the valley and over a vast open plain. Here the trees began to thin out and clumps of sun-bleached grass and wizened shrubs shared the dry, dusty earth with boulders and stones. Away in the distance, wrinkled skirts of rock gathered around the flat-topped mountains.

Skipper turned the fly around and set it down at the edge of the forest, walking it forwards until it was partially hidden by branches. Now that they were up close, Sam began to appreciate the sheer size of the trees. Each one towered at least fifty metres into the air and was covered in a thick, spongy, reddish-brown bark. The massive trunks were anchored to the ground by thick aerial roots which curved outwards from the base of the trees before plunging through a thick layer of pine needles into the soil beneath. The lower third of each trunk was punctured by dark holes, sockets that had been left where branches had fallen or been torn off by winter storms.

'They'll extend their search out here soon,' Skipper said. 'If we hide it in the trees there'll be less chance of them spotting us from the air. They'll probably be expecting us to fly straight to Vahlzi. But if we stay here overnight, we can get some rest and head for Vahlzi first thing in the morning.'

Sam wasn't looking forward to climbing down the fly's leg and was relieved to see Skipper throw out a rope ladder. As he descended he caught the scent of pine needles on the breeze and watched the dappled patterns of sunlight on the forest floor below.

By the time he reached the bottom, Skipper was already scurrying around collecting armfuls of bracken and dried grass.

'Give us a hand, will you?' she called.

'Sure,' said Sam. 'Of course.' He began pulling up big clumps of the crackly brown and green bracken that grew where sunlight filtered through the canopy. After a while he had made a pile that came up to his waist. He stood proudly next to it for a while, watching Skipper diligently adding to her own growing collection, and then called out, 'Skipper – what are we doing exactly?'

Skipper looked at him in surprise. 'We're collecting bracken,' she said.

'Well, I know *that*,' said Sam, 'but what I really want to know is – why?'

'Because we're going to need some shelter tonight,' replied Skipper, 'so I'm going to build us a tree house.'

Sam looked at Skipper, tilted his head back to look at the top of the nearest pine tree, then turned to look back at Skipper again.

'A tree house,' he said. 'Up there?'

'Well, it's a tree, isn't it?' said Skipper patiently. 'And I'm going to build a house in it. So that makes it a tree house.'

'But,' protested Sam, twisting his neck to look back up

at the top of the tree again, 'that's impossible. It's too high.'

Skipper threw her bundle of bracken down at the base of the tree and put her hands on her hips. 'For someone who's gone from riding his bike down the road to getting locked in prison, thrown in a tank of mosquito larvae and escaping from giant ants in a horsefly, I'd have thought you'd have learned to be a bit more cautious with your use of the word "impossible".'

Sam had to admit she had a point.

Ten minutes later he watched in admiration as Skipper raced quickly and easily up and down the huge tree trunk carrying bits of wood and bracken tied to her back with lengths of vine. He tried to help at first, but after several failed attempts at climbing the tree, Skipper suggested he collect materials on the ground while she got busy with construction up at the top.

To watch her work was, quite simply, breathtaking. She had no fear of heights and leapt from branch to branch fifty metres or more above the ground, apparently unconcerned that one slip would almost certainly result in death.

In less than an hour, she had constructed a wooden platform wide enough for two people to lie down on comfortably and a canopy of bracken which curved over the top to provide shelter from the elements. She then helped Sam find footholds in the tree trunk and showed him how to pull himself up by the thick aerial roots until he reached the rope ladder which she had taken from the horsefly. Helped by Skipper's shouts of

'That's it!' and 'Don't look down!' he carefully made a slow and cautious ascent to the top of the tree.

'This is amazing,' said Sam. He bit into the mushroom-like flesh of one of the wild truffles that Skipper had unearthed from the forest floor and savoured its rich, musky flavour. 'Is there anything you can't do?'

They sat cross-legged on the platform of thick branches, a woven tapestry of wood that Skipper had broken from the upper canopy and collected from the forest floor. A soft breeze ruffled Sam's hair and as the sun began to set the clouds that hung over the horizon coloured a deep red. He looked out across the treetops towards the mountains that lay like sleeping beasts in the gathering darkness.

It was silent for a while and then Sam tapped the newly constructed platform with his knuckles and looked across at Skipper. 'Where did you learn to make something like this?' he asked.

Skipper swept her arms out, indicating the trees that surrounded them. 'Right here,' she said. 'This is my home.'

Nineteen

'Some years ago, men from one of the forest tribes were walking through the trees looking for food when they heard a sound that made them stop and listen. It was quite faint at first, but the more they listened, the more they realised that it wasn't a normal forest sound. Eventually they tracked it down to the foot of a tree.'

'What was it?' asked Sam, intrigued.

'It was a baby in a basket,' said Skipper. 'Left there by its mother in the middle of the night.'

'That's terrible,' said Sam. 'Why would anyone do a thing like that?'

'Well, there was a war on,' said Skipper, 'and a lot of bad things were happening in the villages and towns. Perhaps she was in danger and wanted to try and save the baby's life. Maybe she hoped to come back for the baby when things quietened down.'

'Did she come back?' asked Sam.

'No,' said Skipper. 'She never came back.'

'What happened?'

'The tribal elders agreed that they would look after the baby until it was old enough to fend for itself.'

Sam nodded thoughtfully. 'It was you, wasn't it?' he said.

'Yes,' said Skipper. 'It was me.'

There was silence for a moment, broken only by a breath of wind that moved softly through the forest like a sigh.

Skipper drew her knees up under her chin and looked out across the treetops to the dark plain and the mountains beyond.

'I became one of them,' she continued. 'I learned how to forage for food, to climb trees and to move quickly through the treetops when there was danger. I learned how to disappear into the foliage and blend in with the bark so that no one even knew I was there. And I learned how to build a tree house that would keep me warm so that when the winter storms came howling through the forest I would be safe and dry.'

She was quiet for a moment and Sam could see her blue eyes fixed on some point far away in the past, staring down the telescope of years at the way things used to be.

'The men told me I was a gift, a blessing bestowed upon them from out of the darkness, but something made me think that they didn't know the whole truth. I saw Arbous, the tribe elder, watching from the shadows when I asked questions and I felt he knew more than he would speak of. The men were dark-skinned, but when I drank from the woodland pools all I saw was a reflection of blonde hair and blue eyes. I knew that I was an outsider, that I didn't really belong.

'One night, while the others were asleep, I looked down from my sleeping platform and saw Arbous beckon to me from the foot of the tree. I followed him and we walked for nearly an hour until at last we reached the edge of the forest. We crossed into the fields and eventually came to a small grassy mound where a patch of white daisies were scattered like snow. Arbous said, "This is where I buried your mother." I remember I cried then. I don't know why really, because I never knew her, but he put his arms around me and we talked until morning.'

Sam found that he had stopped breathing in case his breaths should disturb Skipper's memories, like pebbles thrown into a pool.

'Do you know how she died?' he asked at last.

'She was shot by Odoursin's army. As they retreated from Vahlzi they plundered many Mazrian towns and villages, including my own. My village was burnt to the ground and, as far as I know, I am the only one to have survived. Arbous told me that I must have been spared for a reason and that it was my destiny to find out what that reason was.'

'But why did Odoursin want a war in the first place?' asked Sam.

Skipper tucked a stray wisp of blonde hair behind her ear and smiled. 'Time for a quick lesson, I think. Let's start with geography.'

'OK,' said Sam.

'Aurobon – the world we're in now – has secret pathways leading to your world through a series of what we call "fabric gaps" in the universe. The people of Vahlzi – who are descended from the Olumnus tribe – work as part of a large force which operates secretly on Earth to ensure that things in your world don't get knocked out of kilter.'

'How?' asked Sam.

'Well, for example, there's a huge department that operates deep in the oceans to remove poisonous toxins from the water. They run breeding programmes to restore the numbers of fish that have reached dangerously low levels and introduce predators to feed on other predators that have become too successful.'

Sam was amazed and also a little sceptical, but he had learned that he could no longer take anything for granted. 'But surely the world can do that for itself,' he said. 'That's what nature's all about, isn't it? Natural selection and all that. We learned about it in science.'

'Well, yes and no,' replied Skipper. 'That's what it *used* to be about. Your world used to run itself much more than it does now and it needed much less maintenance. But in the last hundred years or so, everything has changed. Now our secret forces have to operate round the clock just to stop the whole place from self-destructing.'

'Why?' asked Sam. 'What's changed?'

'Your people have,' said Skipper. 'They've become

greedier. Well, no, that's not strictly true. They were probably always this greedy, but now they've developed the tools that allow them to plunder and poison the Earth to their heart's desire. They're killing it in the process, but for the most part they don't even realise it.'

Sam looked dubious. 'Sounds a bit far-fetched. If all this is true, how come I've never heard of these secret forces?'

'Because, Sammy boy,' said Skipper, winking and tapping the side of her nose, 'they're secret.'

'Oh,' said Sam. 'Right.'

Skipper smiled. 'I know it's difficult to understand.' She looked thoughtful for a moment and then suddenly brightened. 'I've got an idea,' she said enthusiastically. 'Think of yourself as a flea on a dog.'

'Must I?' Sam asked.

'Seriously – think of the dog as the world on which the flea lives. Inside the dog's bloodstream is a whole other world where white blood cells fight with viruses and bacteria, where every second there is a battle between opposing forces to decide whether the flea's world – the dog – survives or is destroyed. But the flea has no knowledge of this world within a world. It exists in a place beyond the flea's understanding.'

'So you're saying that this world – Aurobon – is like the bloodstream of my world? It's hidden from Earth but still part of it?'

'Sort of, although it's a bit more complicated than that. But yes – the two worlds are linked and – like the dog and the world inside it – they depend upon each other for their survival. And that's also why the insects we fly here are so huge. Their eggs are harvested from your world and so the scale of things is different.' She paused for a moment as if considering something. Finally she said: 'I think I'll leave it to Firebrand to explain about your size. I got a bit confused when he tried to tell me about that one.'

'I know the feeling,' said Sam. 'But what about the war?'

'Right,' Skipper replied, 'history lesson now. About fifteen years ago, fly populations on Earth had been going absolutely crazy with the huge rubbish tips that were being created and a change in the climate that brought milder winters and hotter summers. Flies have always been an important factor in the spread of disease and it became a priority to try and control their numbers. But at the same time it was recognised that flies had an important role to play both in clearing away dead material and as food for other creatures higher up the food chain. So a way had to be found to control them without killing them all off.'

'What did they do? Build a big fly swat?'

Skipper smiled. 'Well, biologically speaking, yes. Remember what I told you back at the factory, about them interrupting the development of the fly larvae so that they could pilot the adult creatures?'

'How could I forget?' replied Sam. 'I went swimming with them.'

'Oh yeah,' said Skipper. She giggled at the memory.

'So you did. Anyway, Odoursin and Firebrand were part of the team that developed the first Insect Pilot Programme. Until then, operations had concentrated on trying to curb the flies' breeding capabilities, with mixed results. The success of the pilot programme meant that they could now go on the offensive.'

'You mean they put pilots in flies to attack other flies?'

'Not exactly. The first Pilot Programme used wasps. Not only were they fast and manoeuvrable, but they already had built-in systems which made them excellent hunters. Once they were piloted, their kill rate immediately increased a hundredfold and squadrons could be deployed in high-population areas much more quickly.'

'Wow,' said Sam, impressed. 'Attack of the Killer Wasps!'

'Something like that,' said Skipper. 'Anyway, they also flew protection missions around newly hatched queens to ensure that more nests were created in the summer. If you think that each queen is worth anything up to ten thousand new wasps, you can see what the advantages of such a strategy are. The result was a huge increase in wasp populations, which took out literally millions of flies and kept the numbers down to manageable levels.'

'That's incredible,' said Sam. 'So what went wrong?'

'Well, Odoursin was a big player in the whole Insect Pilot Programme. He and Firebrand were both brilliant fliers by all accounts, but Odoursin was the one who always took the biggest risks. Apparently he once flew into a can of Coke and did ten circuits inside while the guy was still holding it, just for a dare. He flew out just as the fella was taking a swig and ricocheted off his top lip. Pilots still talk about it in the mess. But then, just as it seemed as though they were winning the battle, tragedy struck.'

Skipper chewed her bottom lip thoughtfully.

'Go on,' said Sam.

'Odoursin had a younger brother who dreamed of becoming a pilot just like him,' Skipper continued. 'So on the boy's birthday, Odoursin smuggled him into the cockpit of his wasp and took him for what was supposed to be a routine flight.' She paused. 'Only it wasn't.'

'Why?' asked Sam. 'What happened?'

'They were supposed to be hunting down a swarm of flies on a domestic compost heap somewhere in England. Nothing dangerous, just taking out a few egg-laying females to keep numbers down. But Odoursin wanted to make it more exciting for his little brother; he wanted to give him a day to remember. So instead of just doing the mission and returning to base, he flew in through an open window and took him on a tour of a nearby house. Against all safety regulations, of course, but that was Odoursin all over. Always taking risks.'

A faint smile appeared on Skipper's lips and Sam guessed why. It was, after all, exactly the kind of thing that she would have done.

'Everything was fine until he got to the kitchen, but as he banked the wasp round to go back the way he had come, a woman shut the door and zapped him with a can of fly spray. That was it, of course. He lost control of the aircraft and crashed it into the gas ring of the cooker. The whole thing burst into flames and Odoursin was horribly burnt. His brother was killed instantly.'

'How did Odoursin get out?'

'Well, normal procedure in the event of a crash is for the search-and-rescue teams to go in and retrieve the pilots. But then normal procedure is for all missions to be flown outside apart from in exceptional circumstances, in which case search-and-rescue teams go into the building prior to the mission taking place.'

'Who are the rescue teams?' Sam asked.

'Ant squadrons,' said Skipper. 'Just like the ones in the factory, except ours are black and a bit smaller. Whenever an aircraft goes down, a homing beacon is activated and the nearest squadron moves in to retrieve the aircraft and rescue the pilot.'

'Oh, I've seen that!' Sam shouted excitedly. 'I've seen ants pulling a dead butterfly along the pavement! Was that a search-and-rescue team then?'

'Unlikely,' said Skipper. 'We don't tend to pilot butterflies. Very pretty and all that, but dreadful to fly. They're all over the place.'

'So what were the ants doing then?'

'Probably just ordinary ants dragging a dead butterfly home for tea,' said Skipper. 'That's the beauty of our secret operations, you see. Everything we do looks perfectly normal.'

'You've certainly thought this through,' said Sam.

'Nothing to do with me,' said Skipper. 'I just fly the things. Anyway, picture the scene: Odoursin escapes from the burning wreckage, horribly injured, and there he is, a tiny speck on top of the cooker, watching this woman pick up the charred remains of the wasp with his little brother inside it and put it in the bin. That was the moment he turned.'

'What happened to him?'

Skipper shrugged. 'He decided that all the things he believed in – the importance of Earth and the need to protect its people from themselves – were nothing but a lie. He became bitter, full of hatred. You see, the one person whom he loved more than anything in the world had been killed by the very things he had spent years trying to protect. From that moment on, Odoursin turned his back on trying to preserve human life. He decided that your world was too good for the people who lived there.'

'Us, you mean?'

Skipper nodded. 'He vowed to rid the Earth of all human life for the good of the environment. He was a powerful, persuasive man with many followers. Over the next few years he secretly built up an army of people from both inside and outside the organisation who were excited by the idea of ridding the world of its human parasites. Odoursin promised his followers a new world order. They were the chosen ones who would safeguard the Earth's resources and become its proper guardians.

'After months of planning, his forces struck during the night and many of those loyal to the President of Vahlzi were killed as they slept. But the President's remaining forces recovered quickly and under Firebrand's command they fought back with great courage, forcing Odoursin to retreat into the east through Mazria. It was during this withdrawal that my village was destroyed. I was the only survivor.'

Sam thought for a moment of all those lives lost, all that death and destruction resulting from the simple act of one woman with a can of fly spray. 'Incredible,' he said. 'What happened next?'

'Once his army had overrun Mazria, Odoursin transported thousands of prisoners east to remodel the city of Kilvus. The skills learned by many of his followers during their time in Vahlzi, together with the huge numbers of prisoners forced to work for nothing, meant that the new city of Vermia was built very quickly. Odoursin then used the experience gained from his work on the Insect Programme to begin one of his own. But instead of wasps, he concentrated on biting insects, which he hoped would eventually provide him with the means to wipe out the people on Earth.'

Sam nodded as his mind began to make links between the different bits of information. 'Hence the mosquitoes,' he said.

'Hence the mosquitoes. But Odoursin used horseflies as his main reconnaissance craft as they were fast, manoeuvrable and excellent at finding and tracking human subjects. His observations of recent events on Earth have led him to believe that an ancient prophecy is about to be fulfilled. The reports all indicate that he is on the verge of a major breakthrough with a new and terrible disease. If this information is correct, then he may be about to achieve his ambitions.'

Sam frowned. 'But where do I fit into all this?'

'Odoursin originally believed that he needed to bring you to Aurobon so that the prophecy could be fulfilled and he would be victorious. But his Council saw things differently; they wanted you dead. And from the way those ants went after us in the factory, I'd say things have changed and that Odoursin wants you dead too. Along with the rest of them, he now believes that you pose a serious threat to Vermia's plans.' Skipper winked. 'And that's what we believe too. Which is why I came to get you.' She shook her head and smiled. 'You know Sam, you are one important individual. How does it feel to be so popular?'

Sam frowned. 'But why do they think I could possibly be a threat? I just don't get it.'

He waited for Skipper's answer, but she had stopped smiling and was staring over his shoulder.

'What?' said Sam.

Something was wrong.

Suddenly there was a rustling sound behind him and without warning Skipper sprang forward like a wildcat. As she leapt into the air, Sam felt the wind from her foot as it kicked past his ear and there was a loud smack followed by a shriek, as whatever she had connected with fell backwards out of the tree.

Branches snapped and cracked, there was a dull thud from below and then Skipper was up and kicking back from the tree trunk, spinning round through 180 degrees to face a new threat. Sam watched in horror as the glowing yellow eyes of marsh dogs began to appear all around the platform, gripping onto the bark with their razor-sharp claws. He stood momentarily frozen in terror as Skipper scissor-kicked three more of them back into the darkness.

'Come on, Sam,' she yelled. 'I need some help here!'

Taking a deep breath, he turned to face one of the dark shapes climbing over the lip of the platform. He drew his leg back but before he could deliver a kick his foot was seized from behind and he fell flat on his face. He reached out to grab hold of the woven branches beneath him, but the grip on his foot was too strong and his fingers scrabbled helplessly as he was dragged back towards the edge.

In front of him, a marsh dog had successfully climbed onto the platform and now it growled menacingly, snapping its jaws together as it crouched low and crawled towards him. Feeling himself being pulled backwards with increasing speed, Sam made a desperate grab at a branch stub that was protruding through the platform. His fingers locked around it, stopping his slide with a sudden jolt, and he was rewarded by a startled yelp from behind as his assailant lost its grip and slid off into the darkness below.

Sam now hung with his legs dangling over the side, saved from falling only by the branch that he clung to. A sharp pain in his fingers made him gasp and he looked up to see that the creature on the platform was clawing at his hand in an effort to loosen his grip on the branch. Ignoring the pain, he squeezed his hand more tightly still. Then, summoning all his strength, he placed his other hand on the lip of the platform and swung his legs upwards and sideways like a gymnast on a horse. The momentum brought him onto the platform with such force that his snarling attacker was knocked clean off its feet. Sam just had time to register the shock and disbelief on the creature's face before it crashed into the tree trunk, bounced once on the side of the platform and disappeared over the edge.

Sam glanced across at Skipper and saw that she was looking back at him approvingly. 'Nice one,' she said.

Then, without turning round, she added, 'Down boy,' thrust an elbow quickly backwards and the last of the marsh dogs went yowling over the edge into the darkness. She dusted her hands together as if she had just thrown a piece of rubbish into the bin. 'Good dog,' she said.

Sam was about to speak, but Skipper held up a hand and he stopped.

They both listened. A lone, eerie howl echoed through the forest, quickly joined by others. The hunters, it seemed, were gathering.

Sam shivered. The idea of staying the night here had suddenly lost its appeal.

'I don't know about you,' said Skipper, 'but I'm bored with kicking marsh dogs out of trees.'

Sam smiled in spite of the fear he felt inside. 'I know what you mean,' he said. 'The fun's gone out of it somehow.'

'Shall we go then?' Skipper suggested.

'Yes,' said Sam. 'Let's do that.'

They looked at each other and laughed nervously. Then they scrambled down the trunk and ran for their lives.

Twenty

Somewhere in his dreams, Sam became aware of a tugging sensation on his chest and awoke to find Skipper pulling his seat belt tight with one hand while piloting the fly with the other. He blinked, yawned and rubbed his eyes. There was a lightening of the sky away to the east and he could see that they were travelling at speed across the dry, sun-bleached plains.

'There,' said Skipper, giving a final yank on his seat belt, 'that's better.'

Sam looked down at the straps that pinned him firmly to his seat. 'Should I be worried?' he said.

'Just a precautionary measure.'

Sam looked at her sideways and narrowed his eyes. 'Against what, exactly?'

Skipper pushed forward on the joystick and Sam felt his stomach flip as they pitched forward and rapidly began to lose height. The humming of the insect's wings became louder as they went into a steep dive.

'The thing is,' said Skipper, raising her voice slightly against the sound of the wings, 'we need to fly low from now on to avoid detection. We're only about ten minutes from the airbase and it would be really annoying if we got shot down.'

'Annoying?' said Sam. He noticed his voice was rather high and he fought to return it to its normal register. 'Well, that's one way of putting it.' He rubbed his eyes with his hand. It was unsettling having people try to kill you all the time. Tiring too.

'So this would be the airbase where Firebrand and his forces are anxiously awaiting our safe return, would it?'

'It would,' said Skipper.

'In which case,' said Sam, 'why on Earth would they want to shoot us down?'

'Because they won't know it's us,' replied Skipper. 'We can't use the radio to identify ourselves because it's code-locked onto Vermian frequencies. So all they'll see is a whopping great horsefly zooming towards their airbase and their natural reaction will be to destroy it.'

Sam paused for a moment to digest this information. 'Can I make a small suggestion?' he offered, watching the dry, boulder-strewn landscape zip beneath the cockpit at an alarming speed.

'Please,' said Skipper, 'be my guest.'

'What do you say we turn around and fly very fast in the opposite direction. With any luck they won't see us. Then – who knows – we may not die.'

'You really *are* a worrier, aren't you?' said Skipper.

'Yes,' said Sam. 'In this case, I am.'

'Well, there's no need,' said Skipper in a voice that was meant to sound reassuring. 'I can outmanoeuvre a few wasps, no problem. By the time they've caught up with us we'll be sitting down having a nice cup of tea with the Commander. Just you wait and see. I'll look after you.'

'That's what I'm afraid of,' said Sam.

Skipper smiled. She flicked the joystick slightly and they banked around to the right. The wings tipped back to the horizontal and Sam saw that they were now skimming over the surface of a river.

'Look, there it is,' said Skipper, pointing up ahead. In the distance to the left of the river Sam could just make out a group of buildings in the middle of a huge expanse of concrete and tarmac, surrounded by tall fencing. It reminded him of the airfield that they had escaped from the day before and he shivered.

Skipper pulled back on the throttle and Sam felt himself pushed back into his seat as they accelerated hard. The surface of the water beneath them blurred to a silver-grey strip and Sam gripped the armrests to steady himself as the fly banked sharply round again.

They left the river and flew low, hugging the ground. Sam could see the dust blowing up beneath their wings and watched the tiny particles swirl into random patterns, catch in the slipstream and then twist and blur out of sight.

'Hold on, Sam!' Skipper shouted suddenly. 'Here they come!'

Sam looked up to find that they were approaching the perimeter fence at incredible speed. Beyond it was the unmistakable, horrifying sight of twenty or thirty enormous wasps taking off from the airfield. He saw the thin-waisted, yellow and black shapes so familiar from summer picnics, watched as the sun glinted on the tips of the silver stings that protruded from their pointed abdomens and just had time to register the inscrutable menace of the black and yellow painted faces before Skipper pulled back hard on the joystick and the scene blurred into clear blue sky.

The g-forces were so strong that it felt to Sam as though invisible hands were grabbing him and pulling him back through the fabric of his seat. His cheeks were dragged backwards and his eyes felt as though they were burrowing down into their sockets.

'Yeeeeeehaw!' shouted Skipper as they levelled out again and Sam's mind gradually emerged from a mist of confusion, trying to work out what had become of his body and whether there were any bits of it left worth worrying about.

Looking down, he realised they must have gained height rapidly, because the airbase looked much smaller and the wasps appeared as black dots far below. But the dots were quickly getting bigger and Sam knew that the wasps had seen them.

'Skipper,' he said, unable to keep the nervousness out of his voice, 'they're getting nearer.'

Skipper leant forward to get a better view. 'So they

are,' she said. 'Well, this should be fun.'

'Fun?' retorted Sam. 'Skipper, they're going to kill us!'

'Relax,' Skipper replied with a nonchalant air that suggested they were setting out for a Sunday afternoon drive. 'They're not going to kill us. They're going to *try* and kill us. And that,' she added, reaching over to flick a couple of switches, 'is a very different thing.'

'But there are hundreds of them!' protested Sam. 'We haven't got a chance!'

'Twenty-five to be precise,' Skipper corrected him, 'and I know for a fact that it's B Squadron, who have only just finished their basic training. They might scare Odoursin's lot, but they're no match for us. Watch this.'

She thrust the joystick forward and the horsefly dropped like a stone. Sam's stomach flipped over again and felt as though it was disappearing off through the top of his head. The formation of wasps was now directly ahead of them, climbing steadily through the sky, and Sam watched in horror as the lead wasp loomed up large, filling the screen as they hurtled towards it. For a split second it seemed certain that they would collide, but in the final moments the pilot must have panicked, because it veered off suddenly to the left, leaving the rest of the formation to be split in half as Sam and Skipper scorched through the centre, sending several wasps tumbling away into the distance. But one wasp at the very end of the formation held steady and Sam could feel the insect's eyes fixed directly on his own as they bore down upon it.

He shot a sideways glance at Skipper and saw that her face was drained of colour. Her hands gripped the controls tightly and she seemed transfixed by the wasp that was rushing headlong toward them.

'We're going to crash!' yelled Sam. 'Get out of the way, Skipper! We're going to die!'

'Not yet!' shouted Skipper with grim determination. 'Not yet!'

'Skipper, no!' Sam screamed. He shut his eyes and covered his face as the inscrutable features of the wasp appeared close up on the monitor, its jaws open to reveal a terrible blackness inside. There was a tremendous thump, followed by a tearing sound, and Sam was thrown hard against the restraints of his seat belt as the whole world turned upside down.

Opening his eyes, he saw Skipper hanging from her straps and desperately struggling with the controls. Her face was pale and she looked very frightened. The fly slowed, shook violently for a few seconds and then went into a sickening spin.

'What's happening?' he shouted. 'Skipper, what's the matter?'

'The wing,' gasped Skipper. 'He ripped one of our wings off.'

Sam felt the safety restraints begin to cut into his shoulders as they plummeted towards the ground. He watched helplessly through the screen as the view flipped sickeningly from sky to ground and back to sky again, all the blues and the browns mixing and merging together as the fly spun out of control.

A sudden memory was triggered in Sam's mind. He was on a bike, riding through a country lane in summer, the scent of wild garlic rising from the hedgerows and the sound of a car somewhere in the distance. There was a pain, a splintering sound, and then all the colours were spinning and screaming and everything was falling away like a stone thrown into the deepest ocean. In a split second Sam thought, *I have been here before and this is what it feels like to die because . . . because I remember it all and now everything will be lost –*

'Hold on!' screamed Skipper. There was a noise so loud that it seemed to rip through the whole world, followed by a scraping, squealing and grinding, a violent juddering and an incredibly loud bang. Then silence.

Sam had just worked out from the thumping of his heart that he was still alive when there was the sound of a metal catch being released, a loud clunk from somewhere below him and an even louder 'Ow!'

He opened his eyes to find he was hanging upside down in his straps. Below him, Skipper was crawling around, scowling and rubbing the top of her head.

She looked up and gave him a cheery wave. 'Hi, Sam. Stay there and I'll come and get you out.' She clambered up underneath him and grabbed him by the shoulders. 'I've got you,' she reassured him. 'Release your safety catch and I'll help you down.'

Sam did as he had been instructed and they were soon crouched together looking up at the seats and the control panel, which were fixed incongruously to what was now the ceiling.

Sam whistled. 'I thought we were goners that time,' he said.

'Me too,' agreed Skipper. 'Those guys were sharper than I thought. Basic training has obviously moved on since my day.'

Sam raised his eyebrows. 'Since your day? You sound as though you're about to retire.'

'Yeah, well, after today I might just do that. I tell you, it's the first time I've ever used a single wing as a rudder *and* a brake. Hope it's the last too. I thought it was going to snap off.'

Sam nodded through the splintered screen towards the smoking remains of what was once a wing, now bent and twisted on the ground outside.

'It *did* snap off,' he pointed out.

'Not before we landed though,' said Skipper. 'If it hadn't been for that wing, we wouldn't be here.'

'Correction,' said Sam, 'if it hadn't been for *you* we wouldn't be here. That was an amazing piece of flying.'

Skipper almost blushed. 'Well, my crashes are becoming more stylish at any rate.' She fished the CRB out of her hip pocket, pointed it in front of her and the side of the fly dissolved in a flash of blue light.

The first thing Sam noticed as he crawled blinking into the bright sunlight was that they appeared to have landed on some sort of roof. The second was that a pair of light blue, perfectly pressed trousers with a crease as sharp as a razor was standing right in front of him, blocking his way. Squinting, he looked up to discover that their owner was a lean, powerfully built man in his late forties or early fifties. He wore a tunic and cap made of the same light blue material as the trousers, and circles of gold braid were embroidered around the sleeves. A column of highly polished brass buttons glinted in the sunlight and a row of golden pips shone from the top of each shoulder. His skin was the colour of old pine and he had the weathered look of someone who had spent a good deal of his time outside facing the elements.

He studied Sam for a few seconds and then shifted his gaze towards the wreckage. He watched as Skipper crawled out onto the roof and then raised one eyebrow as if only mildly surprised that an enormous horsefly should have crash-landed on his control tower.

'Ah, Skipper,' he said. 'Rather thought it might be you.'

Skipper tried somewhat shakily to get to her feet, then decided against it and sat down again. The man paused and looked around wistfully, as though taking in the amount of damage for the first time. In the distance, Sam could see the squadron of wasps returning to base and, beyond the perimeter fence, the wreckage of five or six insects that had crashed following Skipper's unorthodox manoeuvres.

'I suppose we should be grateful that you're on our side,' he added dryly. 'One can only imagine the kind of damage you'd do if you were actually fighting against us.'

'I know,' said Skipper ruefully. 'Sorry about that.'

'And without wishing to sound petty or indeed state the obvious, most pilots tend to avail themselves of the airfield's extensive touchdown area when coming in to land. You, however, have to use the roof.'

Not for the first time today, Sam was worried. This man was obviously extremely important and they had just smashed up his nice building and several of his aircraft.

'I therefore have only one thing to say to you,' the man continued.

Now we're in for it, Sam thought. Expecting trouble, he turned his face back to look up at the man and was amazed to see that he was smiling broadly. The man reached out a large hand and helped Skipper to her feet.

'And what might that be, Commander?' asked Skipper with a twinkle in her eye.

'Welcome home,' said Commander Firebrand. 'It's good to have you back.'

Twenty-one

'It sounds as though we were lucky to get you here in one piece,' said Firebrand after listening to Sam and Skipper recount the events of the past few days. Sam nodded and looked around the large study with its richly patterned carpet, dark wooden bookcases and button-backed comfortable chairs. There was a timeless feel to it, as though its quiet atmosphere of dust and old leather provided an invisible barrier against the outside world. Skipper sat opposite him on a battered old sofa with her legs tucked underneath her, sipping from a mug of hot, sweet tea and tucking in to a thick slice of bread and butter. Sam took a swig from his own mug, leant back in the armchair and listened to a clock ticking somewhere behind him. *This could be England*, he thought.

Firebrand drew deeply on his cigar and the end glowed a deep red. He held it between his finger and thumb and watched the smoke drift up from the tip in thick, aromatic wisps.

'Odoursin wants to get his hands on you pretty badly, Sam.' He tapped the end of the cigar so that the ash fell into the silver ashtray on his desk. 'So right now, you're in the best place. Believe me.'

'I don't wish to be rude,' Sam ventured uncertainly, 'but why am I here?'

Firebrand narrowed his eyes and stared at Sam through the smoke that curled from the end of his cigar. 'You're here because of the prophecy,' he explained. 'Odoursin believed that bringing you to Aurobon was crucial to his future success.'

'I still don't get it,' said Sam.

'After their attack failed at the start of the war, Odoursin's army retreated into the mountains and vented their anger on our ancestors – the Olumnus – virtually wiping them out. And when they took over their caves, they found the Book of Incantations.'

'The Book of what?'

'Incantations,' repeated Firebrand. He got up from his desk and walked across to the window overlooking the airfield. 'It was previously thought of as a legend, a magical book containing prophecies which accurately foretold the future. Its discovery was of enormous significance to us all, and strengthened Odoursin's belief that his destiny was to rescue Earth from what he saw as its human parasites. He began to believe that his defeat in battle was fate's way of bringing him to the book in order to prepare him for future victory. After having the book translated, he was convinced of it.'

'But what does it say?' asked Sam.

'Well, there's a lot of pretty general stuff about the fall of kings and empires and the conjunction of planets and constellations and suchlike. But take a look at this.'

Skipper flipped off the lights as Firebrand pulled a cord to draw the curtains. He picked up a small handset from his desk and a screen lit up on the end wall.

Sam peered through the darkness as words appeared on the screen. He read:

> **. . . and so it is written that there shall be seven states of darkness; the decay of religion, revolution, famine, earthquakes, war, the poisoning of the Earth and plagues and diseases. When these prevail, the Great One shall come from the sky and Earth shall be saved.**

'Now, if you think about it,' said Firebrand, 'that just about sums up the state of the Earth at the moment. The planet's been polluted to such an extent that it's become a huge rubbish tip. People are either turning their backs on religion or using it as an excuse to persecute others – you don't have to look very far to find people fighting each other. Add earthquakes into the equation, and the fact that there are millions dying because they haven't got enough food to eat, and you're nearly there. Just toss in a plague or two and everything's in place for the Great One to arrive. Simple really.'

'The Great One being Odoursin,' said Skipper.

'Well, that's what he believes himself to be.'

'Don't you?' asked Sam.

'I have to admit, I was sceptical,' Firebrand replied. 'Most of the prophecies in the book are so general that you could use them to predict almost anything. But then something happened which changed my view completely.'

Firebrand glanced around and lowered his voice, despite the fact that there were only the three of them in the room. 'One night we were secretly observing some of Odoursin's men on patrol in the forests when we saw a young woman wandering alone and barefoot through the trees. She was distressed and appeared to be searching for something. The patrol followed her for several minutes until she reached the edge of the forest and watched as she climbed over a ditch and into an open field. Here she walked a little way and then stopped as if unsure what to do next. Odoursin's soldiers shouted to her to stay, but she gave no indication of having heard them. The patrol then entered the field and walked towards her, at which point, much to everyone's surprise, she simply disappeared.'

'Disappeared?' Sam echoed.

'Vanished into thin air. But after that she began to appear at irregular intervals, always at night and always disappearing before anyone could get near her.'

'Did you find out who she was?' Sam asked.

'Not at first. But her appearance coincided with a huge increase in activity from Odoursin's forces and we began to suspect that this figure was of great importance to him. We began to see much greater concentrations of horseflies in the towns and cities of your world. Their deployment could only mean one thing: they were searching for her.'

'But why?' Sam tugged at his lower lip. 'Why did they want her so badly?'

'It wasn't her they wanted,' Firebrand went on. 'It was something that belonged to her. Fortunately, we were able to get our hands on a translation of the prophecy and find out what that was. We moved fast and managed to find her before they did. Unfortunately, despite our best efforts, it wasn't enough to stop them.'

'But who was she?' asked Sam.

By way of reply, the handset clicked quietly and the words on the screen dissolved, to be replaced by an image of a woman of about thirty-five. She was standing in a summer meadow, her auburn hair held out of her eyes by her left hand as she waved to someone with her right. Behind her was a low hedge and beyond it a red-brick house. It was a beautiful summer's day.

Sam gave a cry of shock, longing and recognition.

The house was his own and the woman standing in the field was his mother.

The handset clicked again and the image faded to black. The following words appeared in its place:

When the Dreamwalker's Child walks in Aurobon, then shall the East be in the

> **ascendant; a plague shall descend from the sky and the Earth will fall into shadow . . . but the Dreamwalker's Child shall rise up against the Darkness.**

Sam looked at Skipper and saw that she was staring at him.

'Guess who,' she said.

Twenty-two

A small flame of fear and excitement began to burn in the shadows around Sam's heart.

'Me?' he said.

Firebrand nodded. 'That's why they're so keen to get hold of you. They think you're the Dreamwalker's Child – the one who's going to spoil the party.'

'And with our help,' added Skipper, 'that's exactly what you *are* going to do.'

Sam's mind was racing. Suddenly everything around him seemed to come into clear, sharp focus, as though someone had twisted a camera lens and transformed the blurred edges of his new world into hard, precise lines. He saw the red heat as it crawled slowly down the crisp brown sides of the cigar, saw the rough, hard calluses on Firebrand's hands and saw the light from the screen reflected in Skipper's eyes, shining like a pool full of sapphires.

'But why didn't they just kill me?'

'Because of the first part of the prophecy. Odoursin believed he needed you alive in Aurobon so that his forces would be victorious. He saw the people on Earth as the Darkness and believed that in some way you would help him to defeat them. But Hekken and the rest of the Council disagreed, suspecting that the Darkness referred to their own forces. They believed that once you were in Aurobon, it would be safer to kill you. We've recently learned that they have been successful in persuading Odoursin to believe this too.'

Sam blinked and tried to focus on what Firebrand was saying.

'When we realised that Odoursin's forces had made a connection between the woman who walked in the forest and the Dreamwalker of the prophecy,' continued Firebrand, tapping another column of grey ash into the ashtray, 'we couldn't be sure that the connection was a correct one, but neither could we take any risks. So we threw all our resources into finding her before they did.'

Sam shifted in his seat and thought how strange it was to hear his mother talked of in this way, hunted like some fugitive on the run. But he listened and said nothing.

'We programmed her image into our most powerful computers, which analysed every scrap of data we had – hair colour, skin tone, height, bone structure – you name it, we analysed it. The most we got from that was a 78 per cent probability that the woman was of English descent, although for all we knew she could have moved to the other side of the world or been born to English parents who lived in Africa. We had no way of knowing for sure.'

Another image of Sam's mother appeared on the screen, although at first he didn't recognise her. It was night-time and she stood alone in the middle of a field, clearly terrified. She stared wildly at something in the distance and her face was smudged with dirt and tears. All she wore was a simple nightdress. Sam swallowed hard, then felt a small hand close around his own.

'Don't worry,' whispered Skipper. 'It'll be all right, you'll see.'

And although Sam couldn't see how anything could be all right any more, her words calmed him and he squeezed her hand tightly in the darkness.

'We took a chance and focused on England,' Firebrand continued. 'Every single piloted insect that we could spare was taken off normal duties and transferred to search squadrons. Fly populations soared that year, but luck was on our side. After seven months we found her.'

The handset clicked and the face on the screen merged smoothly into a much happier version of the same person. Sam's heart leapt as he saw his mother smiling once more, stretching up in the sunlight and pegging clothes onto a washing line.

'We don't know why she walks through Aurobon in her dreams. But knowing that Odoursin was desperate to find you, we flew round-the-clock wasp patrols for your protection.'

The image changed to one of Sam's face next to a dead wasp. Stretching away into the distance was a line of ants.

'We've been watching you for quite a while, Sam. Remember this?'

Sam gave a half-smile and nodded. He had watched fascinated as the ants tugged the fallen insect across the patio towards their dark holes in the earth, little knowing that he too was being watched.

'That wasp had one of our pilots in it, so the ant squadrons mobilised immediately. Standard search-and-rescue procedure. Got it down to a fine art, we have.'

Sam detected a hint of pride in Firebrand's voice.

'We knew that, sooner or later, Odoursin's lot would find you. In the event, it turned out to be sooner.'

Sam watched as the picture on the screen cut away to a film shot at night from the cockpit of a wasp. The screen was filled with the image of a house approaching at high speed and Sam winced involuntarily as it seemed they must crash, but at the last moment the pilot climbed sharply and shot through a gap in an open window.

Sam recognised his own bedroom curtains just as two black lines appeared at the sides of the screen, pulsated once and then raced to the middle, shrinking themselves into a small, bright square beneath which the words 'TARGET LOCK' glowed fiery red. He just had time to register the unmistakable shape of a mosquito in the middle of the square before there was a sense of incredible acceleration and the mosquito was hit full on, bits of its legs and wings disintegrating beneath like grey, ghostly confetti.

'Nice,' said Skipper.

The screen flickered again and Sam saw himself standing on the lawn. A grey fly was circling above his head, although the Sam on the screen didn't appear to be aware of it.

'Ooh, horsefly!' cried Skipper excitedly. 'Go on, take him down!'

As if in response to Skipper's instruction, the screen was quickly filled by the unfortunate insect as the electronic display locked onto its target once more and the wasp hit the horsefly dead centre. This time the large fly was brought crashing down to the ground, struggling among the long grass beneath the hedge until there was a glint of silver sting, a crunching of jaws and the struggle was over.

'Isn't nature a wonderful thing?' said Skipper as Sam shut his eyes and tried to ignore the queasy feeling in his stomach.

'Red in tooth and claw,' agreed Firebrand as the wasp flew away from the lifeless insect lying broken in the long grass and up into a clear blue sky. 'There were some bloody battles on Earth that summer, Sam, I can tell you.' He got to his feet and rubbed the back of his neck. He suddenly looked very tired.

'It was our belief that Odoursin would try and use mosquitoes to infect your Earth body with some deadly virus, so that they could bring your essence to Aurobon. They may not have developed the virus that will destroy all human life yet, but there are plenty of existing ones that will kill you quite effectively – yellow fever, for instance. We know that they've piloted *Aedes aegypti* mosquitoes in the past to infect key people with the yellow-fever virus – usually scientists in the tropics who are on the verge of some major breakthrough.'

'They killed them?' asked Sam in amazement. 'Why?'

'Because they're afraid that the success of the new virus they're developing might be threatened by these people. So they watch them in the labs and they wait. Then when a breakthrough cure is imminent, a few ants quietly come and bite a hole in the mosquito net. Night comes, the mosquitoes go in and no one knows anything until the target gets sick and dies. Just another unfortunate accident in the name of medical research.'

Sam gave a low whistle. 'Does that sort of thing happen a lot then?'

'Well, they've always done it,' said Firebrand, 'and in the past they've always been quite subtle about it. A scientist dying quietly in some tropical country isn't the kind of thing likely to cause much of a stir in the wider world. But recently they've been more brazen about it, to the extent that we've had West Nile virus turning up in New York, for goodness' sake. Which made us think that they wouldn't worry too much about a case of yellow fever in rural England if it meant that they could bring their number one target back to Aurobon.'

'That being you of course,' added Skipper helpfully.

'But I didn't get yellow fever,' protested Sam. 'I didn't get anything. I was fine. I was riding my bike. So please, someone tell me – how did I come to be here?'

Firebrand sighed. 'We got it wrong, Sam,' he said simply. 'Unfortunately for us, it was not only knowledge of the prophecies that Odoursin gained from the Book of Incantations. In his obsession with finding the Dreamwalker, he learned a great deal about human consciousness and discovered what had long been suspected – that to destroy a body is not necessarily to destroy a person. Tell me something, have you ever owned a balloon, Sam? A balloon on a string?'

'Yes,' replied Sam, rather taken aback by the question. 'I have.'

'Good,' said Firebrand. 'Then imagine for a moment that you are that balloon.'

'What?' asked Sam. This conversation was becoming stranger by the minute. 'But I don't look anything like a balloon.'

'Forget about what you look like. Think about who you are: your thoughts, feelings, dreams and desires.'

Sam gave Firebrand a doubtful look, not unlike the one he had once given a supply teacher in drama who suggested he pretend to be a tree. He looked at Skipper for support.

'Go on, Sam. You'll see.'

'Right,' said Sam. 'I am a balloon.'

'Good,' said Firebrand again, 'very good. Now imagine

that you are put into a box with a small hole in the side and your string is taped to the bottom of the box. The box is locked shut and taken into a room in a house. Can you picture it?'

'Yes,' said Sam, 'I think I can picture that one.'

As Sam spoke he detected a hint of sarcasm in his own voice and hoped that Firebrand hadn't noticed. If he had, he didn't show it.

'So you are the balloon in a box, in a room, in a house. You can see parts of the room through the hole in the box, but your view is quite narrow. What happens when the box is opened?'

Sam shrugged, resisting the temptation to point out that he had never come across a balloon that could see, hole in a box or not.

'The balloon floats out into the room I suppose.'

'That's right. But the string remains attached so that it can be pulled back into the box at any time. Correct?'

'Correct,' agreed Sam, still wondering where this conversation was leading.

'All right,' said Firebrand. 'Now think of your body as a box which contains all your thoughts and desires – your balloon. When you dream, the box opens and the balloon can float into the room – your world – and see it in a new way, although you are still tied to the box and must return to it.'

'So the room is a world which I see differently in my dreams?' said Sam, becoming interested in spite of himself.

'That's right,' said Firebrand, 'but it's still only one room – *your* world. The balloon stays in one room, usually in its box but sometimes floating above it. But just suppose that the house has more than one room, maybe ten, maybe a thousand . . .'

Sam shook his head. 'I'm lost,' he said.

'Think of Aurobon as another room in the house,' explained Firebrand. 'By rights you shouldn't be here, because normally the door of your room is kept shut and you are tied to your box. But for some reason, your mother is able to open a door in your world and enter this one while still remaining tethered to her body. She simply dreams – or floats – in a different room from the one in which she lives and then returns to her own world. Why, I don't know.'

'But if she can get back then why can't I?' asked Sam. 'If this is some sort of dream, why can't I wake up?' He looked up at Firebrand, noticed in that moment how sad he appeared and suddenly began to feel very, very afraid. 'Why can't I wake up?' he repeated, his voice a whisper in the darkness. 'Why?'

Firebrand placed a hand on his shoulder. 'Because I'm afraid your string has been broken,' he said simply.

Twenty-three

For a long time the words hung in the silence like frozen rain and Sam shivered beneath their shadow. At last, somewhere a long way off, he heard Firebrand say, 'Look at the screen, Sam. You must face the truth before we can go on.'

Skipper put a hand on his shoulder. 'Be strong, Sam.'

Sam looked at the screen.

'This footage was taken from the cockpit camera of the lead wasp,' said Firebrand.

A bright summer's day.

A view from the air of open countryside and a red-brick house below.

Several passes at high speed, the camera searching for something.

A sensation of losing height rapidly.

A boy standing outside a house, holding a bike.

Sam.

Suddenly the air is alive with yellow and black, a

swarming squadron of wasps spreading in all directions, the camera following them, climbing, sweeping, searching the blue sky.

The crackle of static and a voice fighting to stay calm: 'Situation red, repeat, situation red. Enemy fighters engaged and destroyed, but others present, location unknown. Repeat, location unknown. All units, search and destroy. Situation critical. Repeat, situation critical.'

The cloud of black and yellow clears and the horizon tilts, climbing as the wasp dives. Trees, fields and a grey ribbon of road with two specks moving across it, converging: closer now, a white van and a boy on a bike.

Static crackles and roars. A voice, screaming now, 'Enemy attacking! Repeat, enemy attacking!' The horizon flips and turns, a green blur of leaves and tarmac, a flurry of smoky wings, blood, skin, metal and then blue sky once more.

'Subject down,' the voice is saying. 'The subject is down!'

Silence follows.

The wasp turns and makes a final pass over the scene.

A bicycle, crushed beneath the wheels of a white van.

A boy lying still and quiet in the dry, dusty heat of the day and a man running down the road towards him.

Blood and glass.

Bright green flies begin to settle in the sunshine.

The screen fades to black.

Sam stared into the darkness for a long time and no one spoke.

At last he said, 'I'm dead, aren't I?'

Firebrand shook his head. 'No, Sam. You're not dead.'

'But I saw it all. The crash. Me lying in the road. Please, tell me the truth.'

Firebrand glanced at Skipper and gestured towards the window. Skipper got up and drew back the curtains. Warm sunshine poured into the room. Sam rubbed his eyes and realised that they were wet with tears.

'This is the truth,' said Firebrand. 'We thought we had the whole area covered, but then all hell broke loose. About thirty horseflies were sighted swarming a couple of miles down the lane from your house. A squadron of wasps was immediately scrambled to intercept them. Another twenty or so came in from the north, flying low over the fields, while a third group, maybe forty or thereabouts, came at us out of the sun. It was bedlam, but at that stage we still felt reasonably confident. There were four wasp squadrons operating in the area and we thought we could handle it.' Firebrand sighed heavily. 'But of course, it turned out to be a diversion.'

Sam remembered the huge swarm of wasps he had seen that morning, just before he set off on his bike.

'What happened?' he asked.

'One of Odoursin's horseflies had camouflaged itself on a telephone wire and somehow we missed it. It watched you cycle down the road, waited until the van came round the corner and then dropped like a stone onto your neck. It bit suddenly and viciously, causing you to lose control of your bike. At the same time, a whole squadron of horseflies flew through the open window of the van and attacked the driver, who panicked and crashed into you. We now believe that it was a scenario they had practised and planned for many times. But this time they had the element of surprise and all the conditions were exactly right: the van, the bike, the concealed horsefly – there was nothing we could do.'

'But they didn't kill you, Sam,' said Skipper quickly, anxious to provide what reassurance she could.

'Then what am I doing here?' asked Sam.

'In his obsession to find out everything he could about the Dreamwalker, Odoursin discovered something about human consciousness which enabled him to drag you out of your world and into this one,' explained Firebrand. 'You remember what I told you about the balloons?'

'Yes, of course,' said Sam. 'When you dream, it's like a balloon floating out of its box.'

'Exactly. From his readings of the Book of Incantations and his cruel interrogations of the Olumnus tribe, Odoursin learned that death breaks the bond between the spirit and the body in which it resides. The string is cut and the balloon is separated from its box.'

'You mean, like when people die they go up to heaven?' asked Sam.

Firebrand smiled. 'Well, quite *where* they go is anyone's guess. Once their strings are cut they simply float out through an open window.'

'Couldn't they just float into one of the other rooms in the house that you talked about?' asked Sam. 'Like my mum did?'

'Normally, no,' said Firebrand. 'As I said earlier, the door – if we can describe it as such – is always shut. But the fact that your mother somehow found a way into this world through her dreams convinced Odoursin that he could bring you here too. He believed that if he moved fast enough, he could cut your string, grab you before you disappeared off through the window and bundle you back through the door into Aurobon.'

'Kill me, you mean?'

'Well, your physical body, yes. But he wanted to bring the essence of you to Aurobon and make sure that it stayed here.'

'But you told me I wasn't dead!' Sam shouted furiously, feeling the tears pricking at his eyes once more. 'You promised me!'

'And my promise holds true,' said Firebrand. 'As you have seen, Odoursin was able to take advantage of what we might call "the separation of spirit from body" at the moment of your unconsciousness. Somehow, at precisely the right moment when the van hit you, a gap in the fabric between our worlds was opened up and – how shall I put it? – the non-material essence of Sam was dragged violently through it.'

'They got the balloon to go through the door instead of the window,' said Skipper helpfully.

'Quite so,' said Firebrand. 'Exactly that. And as far as

we can understand it, a new physical body formed around your essence as you approached Aurobon – a bit like a photograph developing in a darkroom. Somehow, someone – maybe the Olumnus – managed to change the image for a while, but basically your body was identical to the one you left behind, only smaller because of its new environment.'

'So if I'm not dead,' said Sam, 'then what am I?'

'Good question,' said Firebrand. 'Your Earth body is, at this moment, lying in the intensive-care unit of Queen's Hospital. Heard of it?'

'Yes, I think so,' said Sam, finding it almost impossible to believe what he was hearing.

'You were flown there by helicopter and have remained in a coma ever since,' Firebrand continued. 'It seems the doctors don't hold out much hope for you.'

Skipper squeezed Sam's hand again. 'What do they know?' she said dismissively.

'Now, I'll be honest with you, Sam. Although we've been able to move between Aurobon and Earth for generations, none of us has ever had experience of anything like this. As far as I'm aware, no one from your world has ever strayed into ours before. It was never thought possible, at least not that a person could be in both worlds at the same time. We have watched people die in your world many times, seen their strings finally break and their bodies fade to dust. But we've been watching you up there, in your hospital bed, breathing through all those tubes. And here's the thing: you don't look like those others did. Not at all.'

'What do you mean?' said Sam.

'Usually when separation occurs – when the string is cut – the body gives up. The life goes out of it and it withers away to nothing.'

He paused for a moment, as if trying to make sense of what he had seen.

'But in yours, the life force is still strong. Despite Odoursin's best efforts, it seems that there is an even greater power somehow keeping your Earth body alive.'

Sam shook his head. 'I don't understand,' he said at last. 'What are you saying?'

Firebrand leant closer and, when he spoke, the words came like sunshine after a storm.

'I'm saying that the doctors are wrong, Sam. I'm saying that your body is still alive, it wants you back and that is where you belong. But first we have some unfinished business. Let us not forget the words of the prophecy: "*The Dreamwalker's Child shall rise up against the Darkness.*"'

Firebrand paused and then nodded.

'And so you shall, Sam. We will begin our preparations immediately. But if the prophecy is correct, then your role in any attack against Vermia must be a key one. And for that, I think, you are going to need some training.'

Before Sam could ask any questions, Firebrand leant forward and pressed a button on his desk. 'Mr Palmer will be requiring his room now, Sanderson.'

The long white corridor seemed to go on for miles and after a while the blank, featureless walls made Sam feel quite dizzy. His feet were aching by the time they finally came to a halt, but they didn't appear to have arrived anywhere in particular. The corridor continued on in both directions.

'Your room, sir,' said Sanderson. A slight, dignified inclination of the head gave the impression that serving others was a lifetime's ambition he had been lucky enough to achieve.

Sam looked at the smooth, creamy walls and then back at the silver-haired Sanderson, impeccably dressed in a black suit with trouser creases you could cut your fingers on.

'Hmm,' said Sam. 'OK.'

He looked again. Nope. No door. There was an uncomfortable silence. 'And the room is . . . where exactly?'

Sanderson looked at Sam, looked at the corridor wall, looked back at Sam. A confused expression momentarily clouded his face, but then realisation dawned and the expression evaporated.

'Oh, I'm sorry, sir,' he said, 'my mistake. I'd forgotten you were a new arrival.' He touched the wall with a white-gloved hand. 'It's simply a matter of voice activation,' he explained, 'to ensure extra security. Just say your name to gain entry.'

Sam raised his eyebrows and looked doubtfully at the wall, then stole a sideways glance at Sanderson to see if he was serious. Apparently so. Sanderson did not look the sort to indulge in practical jokes. A white glove gestured in the direction of the wall.

'Please.'

Sam cleared his throat. 'Sam,' he said.

Nothing happened.

Sanderson tilted his head to one side and whispered from the corner of his mouth, 'If I might suggest your full name, sir.'

'Oh. Right,' Sam replied, 'of course.' There was a pause as once again he mentally prepared himself to speak to a wall. 'Sam Palmer,' he said.

Immediately a blue rectangular line appeared, glowed once and then disappeared along with the rectangle of wall inside it.

'Oh, I get it,' said Sam, suddenly understanding, 'that's like the cellular-restructuring beams, the ones they use to make the doors on insects and stuff.'

'I believe the technology has some similarities, sir,' agreed Sanderson. 'Shall we?'

They walked through the newly formed doorway into a light, open room with a long, curving window at the far end. Part of the window had been opened to allow access to a balcony. Sam felt the heat of the afternoon wafting through and watched a group of three wasps come in to land on the airstrip in front of them.

The floor was covered in a thick white carpet and to his left Sam noticed that a blue uniform of some kind had been laid out on the bed. On the floor beneath it was a pair of shiny black boots.

'I assumed you would be tired after your long journey,' Sanderson explained, 'so I have taken the liberty of drawing a hot bath and will arrange for some food to be sent up presently.'

Sam glimpsed a brightly lit bathroom through a half-open door to his right. He realised that he hadn't washed for days and felt a pleasant tingle of anticipation as he pictured himself sinking happily into the warm water.

'I hope everything will be to your liking, sir,' said Sanderson, 'but if there is anything you need, please do not hesitate to call me on this.' He indicated a small metal grille on the wall with a red button beneath it.

'Great, thank you,' said Sam, still slightly stunned by the luxury of his new surroundings.

'I will wake you at six-thirty tomorrow for breakfast at seven,' said Sanderson. 'I have taken the liberty of laying out your flying suit for the morning.'

Sam looked across at the clothes on the bed. 'Flying suit?' he said.

'Of course,' said Sanderson. 'Your training starts tomorrow.'

Much later, Sam opened his eyes and realised two things: one, that he had fallen asleep in the bath and two, that the water had gone cold. Clambering out, he towelled himself dry and pulled on a warm robe that had been left for him on the radiator. His shoulder wound still hurt, but it was healing up nicely and the warm water had definitely helped to ease his aches and pains.

He padded out of the bathroom onto the thick white carpet and spotted a plate of sandwiches on the table.

Realising how hungry he was, he bit into one and discovered that it was filled with a deliciously smoky cheese. He wolfed it down and then, picking up another one, he wandered out onto the balcony and looked out across the airfield. Although it was still quite warm, the sun had gone down and a gentle breeze blew in from the west. He had obviously been asleep for some time. A solitary wasp took off from the far side of the airstrip, its low hum fading as it rose above the perimeter fence and turned away towards the distant mountains.

Sam thought about all the things that Firebrand had told him, about the prophecy, the threat to the Earth, the accident. About him being a balloon that had floated into the wrong room. He thought of his mother and father, watching over his broken body in a world that was now lost to him, a world that had once seemed so permanent and secure. 'Don't give up on me,' he whispered into the darkness. 'Please don't give up.'

Then he turned and walked back inside, carefully closing the window behind him.

Twenty-four

Sam stood on the edge of the long swimming pool and peered down into its blue depths. The crisp new uniform that he had put on so proudly that morning, with its yellow and black stripes on the cuffs and shiny silver buttons, was now hanging on a peg in the changing rooms. Instead he wore a green T-shirt and a pair of grey cotton shorts which came down to his knees.

'Looks inviting, don't it?'

The young man standing next to him was about eighteen, with closely cropped black hair and an easy smile. He was tall and rangy and looked as though he could run like a whippet.

'Hope you don't mind me saying this, but you seem awful small to be a pilot. Maybe you should've ate up them vegetables when your mum told you to.'

Sam looked at the row of men standing along the side of the pool and realised that he was the youngest and shortest person there by a considerable margin.

The man had a point.

'It isn't the vegetables so much,' replied Sam, 'it's more to do with how long I've actually been eating them. I'm still at school, you know.' He thought for a moment. 'At least, I was . . .'

'Well, I ain't wet or nothing, so I guess I ain't been swimmin',' said the man, with a look of mock disbelief on his face, 'but I think my ears still got stuffed up with water, cos I'm damn sure you jus' said you was still at school.'

'That's right,' said Sam. 'I am.'

The man made a big show of sticking his little finger in one ear, wiggling it about and then thumping it with his palm to remove imaginary water.

'Say that again?'

'I'm still at school,' Sam repeated, unable to stop himself from smiling at the pantomime being performed in front of him.

The man stopped, raised his eyebrows and looked Sam up and down, like a farmer who can't decide whether to buy a horse.

'Well now,' he said at last, 'either they're getting desperate or you must be one hell of a flier.' He scratched the back of his head and then nudged the man standing next to him, a stocky, muscular youth of a similar age who had been on the receiving end of a similar haircut to his friend.

'Did you hear that, Zip?' he said. 'This one's still at school.'

Zip nodded and gave a slow, relaxed smile. He struck Sam as someone who would remain fairly calm even if his shorts caught on fire. 'Age doesn't matter,' he said, and tapped the side of his head. 'It's wisdom that counts.'

He stepped forward and offered his hand to Sam, who shook it and said, 'Sam Palmer. I just arrived yesterday.'

'Good to meet you, Sam. My name's Zip and this here's Mump.'

Mump nodded and grinned like a child, showing a mouthful of sparkly white teeth.

'So how come you've just joined the programme? I know we're the newest squad on the base, but we've been training a few weeks already.'

Sam thought about the secret briefing he'd attended earlier that morning, thought about the imminent attack that was planned against Vermian airbases and realised that these young pilots were still unaware of the dangers that lay ahead. So he just shrugged and said, 'All I know is I have to take this evacuation drill today and then I'm on something called dual-flight training tomorrow.'

'Ah, OK,' said Zip, seeming to understand. 'They must have you in mind for something pretty soon. That's why you're getting a crash course in the basics.'

Mump sniggered. 'Crash course,' he said. 'You got that right.'

At that moment an abrupt order was shouted from the far end of the pool. Everyone snapped to attention – shoulders back, eyes straight ahead – and Sam turned to see a short, powerfully built man with close-cropped red hair step up to the water's edge and bang the tiled floor with a long, gold-topped cane. Sam noticed he walked with a slight limp.

'That's Brindle,' whispered Zip, 'survival expert and official nutcase. He was shot down over the forest and got his leg blown off in a minefield. Sort of thing that would set a bloke back a bit, you might think. But not Brindle. When the ants picked him up he was busy carving himself a new leg out of a tree stump. Give him another week and he'd have been attacking them with a machete made out of twigs.'

'Just look at him,' said Mump. 'I'd surrender. No question.'

Sam looked at Brindle, with his small hard eyes and short bristling red hair. 'Me too,' he said.

Next to Brindle was a high metal tower with a set of steps leading up at the back. At the top of the tower was a metal box in the shape of a wasp's head, with glass screens where the eyes would normally have been. There were gaps at the side and through them Sam could just make out a single seat of battered brown leather. A length of steel track - not unlike the rails of a rollercoaster – sloped steeply down from the front of the tower into the pool, where it continued all the way to the bottom before finally straightening out again.

'All right, now listen up,' Brindle shouted. 'If you pay attention to every word I say and follow my instructions to the letter, then you will not get hurt. Do you understand?'

'Sir, yes sir!' everyone roared back.

Sam jumped at the unexpected volume of the reply, then recovered and quickly stood to attention, staring straight ahead and watching the early-morning sunlight dapple the water with bright intricate patterns.

'Upon my command you will enter the capsule and the safety officer will check that your harness is secure. The capsule will then be launched. Upon impact with the water the capsule will immediately turn upside down. Only when it is fully inverted and stationary should you attempt to release the harness and swim to the surface. Rescue divers will be on hand should you encounter any difficulties, but follow my instructions and they will not be necessary.'

'Too right they won't be necessary,' hissed Mump out of the corner of his mouth, 'cos I ain't going anywhere *near* that damn thing.' He grinned and winked in Sam's direction.

There was a long pause, then the slow, steady tread of footsteps over tiles as Brindle's boots echoed their way up the side of the pool towards them. Heads automatically turned to face the front.

'Uh-oh,' said Mump. 'Now I gone and done it.'

Sam heard the boots pass behind him and then squeak once as Brindle swivelled around to look at Mump. Sam watched from the corner of his eye as the instructor leant his face in close.

'Did you say something to me, boy?' he said with quiet but unmistakable menace.

Mump swallowed so hard that the gulp was audible, but he followed it quickly with a shout of, 'Sir, no sir!'

'I'm sorry,' said the instructor, 'I didn't quite catch that.'

'Sir, no sir!' shouted Mump again.

'No. Well then, I must have been hearing things. Do you think I was hearing things, boy?'

'Sir, yes sir.' Here Mump glanced at the amazed face of the instructor and then quickly changed his mind, 'I mean sir, no sir!'

Brindle leant back so that his boots squeaked again. He cocked his head on one side and stared at Mump as if contemplating something he had almost stepped in.

'It seems to me, boy, that you don't have an idea what to think. So I'm going to straighten out your mind a little with a nice cold wake-up call. Would you like that?'

It seemed for a moment that Mump wasn't going to answer, but then finally his expression seemed to change to one of unbridled enthusiasm and he shouted, 'Sir, I would love it, sir!'

The instructor seemed momentarily taken aback by the apparent glee with which Mump had reacted to his question, but quickly recovered and began to lead the way back towards the tower. Sam watched Mump follow and noticed how he almost skipped along behind as if he had been singled out for a special treat.

He stood beneath the tower with his head back and mouth open, looking up at it. Zip sucked air through his teeth and Sam saw a look of concern cross his face.

'Could be a bit of a problem here,' he whispered at last.

'Why?' asked Sam.

'Mump can't swim.'

Sam could see that Mump was quite excited now, shifting his weight rapidly from foot to foot like a small child who has discovered that the toilet door is locked.

'OK, ladies,' bellowed Brindle, 'listen up.' He lifted his cane and brought it up to rest against Mump's chest, which seemed to calm him a little. The hopping became less frantic.

'What we have here is a *brave* volunteer who is going to show you all how it's done.' He turned to Mump. 'Isn't that right?'

Mump nodded furiously.

'Good. What's your name, son?'

'Sir, my name's Mump, sir.'

Brindle considered this for a moment. 'Well that's not your fault. Now this here's your opportunity to be a shining example to your fellow fliers. You, Mump, are to be a beacon that lights the way so that all who witness it experience a perfect vision of how this thing should be done. What you are about to do is an honour and a privilege. How does that feel?'

Mump was beaming happily now. 'Sir, it feels good, sir!'

'Of *course* it does!' Brindle pointed up the metal steps with his cane. 'OK, son. Up you go.'

'I thought you said he couldn't swim?' whispered Sam as Mump clambered unsteadily up the first few steps under Brindle's watchful gaze.

'He can't,' replied Zip. 'Sinks like a stone every time.'

'He looks pretty confident to me,' said Sam.

'That's the trouble,' said Zip. 'Bags of enthusiasm, acres of self-belief, but no grasp of reality. The thing is, you see – as with everything else – he thinks he *can* swim.'

'Oh,' said Sam. He watched as Mump stepped cheerfully into the cockpit high above the water and allowed himself to be strapped in. 'Oh dear.'

'Oh, well,' said Zip with a half-smile that seemed to suggest he was not unduly worried about his friend. 'Bring on the divers, I say.'

Up on the tower, Mump put his thumbs up.

There was a sharp, warning blast on a horn, the hiss of an air brake being released and then a loud clattering and clunking as the cockpit gathered speed and descended the rails towards the calm blue surface of the pool. With a tremendous smack, it hit the water and Sam just had time to see Mump's eyebrows raised in surprise before the entire cockpit plunged beneath the surface and turned upside down. The force of the impact sent a wave racing towards the poolside, where it splashed over the edge and slapped onto the cold tiles around Sam's feet. As it receded, he stepped forward to get a better view and noticed that everyone else was doing the same.

The surface of the water remained choppy for a while, but as it began to settle Sam could clearly see the cockpit lying upside down at the bottom of the pool. There did not appear to be any movement under the water.

'Shouldn't he be up by now?' asked Sam. He imagined Mump's pale, surprised face hanging upside down, shouting for help in the blue and watery silence.

'Yeah, he probably should,' said Zip. 'But then he's late for everything. Look – here come the divers.'

Sam watched the rubber-suited figures push smoothly away from the side of the pool and flipper their way down towards the sunken craft, trailing lines of silver bubbles behind them.

Zip patted Sam's shoulder reassuringly. 'Don't worry about Mump,' he said. 'He'll be calmly sitting there, scratching his head and trying to figure out whether he's having a horse ride or a haircut. It'll only be when they pull him out that he'll remember what he was supposed to do.'

Right on cue, Mump's head broke spluttering through the surface of the water and the divers pulled him struggling and coughing to the side of the pool.

'I don't mean to be rude,' said Sam, 'but isn't he a bit of a liability?'

'Oh absolutely,' agreed Zip. 'The guy's a walking disaster. But,' he added, 'you put him in a wasp and that boy'll fly like an angel with a new set of wings.'

Zip leant forward and extended his hand to Mump, who grabbed it and pulled himself dripping from the pool. He stood in front of them both, bedraggled and gasping for air.

'So how was it, Mump?' grinned Zip. 'How does it feel to be a shining example to us all?'

Mump smiled weakly. ‘It feels great,’ he said. ‘Piece of cake.’ Then he burped up several pints of chlorinated water and fainted.

‘OK, son. Is that tight enough for you?’

Sam nodded as the safety officer gave a final pull on the seat restraints.

‘All right. Good. Now, remember the drill: deep breath as you hit the pool, then wait until the capsule inverts and fills with water. When everything stops moving, release the buckle and swim up to the surface. OK, now you. Talk me through it.’

Sam narrowed his eyes and squinted through dark lashes at the blue rectangle far below. It felt as though a million butterflies had suddenly hatched in his stomach and were flitting madly into his fingers and toes.

‘Right. I take a deep breath as I hit the water, I wait until I’m upside down, then I release the buckle and swim out.’

‘Excellent.’ The safety officer had a kindly face and Sam guessed he wasn’t used to watching a young boy ditch an aircraft, even if it was only a drill. He put a thumb up. ‘Show ’em how it’s done, lad.’

Sam raised his own thumb briefly and then quickly dropped it again, gripping the metal bar in front of him as the man moved towards the brake-release mechanism at the rear of the tower.

‘Prepare to ditch,’ called the safety officer.

There was a loud blast from the horn, a hiss from the

brake and then Sam's stomach flipped and headed north as he dropped like a stone towards the pool. It was like the moment when a rollercoaster reaches the very highest point of its track and then tumbles over the edge, but worse – like stepping off a cliff and falling into an abyss. It was terrifying, but Sam only whimpered quietly as he hurtled towards the pool at a speed that seemed to him quite unbelievable.

He took a deep breath and closed his eyes.

With a smack and a roar, the capsule plunged below the surface and a whirlwind of water tore into the open cockpit, flooding everything with its cold, wet light and pulling Sam down into a churning chaos of sound and confusion.

Sam listened to the shriek of bubbles and the eerie creak of straining metal. He held his breath close to his heart and counted – one, two, three. There was a final clunk as the chains and the gears of the machinery slotted into place and then the capsule came to rest upside down.

The flurry of bubbles subsided and Sam felt his lungs straining, crying out for air. He opened his eyes and, looking down through the haze of blue, saw the silver buckle gleaming in the centre of his chest. He pulled at the clasp and felt the tension in the straps disappear as they fell away. Rolling forward towards his knees, he pushed away from the seat with his feet and found his hands were on the edge of the doorway. Water filled his nostrils and stung his eyes. Pulling hard, he kicked his legs and swam up towards the surface. With a last desperate pull of his hands he broke through and suddenly he was splashing to safety, gulping down lungfuls of fresh air and staring up at the pools of light that bounced and shimmered around the walls of the building.

'You know,' said Mump as they towelled themselves dry and prepared to change back into their uniforms, 'if they'd only waited a few more seconds, I'd have been out of there no problem.'

Sam and Zip exchanged knowing smiles.

'Of course you would,' said Zip.

'I would!' Mump protested indignantly. 'I quite like it on the bottom.'

There was a slight pause, followed by a loud crack as Singer, another of the trainees, scored a direct hit on Mump's backside with a well-aimed flick from his towel. 'Happy to oblige,' he said, and the changing room erupted into raucous cheers as Singer ran off around the corner with Mump in hot pursuit.

Twenty-five

Jack Palmer reversed his car into an empty parking space and turned off the ignition. The sound of the engine died away, to be replaced by the moan of the wind and the heavy splatter of rain against glass.

August: the great British summer, he thought. Already the windscreen was misting up, and rubbing a clear patch with the sleeve of his raincoat, he peered through at the mass of grey concrete and glass that rose up against the dark sky. Did they deliberately build hospitals to look so depressing, he wondered, or was it just a combination of dust, grime and the despair of the people who came to visit?

High up in one of the lighted windows, he saw a small figure looking out across the city.

Sam? Could it be?

His heart skipped a beat.

But as quickly as the thought came he pushed it away again, ashamed of himself for daring to think such non-sense. He knew it couldn't be Sam. Sam was on the other side of the hospital, surrounded by tubes and machines, and smiling nurses who were always professional, efficient and cheerful.

'Hello,' they would say. 'How are we today?'

'I'm fine,' he would say. 'How are you?'

They didn't know how, with every fragile breath, Sam broke his father's heart a little more.

The rain was a torrent against the windscreen now and Jack turned the wipers back on. As they whirred rhythmically back and forth he watched anonymous silhouettes run across the rain-lashed car park and wondered sadly if his share of life's happiness had all been used up. Could there be an extra parcel for him, hidden around a bend somewhere?

It seemed unlikely. All he could picture now was a featureless grey road, leading away from all that he had loved.

Of course, it hadn't always been so.

He remembered a winter evening long ago when the fields were silver with frost and the moon hung low in the trees; how he had stumbled hand in hand with Sally through the bright doors of the small cottage hospital, their breathless laughter turning to smoke on the cold night air.

As the nurses bustled around her, he had glanced out of the window and seen the orange glow from the street-lamps. They reminded him of the lights on a runway, waiting to guide the planes safely home in the darkness. Then Sally was gasping, calling for him, and their baby was here at last, coming in to land on the brightly lit table, all the way from eternity.

They called him Sam.

Before he met Sally, Jack had never found it easy to say the things he felt. He had been brought up to believe that shows of affection were a sign of weakness. If you hugged people, or kissed them, or told them that you loved them, then you were a feeble sort of person lacking in strength or character. People would take advantage of you and that was a bad thing. His mother and father had been big on teaching him the values of strength and independence, and they rarely cuddled him or held him close. They wanted him to be able to look after himself in the world.

Jack's parents were not bad people, but nobody had ever taught them that love makes you strong on the inside. Without it, you can be as strong as you like on the outside, but one day something, somehow, will find its way through and then you're done for. But Jack didn't know about that, because no one had ever told him.

So he had joined the army to try to be just as strong and tough as he possibly could. He became very fit and he learned how to fight and how to kill and how not to let anyone get too close to him.

But then one day he had found Sally on her knees by the side of a busy road, trying to change the wheel on her little green Mini.

'I'm perfectly capable of doing it myself, thank you,' she had said, politely but firmly.

And so she was. But she had smiled at him with her eyes and all of a sudden he hadn't wanted to go.

So he had sat on the verge instead, handing her the spanners and, when she was finally done, pouring hot coffee from his flask. She told him all about her work as a garden designer, about how she painted pictures with plants and went to sleep dreaming of dandelions and daisies.

'Why do you love me?' he asked on their wedding night, looking up at the square of stars through the skylight above their bed.

'Because you're not who you think you are,' she had whispered mysteriously in the darkness.

'Who am I then?' he asked.

But she had just smiled and held him close.

And although he hadn't fully understood, he knew that he loved her more than anything in the world.

Soon afterwards, he left the army to help her with her gardens, and it was like stumbling out into sunshine after a long winter, the feel of earth between his fingers and the green shoots of new seedlings touching something deep within him that had lain buried all his life. He had never known such happiness.

The business did well, and when Sam was born it seemed as though his life was complete. Sam was an unlooked-for gift and as he grew and held his arms out for Jack, the last of Jack's defences had crumbled away and his heart had fallen open.

Sally was right. He wasn't who he thought he was at all.

Jack turned off the wipers and stared at the blurred wall of water that sluiced down the windscreen.

So he had learned how to love. He had stepped into the world and held it gently in his arms. And now, little by little, it was falling apart.

He remembered the words of advice his father had once given him. 'Don't be taken in by this world, son,' he told him. 'You'll only get hurt.'

Jack screwed up his eyes and quietly, wearily rested his head against the steering wheel.

'I'm sorry, Dad,' he said. 'I'm so sorry.'

Sally Palmer stroked her son's pale cheek and gently squeezed his hand. The only other movement came from the ventilator by his bed as it puffed endlessly up and down, keeping him alive with its mechanical exertions. Next to it, a heart monitor bleeped quietly to itself.

'I bought you a new CD for your computer today,' she told him. 'It tells you all about the stars and planets and everything. I know how you love to look at them. The man in the shop said it's brilliant. He said you just have to put in where you live and then it shows you the whole sky above your house, tells you the names of all the stars and what the constellations are called.'

A nurse popped her head around the door, smiled at Sally and then disappeared back into the corridor again.

'Dad will be here in a minute. He's been busy putting up a new trellis so that we can grow roses round the door – you know, the red ones we saw on holiday last summer.

I always said I wanted roses round the door, didn't I?'

Sam's chest rose and fell in time with the ventilator. Apart from the blue and green bruising around his eyes, his face was undamaged. He looked as though he was asleep.

'Did I tell you we've finished the baby's room now? You'd love it, Sam. Dad went and bought a mobile with little teddies on it and we've put up some nice yellow wallpaper all covered in daisies. It's really bright and summery.'

Sally smiled, trying desperately to think of something else to say. But it wasn't easy trying to talk to someone when they couldn't answer you, when you didn't know if they could hear you, didn't know if they were even there any more. She reached into her bag, took out a small pink teddy bear and placed it on the bedside table.

'You didn't tell me, did you, love?' Sally's smile wavered and her bottom lip began to quiver. 'Dad says you won it for me, that day at the arcade. But you never told me, did you? And so I never said thank you . . .' Her voice trailed off as she lifted Sam's hand and held it tightly against her chest. The tears were running down her cheeks now. They dripped off the end of her chin and made tiny damp circles on the pale blue hospital blanket.

'The thing is,' she said, 'we just want you to come home, Sam. That's all. We just want you home.'

Sally pulled a tissue from her bag to try to stem the tears and as she did so she felt a hand on her shoulder.

Jack stood beside her and she buried her face in his sleeve.

'Oh, Jack,' she whispered when her sobs had subsided a little, 'tell me it will be all right.'

Jack stroked her hair as she wept and looked across at his only son, his gift from heaven that had been so brutally snatched away.

'Of course it will,' he told her. 'We'll get him back, you'll see. Remember what you used to say to me? Everything is for the best in the end.'

He tenderly kissed the top of her head, shut his eyes tight and wished more than anything that what he said was true.

But the truth was, he didn't believe it any more.

Twenty-six

Skipper dropped through the hatch into the seat next to Sam and the CRB flashed blue as she closed the hole up again.

'How are you feeling?' she said.

'I'm fine, thank you,' said Sam. 'And, I am pleased to inform you, fully trained for water-related disasters.'

'Explain?' said Skipper.

'Cockpit-evacuation drill,' said Sam. 'Did it this morning. If we were to crash into a lake this afternoon, I would coolly unclip my safety harness, flip calmly out of the emergency hatch and swim up to the surface with the speed and grace of a dolphin.'

Skipper smiled and nodded. 'Yeah, I heard you did pretty well.'

Sam raised an eyebrow. 'Who told you?'

'Brindle. He reckons you're a natural.'

'Brindle said that?'

'Yeah.' Skipper flicked a switch and the instrument

panel glowed deep red. 'Textbook evacuation, he called it. Brindle may be a bit of a hard nose, but he's a pretty good judge of character. You must have done really well, Sam.'

Sam blushed. 'I think it was more to do with the lack of competition actually,' he said.

'Don't tell me,' said Skipper, 'let me guess. You didn't have Mump on the team there, did you?'

'We did,' said Sam. 'Why, do you know him?'

'Only by reputation. Apparently he's a promising pilot but as soon as he gets out of his aircraft he turns into an almighty accident just waiting to happen.'

Sam frowned. 'He can't be that bad, can he?'

'Don't you believe it. Last week on the infantry course he picked up a drill bomb instead of a hand grenade and threw it onto the practice range. When there was no explosion, the weapons officer climbed out of the trench to have a look. Instead of an unexploded grenade he found a neat little hole in the ground with smoke coming out of it. Just had time to dive for cover before the whole ground erupted and the air was filled with flying cookers.'

'Eh?' said Sam, confused. 'What do you mean, flying cookers?'

'The drill bomb had burrowed its way down into the underground kitchens and blown 'em all to bits. Terrible business it was.'

'Sounds it,' said Sam. 'Did anyone get killed?'

'Luckily not,' replied Skipper. 'Although no thanks to Mump. It just so happened that everyone was changing shift at the time and the only casualty was a chef who had his teeth knocked out by a ninety-mile-an-hour onion.'

Sam tried not to laugh. 'That must have been a shock for him,' he said.

'I'll say. Apparently he has to suck his food up through a straw and gets nightmares about being attacked by vegetables.'

There was a pause.

'I thought they were supposed to be good for you,' said Sam.

Skipper giggled but then the intercom crackled into life and there was a hiss of static followed by a clear, calm voice from the control tower: 'Hunter 437, this is control, do you read me?'

Skipper cleared her throat with a final chuckle, clicked her safety harness into place and said: 'Control, this is Hunter 437 reading you loud and clear.'

'Hunter 437, you are cleared for take-off. Proceed when ready.'

'OK, control. Please be advised that pilot training is now under way, so anticipate slight take-off delay, over.'

'Understood, 437. You have been granted a ten-minute window to complete procedures, over.'

'Appreciate that, control. Hunter 437 out,' said Skipper. Then she turned to Sam. 'Ready?'

'Ready,' Sam replied. He felt a thrill of anticipation run through him like electricity as he looked at the brightly lit control panel. The thought briefly occurred to him that he would soon be flying into action against

Vermian forces, but he pushed it from his mind. He would worry about that later. For the moment, he was determined to enjoy the fact that they were actually going to let him fly this thing.

'Now what we have here,' Skipper explained, 'is a dual-control system.'

'Right,' said Sam, looking at the two identical joysticks and the array of switches and dials in front of him.

'That means,' continued Skipper, 'that any time I think you're about to kill us both, I can take over.'

'And vice versa presumably,' suggested Sam.

Skipper gave him a look. 'Behave,' she said. 'Now this –' here she pointed to a red button '– is the ignition. Basically it does two jobs: First, it feeds a glucose solution through to the insect's wing muscles in order to supply them with enough power to get us airborne. Then it sends out an electrical impulse which fires them up. Go ahead, try it.'

Sam pressed the button and heard the hum of a pump starting up, the gurgle of liquid and then almost immediately a low whirring sound which made the whole cockpit very gently vibrate. He looked through the curve of the screen and saw the wasp's delicately veined wings begin to describe figure-of-eight patterns in the air, quickly blurring into an indistinguishable grey as the wing speed increased. Sam felt lighter, as if invisible hands were holding him up.

'Good,' said Skipper, 'that's very good. Now then. These controls have been designed so that even an

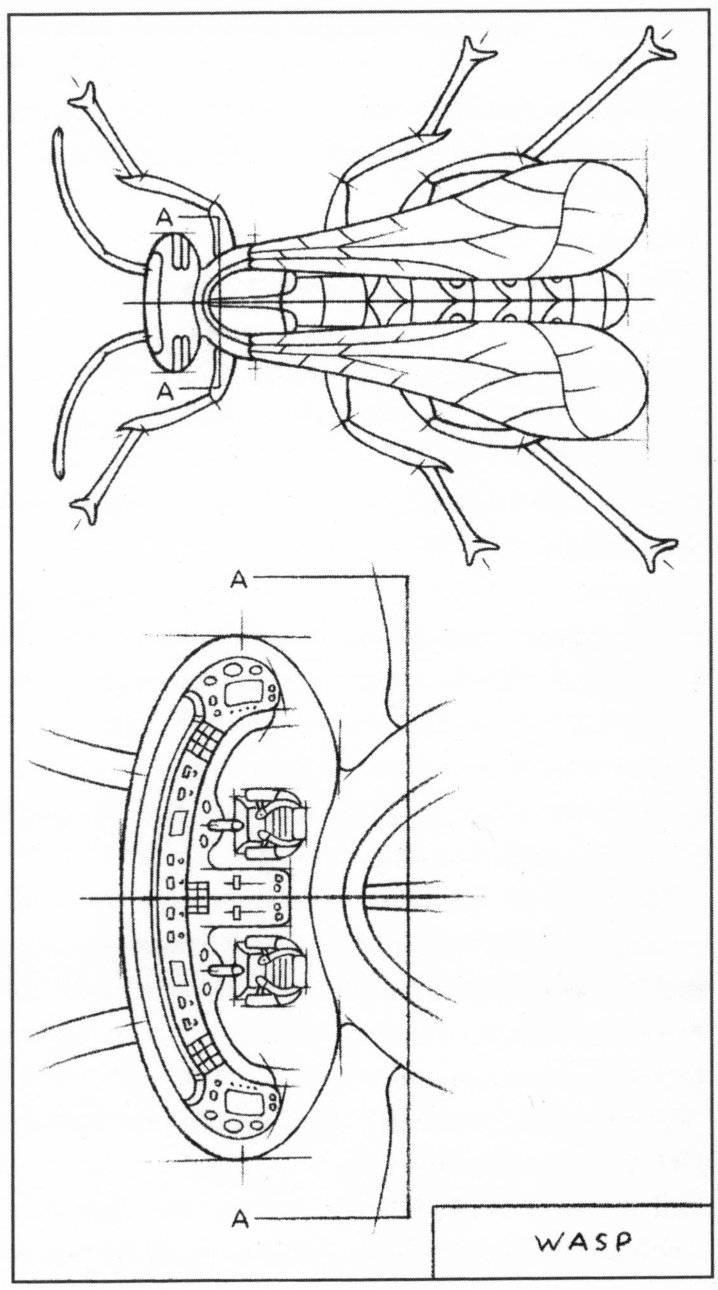
A
A
A
A
WASP

idiot can use them, so you really shouldn't have any problems.'

'Flatterer,' said Sam, peering down at the ground.

'Oi. Pay attention or I'll activate your ejector seat.'

'Has it really got one?'

'It really has.'

Sam imagined himself shooting up into the air at a zillion miles per second. 'Cool,' he said.

'Come on, concentrate. Right. Put your left hand on the grip of the lever down by the side of your seat. Found it?'

'Found it,' said Sam, feeling his hand fit comfortably over the padded handle.

'All right, good. Don't move it yet though. That's the throttle, which controls the speed of the wings and makes you go faster or slower. At the moment we're just ticking over. Now put your right hand on the joystick.'

Sam's fingers closed around the stick and he touched the red button at the top with his thumb. 'Has this thing got machine guns?' he asked.

Skipper shook her head. ''Fraid not, no. This one's kitted out for Earth missions so they generally leave out stuff like that. Wouldn't do for some old chap to see us scorching across his allotment shooting down horseflies with tracer bullets, would it?'

'I s'pose not,' said Sam. 'It'd be fun though. What does the red button do?'

'It deploys the sting,' said Skipper. She flicked a switch on the instrument panel and a red box appeared on the screen in front of them. 'You see that? Well, you get your enemy lined up in there between the front legs and then zap! You bring the sting up and it's all over.'

'What about the blue one next to it?' asked Sam.

'Press it and see.'

'Are you sure?' asked Sam uncertainly. He had visions of a couple of guided missiles flaming off towards the control tower and vaporising it.

'Trust me,' said Skipper. 'I know these things.'

Sam pressed the button and at once there was a loud slicing, grinding sound from outside the cockpit. Sam quickly took his thumb off the button again and the noise stopped.

'What was that?' he asked in alarm.

'Mandibles,' said Skipper. 'That was the sound of this little fella grinding his jaws together.' She patted the top of the cockpit. 'Put that together with the sting and it's Goodbye, Mr Fly. This thing is a killer, believe me.'

'I know,' said Sam. 'It nearly killed us yesterday.'

'What? Oh yes, that.' Skipper gave a half-smile. 'You know who was flying that other wasp, don't you?'

'No. Who?'

'Your friend Mump.'

Sam was amazed. 'That was Mump who flew straight at us?'

'Apparently so. I saw the notes from the debriefing this morning. He was reprimanded for reckless flying and causing unnecessary damage to a squadron aircraft.'

'That seems a bit unfair. Surely he was only defending

the airfield against attack. He didn't know it was us, after all.'

'Oh, that wasn't what he got reprimanded for,' said Skipper. 'It was what he did afterwards that got him into trouble.'

'What do you mean?'

'He buzzed the control tower, did a victory roll over the landing zone and then caught his wing on the top of the perimeter fence while flying upside down. He escaped with just a few cuts and bruises, but the wasp was a write-off.'

Sam grinned. 'Sounds like Mump. Perhaps I'd better leave out the victory roll today then.'

'Better had,' said Skipper. 'Crashing is *so* last year.' She pointed down the airfield towards the perimeter. 'You see that fence?'

Sam nodded.

'Well, in a minute I want you to fly up over it and then keep climbing until I say. We'll then head west and fly up over the mountains, OK?'

'OK . . .' said Sam nervously. 'Um, how do I do that then?'

'Simple,' said Skipper. 'You just increase your throttle speed like this –' here she pushed the throttle forward and the hum in the cockpit increased '– and then move the joystick like . . . so.' The wasp rose a little way off the ground, travelled forward slightly and then, as Skipper throttled back and returned the joystick to its original position, bumped gently down to earth again.

'Easy, isn't it?' she said. 'Now you try.'

Sam's palms were sweating and he rubbed them on the front of his jacket. 'OK,' he said, 'here goes.'

He gripped the throttle with his left hand and pushed it forward until the wings began to whine, then pulled back gently on the joystick. He glanced over to his left and saw to his delight that the ground was falling away beneath him. 'I'm flying,' he shouted excitedly. 'I'm flying!'

'Look ahead of you, Sam,' Skipper warned. 'Not to the side – look ahead.'

Sam looked through the screen and saw that they were rapidly approaching the perimeter fence. He turned quickly to Skipper. 'What do I do?' he asked.

'Try pulling back on the stick,' suggested Skipper.

As it now appeared to Sam that they were about to crash into the fence, he did as he'd been told and pulled back hard on the joystick. In an instant the fence disappeared and suddenly the ground was where the sky used to be and Sam was hanging upside down in his seat, feeling the blood rushing to his head.

'Aaaagh!' he yelled. 'Skipper, help!'

'Relax,' said Skipper, calmly adjusting the joystick with two fingers and restoring the horizon to its proper position. They began to climb gently through the wisps of shredded cloud above the airfield.

Sam had turned pale and was breathing heavily. 'What happened there?' he asked.

'Well, you might want to use a slightly lighter touch on the joystick next time,' said Skipper. 'But on the plus side, that was a really neat little somersault. Victory rolls may yet be within your grasp.'

Sam wiped his forehead and saw that the fence posts below had already shrunk away to matchsticks.

'I'm handing control back to you now, Sam,' said Skipper.

'Is that wise?' said Sam, but he eased the stick back and the wasp soared effortlessly through the blue sky. He felt a sudden, unexpected lightness in himself which came not only from the fact that he was flying but also from his realisation that this strange new world was not so strange any more. Once he had been a lost soul looking for a way out; now he was finding that this new world seemed more and more like home to him. He was growing into himself and adapting quickly to the many changes. Already this new existence was becoming more real than the one he had left behind.

Sam still experienced feelings of guilt and unease about what had been lost. He missed his parents badly, especially in those quiet moments when he was left alone with his thoughts. Last night he had lain awake for hours staring at shadows on the ceiling, trying desperately to picture their faces and recall the sound of their voices. It was at such times that he felt his loss most keenly, like an ache that never really went away.

But his friendship with Skipper was nothing short of a revelation to him. He had never in his life felt so comfortable with anyone, never before met anyone who was so self-assured and yet so completely without vanity. She was wise beyond her years, devoted to putting right what she perceived to be wrong. But at the same time she possessed an innocence which seemed untouched by the many evils she must have encountered during her short life.

He remembered the first time he saw those bright blue eyes, shining in the dark corridor outside his cell and bringing hope where he had thought there was none.

He realised now what it was about her that touched him. Despite the fact that he was probably dead, she made him feel more alive than he had ever been. She took away his fears and made him want to be the best person that he could be, made him think that anything was possible.

'Thanks, Skipper,' he said, before he realised what he was saying.

'Hey, don't thank me – you're a natural. Should've been a bird.'

Sam scratched his head, embarrassed but not wanting to be misunderstood. 'No, I mean thanks for all you've done. Saving my life and everything.'

Skipper looked sad. 'I haven't saved your life, Sam, remember? If I had, you wouldn't be here now.'

Sam thought about that for a moment, about the bike accident and the hospital bed and how confusing it all was. 'I don't mean that. I mean getting me away from Odoursin at the airfield. You saved the life I have now, didn't you?'

Skipper nodded. 'Yes, I did that. But now we need to get your other life back.'

Sam paused and when he spoke again it was with some hesitation. 'What if I don't want it back?' he said tentatively. 'What if I want to stay here? What then?'

Skipper seemed surprised by the question. 'Don't you want your life back?' she asked.

'I don't know,' Sam replied. 'I did. And part of me still does. But part of me – a big part of me – is very happy here.'

There was a long silence. At last Skipper said: 'I think that there are some things we just can't know. When I was a small child, I used to think that my life in the forest was everything. That was how things were and that was the way I thought they would stay. I thought I would always be there. But then, one day, something called to me and I knew I had to go. Maybe it'll be the same for you.'

'You think I'll be called back?'

'I don't know. All I know is, my world suddenly changed and, although it was different, it wasn't bad. Good things have come out of it.'

'Like what?'

Skipper smiled. 'Like saving your life,' she said. 'I'll never forget what Arbous told me just before I left the forest. He said, "Remember, it's not the things that happen to you that are important. It's what you do about them that counts."'

Sam was silent for a while. Then he looked across at Skipper and touched her gently on the arm. 'I'd do the same for you, you know,' he said. 'I'd save your life if I could.'

'I know you would, Sam. And who knows – you may get the chance much sooner than you think.'

Sam wanted to ask her what she meant, but something stopped him. He was learning not to ask too many questions about a future that could never be certain. Pushing the joystick to the right, he banked the wasp smoothly round and saw the sharp, crisp lines of the western mountains spreading out far below them in the afternoon sunshine.

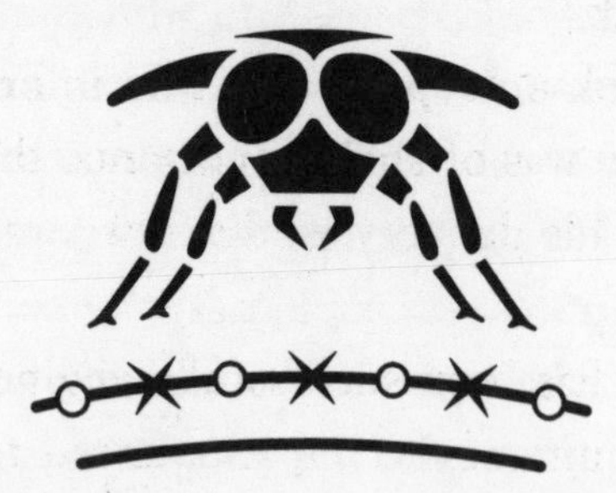

Twenty-seven

As Hekken walked across the marble floor towards the circular table around which the other members of the Council were seated, he was aware of eleven pairs of eyes turning to look at him through the gloom. He returned their gaze with his head held erect, his measured, unfaltering progress betraying a certain amount of arrogance and determination.

Odoursin stood up slowly as Hekken reached the table and Hekken bowed stiffly. The other members of the Council made as if to stand but Odoursin motioned them to remain seated.

'I am sorry for my lateness, Your Excellency. But there have been important developments in the laboratory which I was anxious to relay to the Council.'

Odoursin's eyes glinted in the half-light. 'You have news of the virus?'

Hekken nodded. 'Indeed I do, Your Excellency. And the news is good.'

'Then speak.'

Hekken took a deep breath. The information from the laboratory was of such importance that he wanted to make sure his delivery of the news was equal to its significance.

'The virus has been successfully engineered to meet all of our requirements,' he announced to gasps from around the table, 'and the first batch will be ready for delivery in less than a week.'

Hekken was gratified to observe the looks of shock and disbelief on the faces of several members of the Council, but Odoursin's face had become impassive once more.

'How can you be sure of this, General? Your last report gave the Council the impression that there were still many problems to be overcome.'

'It is true that until recently there were many difficulties,' replied Hekken, 'but, as you know, the team is loyal, hard-working and anxious to achieve success. To this end they have worked day and night to find a solution, and this morning, at last, came the breakthrough that they were looking for.'

Odoursin's thin, papery lips twitched briefly into the shadow of a smile, the movement as fleeting and barely discernible as that of a mosquito moving through the dust of a forgotten room.

'Explain,' he said.

'Well,' said Hekken, 'if you remember, we had isolated a virus which was so virulent that it would kill humans in a matter of hours once it was in their bloodstream. But the problem was that it released a substance so toxic to mosquitoes that it killed them before they could transfer it. We tried coating the gut of the mosquito with a protective material, but realised it would protect only the piloted mosquitoes that we sent to deliver the first batch of the virus. If the plague was to be successful in wiping out humans, it needed to be spread by the billions of wild mosquitoes that inhabit the Earth. To give them protection in sufficient numbers would have been an impossibility.'

Hekken glanced at Odoursin and saw a look of irritation on his face. 'I hope this is not going to be a science lesson in failure, General Hekken. Please get to the point.'

'I am sorry, Your Excellency. The point is, it appears we were coming at it from the wrong angle. What we should have been doing is looking for a way of preventing the release of the toxin in the first place.'

He waited for some encouragement to continue before remembering that he had already been told to get to the point.

'Instead of coating the gut of the mosquito, we coated the surface of the virus instead.'

He paused for dramatic effect.

'The results were even better than we had hoped. Not only did the mosquitoes survive, but the next generation of viruses mutated and produced their own protective coating. This new coating slowed down the initial rate at which the virus multiplied once it was in the human bloodstream.'

'Surely you are not suggesting that this is a positive development?'

The speaker was Martock, the Council Deputy who had embarrassed him previously over the discovery of the Dreamwalker.

'Surely if the virus multiplies more slowly, it slows down the death rate and also increases the opportunity for possible treatment of the subject.'

Martock looked smugly at Hekken with his little piggy eyes, convinced that once again he had managed to score a small yet humiliating victory over him.

Unperturbed, Hekken smiled and felt the warm satisfaction of knowing that Martock was wrong and that he would soon be forced to acknowledge the fact in public.

'That is, of course, an understandable view, if a little simplistic,' he replied, enjoying the look of annoyance that flashed from Martock's eyes. 'But if you think about it, the longer it takes for the symptoms of the virus to appear, the longer the virus can survive and the longer the subject can move around. This in turn increases the opportunities for the subject to be bitten by other mosquitoes, which then allows the virus to spread to others. If the subject dies within hours, the opportunities for the virus to spread are limited. If he lives for a week, however, the numbers infected increase so rapidly that within six months you will have a human population on the verge of extinction.'

He allowed himself the luxury of staring straight into those eyes which a moment ago had looked at him with such supercilious contempt.

'Was there anything else, Martock?'

Martock looked at the floor and shook his head. 'No.'

'Well then.' Hekken inclined his head slightly towards Odoursin and was pleased to note that he was smiling. 'In that case I await Your Excellency's further instructions to proceed.'

Odoursin took a deep breath and his eyes stared fiercely through Hekken as though fixed on an image of the future that only he could see. 'Finally, my friends,' he said, 'the time is at hand. For years we have been patient. We have watched comets cross the heavens and seen wars rage in every corner of the Earth. We have heard earthquakes shake the ground, while famine stalks the deserts and humans pump their poison into sea and sky. And now the plague that we have waited for is about to be unleashed – unleashed with a fury that they have only imagined in their darkest nightmares. The words of the prophecy will at last find their place in reality, for these precursors herald my arrival. The Great One shall descend from the sky.'

Outside in the blackness, thunder rumbled through the dark clouds and suddenly Odoursin began to shout, his voice driven by a wild and terrible joy that was born out of the years of frustration, pain and struggle.

'Gentlemen, loyal members of the Council, the time has come and the Earth shall be rid of its tormentors. Together we shall create the promised land!'

As he raised his right fist with the others in fervent support, Hekken received a short message through a tiny speaker concealed in his ear and allowed himself a discreet smile. It seemed that in all the excitement, everyone had forgotten to mention the Dreamwalker's Child.

Which was very good news indeed.

Particularly as he now knew that by the time the Council met again, the Dreamwalker's Child would be dead.

Twenty-eight

The sun was already high in the sky as they left the cool green woods of the lower slopes behind them. Several weeks had passed since Sam's first flying lesson and now – much as he had enjoyed the training – he was glad to be taking a break from the intensive schedule. As he followed Skipper along the narrow path that snaked up the side of the mountain, he heard the loose stones rattle beneath his boots and tried to ignore the ache that came from muscles he didn't even know he had.

Firebrand had given them some time off and Sam guessed this meant that things were coming to a head. It was likely that a strike against Vermian airbases would take place very soon and Firebrand wanted them to get some 'rest and recreation' before operations commenced. Sam felt nervous when he thought about the days to come, but he also felt excited knowing that he was about to take part in such a dangerous and important mission.

Skipper's idea of r & r was to hike up into the mountains for a day or two. It had seemed like a good idea at the time, but the mountain was a lot steeper than it had first appeared from the comfort of his balcony and the backs of his legs were protesting.

To take his mind off the discomfort, Sam let his thoughts wander back over the events of the past few weeks. The hours of intensive training had left Sam feeling as though he had been flying all his life. Everything had come so naturally to him, twisting and turning through the forest trails or climbing effortlessly into the blue sky and watching the thin wisps of cloud fall away. He no longer had to think about where to move the stick or how much throttle was needed to take him over a ridge or across a valley. It was as easy as having an extra body. You just thought about where you wanted to go and then went there.

It had been a proud moment yesterday, standing there on the parade ground with Mump and all the others. Firebrand had stood on the podium with the sunlight glinting off his medals and had spoken to them of their achievements.

'You have done well,' he'd said. 'Every one of you who stands here today is here not only because you have shown mastery of your aircraft but also because you have shown that you have determination, perseverance, endurance and, above all, courage. These qualities will be essential to you in the days that lie ahead, for in the East there is a darkness that casts a shadow across the future. The time draws near when every one of us will have a part to play.

'But perhaps we should not talk of tomorrow when there is so much to celebrate today. For whatever happens in the future, your present achievements can never be undone. Through dedication and tenacity you have climbed your first hill and already from where you stand the world looks different to you. And as you continue to learn and grow, so your perspective will change with you. Never again will you see things as you once did. It is this which sets you apart from others.'

Firebrand's speech had been followed by a solemn and respectful silence until Mump had gone forward to receive his pilot's badge and tripped up the steps to the podium, landing flat on his face at Firebrand's feet.

The whole place had erupted and Sam had clapped and cheered madly with all the others as Mump struggled to his feet before turning and giving a cheerful wave to the crowd.

Then it had been Sam's turn, and as Firebrand shook his hand and pinned the golden wasp onto his lapel, the tremendous pride he felt was tinged with a sadness that he couldn't quite understand. It was only now that he realised what it was.

His mother and father would have been so proud of him. And they would never, ever know.

A familiar voice broke into his thoughts. 'Are you all right back there?'

Sam looked up to find that Skipper had stopped and was waiting for him on a long, flat rock that jutted out from the side of the mountain. He climbed up to join her and realised with some alarm that behind her lay a thousand-metre drop all the way to the valley floor.

'I'm fine,' Sam replied somewhat nervously. 'Just don't step back any further, that's all.'

Skipper glanced nonchalantly over her shoulder at the dizzying fall that lay just a metre or so behind her.

'Oh, you know me,' she said. 'I'm always very careful.'

Then she jumped in the air, did a quick backflip and landed perfectly with her heels on the very edge of the precipice.

'Whoops,' she said, and put a hand up to her mouth in mock concern. 'That was a bit close.'

Then she proceeded to stick her arms out and rotate them in small circles as if trying to keep her balance. 'Woe, whey, whoe . . .'

'Skipper!' shouted Sam nervously. 'Cut it out!'

Skipper smiled apologetically and cartwheeled back over to him. 'Sorry,' she said. 'Couldn't resist it.'

'You're going to kill yourself one of these days,' said Sam, realising as he did so that he sounded like a sensible, middle-aged aunt. 'Mind you,' he added, 'I'm a fine one to talk. I mean, I killed myself and just look at me now: I'm a qualified pilot, I can escape from a cockpit in five metres of water and I'm halfway up a mountain with a nutty gymnast who wants to chuck herself off the edge.'

He paused. 'So perhaps these things have an upside after all.'

'You didn't kill yourself, Sam,' Skipper reminded him gently. 'You got knocked off your bike, remember? But part of you is still up there, lying in a hospital and waiting for your return. The door's still open, you know.'

Sam picked up a stone and threw it over the edge, watching it arc and fall through the still morning air to the valley below.

'Yeah, maybe. But for how long?'

Skipper shrugged. 'I don't know. But then I suppose, when you think about it, nobody really knows anything.'

'What do you mean?'

The sun was hot and Skipper wiped the sweat from her forehead with the back of her hand.

'Well, we all like things to be predictable, don't we? We expect things to be safe and to keep on happening just the way they always have. We expect the sun to rise in the morning. We expect to get up, survive the day and finish up back in bed at the end of it, ready to start all over again the next day. But maybe that's just a trick we play on ourselves, our way of making life seem ordinary. Because the truth is, life is so extraordinary that for most of the time we can't bring ourselves to look at it. It's too bright and it hurts our eyes. The fact of the matter is that nothing is ever certain. But most people never find that out until the ground suddenly disappears from beneath their feet.'

'Like me, you mean?'

'Well, think about it. You expected to go for a ride on your bike, come back home and then everything would be just as it had always been. Didn't you?'

'Yes.'

'Of course you did. Which is perfectly natural. After all, if you spent your life worrying about all the strange things that might be lurking around the next bend in the road, you'd never do anything. But like thousands of others, on that day and on every day, the life that you were so sure of came to a sudden end. And then you – like the rest of them – realised for the first time that the solid boundaries of your world could dissolve and disappear in a moment. Yet just seconds before, the world was everything to you and the idea that it might not continue didn't even enter your head.'

Sam listened to Skipper as she spoke and wondered how she had gained so much knowledge about things in her short life. Sometimes it was easy to forget that she was only the same age as him, she seemed so wise. And what she said was true. Like most people, Sam had just assumed that his life would follow a pleasant but fairly predictable path. Swimming with mosquito larvae, being hunted by ants and learning to fly wasps had never been signposted anywhere along the route.

But it still irritated him that Skipper never seemed able to give him a simple answer.

'What's your point exactly?' he said.

'My point,' Skipper replied patiently, 'is that if you are meant to find a way back to your other life, then a door will stay open long enough for you to do so.'

'But what if I'm not,' asked Sam. 'What then?'

'Then something else will turn up,' said Skipper. 'These things have a habit of sorting themselves out in the end. But there's no point in trying to guess how exactly. The best we can do is just to keep on going.'

'Keep on going?' said Sam. 'Where?'

'Forwards,' said Skipper simply. 'And in this case, upwards.'

She took his hand and began to pull him up the mountain path again. 'One thing I've learned,' she said as the sun burned hot and the sweat stung Sam's eyes, 'is to never give up until it's over.'

'Is that right?' said Sam, whose legs had already decided it was over about a mile back. 'Tell me, have you ever heard the expression "It's not over until the fat lady sings"?'

'No,' said Skipper. 'What's it mean?'

'This,' he said.

He stopped, puffed out his cheeks and spread his arms wide like a large diva about to deliver her swan-song. Then he took a deep breath and began to sing in a high, loud and extremely wavery voice.

'Isn't that a song from *The Sound of Music*?' asked Skipper. She began to giggle. 'Julie Andrews isn't fat!'

'When have you seen Julie Andrews?' asked Sam.

'When I was chasing a mozzie into a cinema,' replied Skipper. 'I ended up staying for the whole film. Good, wasn't it?'

'No,' said Sam, 'it was soppy. Anyway,' he went on, 'I'm not Julie Andrews, I'm Mrs Banwick, our music teacher, who is the size of a planet. Now shush.'

He continued to sing the song in a high, falsetto voice and Skipper quickly picked several of the yellow, daisy-like flowers which were growing in abundance on the mountainside. As Sam finished with a final flourish she flung them at him and clapped madly. 'Bravo, maestro,' she cried. 'Bravo!'

Sam promptly fell over, announcing in a solemn voice: 'She died doing what she loved best, performing in front of her adoring fans.'

As the two of them collapsed in a fit of the giggles, Sam forgot everything except the sun on his face and the joy of the moment. No one could see them and no one could hear them. Perhaps their brief happiness meant nothing, for it would never be known or, in the end, even remembered.

But there it was. And the sound of their laughter carried on the breeze, over the mountain slopes and across the valley before fading at last into the quiet blue air beyond.

Twenty-nine

It was the middle of the day, and the fierce heat of the sun combined with the steepness of the climb had left Sam weak and thirsty. His throat was parched and he ached all over. He was having difficulty even placing his next footstep. All he wanted to do was lie down and rest.

'Last bit, Sam,' said Skipper.

She reached a hand down from the ridge above where he stood, panting like a dog on a summer pavement. He wiped the sweat from his eyes and realised that he could see nothing above and beyond her.

'Are we at the top?' he asked.

'Well, I am,' said Skipper.

With a final effort, Sam grabbed her hand and scrambled up over the ridge. He stood there blinking, staggered by what he saw.

Instead of the expanse of dry rock that he had expected, it was as if a giant spoon had scooped out the top of the mountain, leaving in its place a vast fertile basin of exotic plants and flowers the like of which Sam had never seen before. Enormous palms spread their fronds into a feathery canopy through which cool green light filtered into thick, lush vegetation beneath. Bright flowers of orange, purple, red and yellow rose up between a jumble of different-shaped leaves. Sam noticed that some of the leaves were covered in a variety of crimson and blue spots which glowed with an eerie luminescence in the warm shadows. Steam rose from the forest floor and he could feel the heat and humidity sweeping past him, carrying with them the rich, heavy perfume of a thousand flowers in bloom.

Sudden flashes of colour between the treetops betrayed the fact that the canopy was alive with small birds and for the first time Sam noticed the warble and chatter of their song filling the air.

'What do you think?' asked Skipper. 'Worth the climb?'

'It's beautiful,' whispered Sam in amazement. 'Absolutely beautiful.'

'You haven't seen the best bit yet,' said Skipper. 'Follow me.'

She led him down past twisting vines and through curtains of waxy leaves the size of elephants' ears until they came to a clear, fast-moving stream which twisted like a silver thread through the dense undergrowth. They stopped and drank deeply, and as the cool water ran down his dry throat and slaked his thirst, Sam felt his strength gradually returning.

They continued to follow the course of the stream for a while until at last they stumbled out into a clearing where the stream gathered pace and disappeared with a roar over the edge of a cliff.

'Look,' said Skipper. 'Lake Orceia.'

Sam joined Skipper at the edge and looked down. He saw that the stream had become a waterfall that tumbled fifty metres down a cliff face into a huge pool of crystal-blue water. The pool formed part of a great lake which shone like a diamond in the sunlight, a secret jewel hidden away in the very heart of the mountain. The water was so clear that you could see straight down to the rocks at the bottom. It was very deep, and Sam imagined himself leaving the heat of the day behind and swimming languidly through its cool waters. But, he reasoned, it was a long way down and the jungle was very thick. It would be at least another hour before they got to it.

Skipper took him by the hand. 'Ready?' she said.

Sam looked at her. 'Ready for what?' he asked. Then he saw the look in her eye. He'd seen that same look on previous occasions. It had been there before the breakout from the larvae factory. It has been there before the crash at the airbase and before the backflip. It was not a safe look. Not safe at all.

Sam gazed down at the pool far below, then back at Skipper, his eyebrows furrowing in disbelief. 'You have *got* to be kidding,' he said.

'After three,' said Skipper. 'One . . .'

'You're not kidding, are you? You're serious.'

'Of course I'm serious. Now come on. Live a little. Two . . .'

'Skipper, no. No, no, no. I don't want to live a little. I want to live a *lot*. Skipper! SKIPPER!'

'Three!'

Suddenly there was space where the ground used to be and Sam's legs and arms were flailing in the air. He felt his stomach flip and had a sense of falling rapidly into a fast cool wind that made his eyes water. At the edge of his blurred and filmy vision he just had time to register Skipper jackknife into a perfect dive before the blue pool rushed up to meet him. With a tremendous smack on the soles of his feet, the world erupted into a shocking cacophony of white foam and bubbles. His toes brushed momentarily against the smooth pebbles at the bottom of the pool before he pulled back with his arms and swam up towards the sunlight once more. Breaking through into the air with a gasp, he flicked his head so that droplets flew from his hair and skittered like tiny crystals across the surface of the pool.

Skipper was busy treading water a few feet away.

'Now be honest,' she said with a grin as Sam fought to get his breath back, 'you can't tell me that wasn't exhilarating!'

Sam stared at Skipper for a few seconds and then he began to growl like an angry dog. The sound was quiet at first, soft and low in the back of his throat, but gradually it became louder and louder.

'Now, Sam,' said Skipper, 'don't get mad. It wasn't as bad as all that. Was it?'

But Sam had his head down now and was swimming towards her as fast as he could. Realising that he was set on revenge, she let out a little scream and struck out for the shore with Sam grabbing at her heels all the way. 'Help!' she shrieked in mock alarm, running up the beach with Sam in hot pursuit. 'I'm being attacked by the fat lady from *The Sound of Music*!'

At which point the fat lady caught up with her, picked her up and dumped her unceremoniously back into the water with a satisfying splash.

The rest of the day was spent sunbathing, swimming and diving into the pool. Skipper taught Sam how to do a backwards somersault off a rock into the water and together they managed to tie a long vine to the branch of a tall tree which grew out from the side of the mountain.

They took turns grabbing hold of the vine and swinging out over the pool, letting go at the last second and flying off at great speed into the water. A couple of times Sam got the angle just right so that he landed on his bottom and went skimming across the surface like a stone.

They were still playing as the sun went down behind the mountain.

'Do you think we ought to stop and get something to eat?' asked Skipper as they dripped their way back up the steep path which led to the swing.

'You're right,' said Sam. 'You can have too much of a

good thing. Just fifty more goes and we'll call it a day.'

Much later, as they lay on a bed of leaves in the warm darkness, Sam looked up at the palm fronds waving gently in the night breeze and realised that he was thinking about Odoursin and what was going to happen.

'Skipper?' he whispered.

'Yes?'

'You know the Darkness that Firebrand talked about?'

'What darkness?'

'You know – Vermia, Odoursin, all of that.'

'What about it?'

'Do you think he'll win?'

'No,' said Skipper. 'Do you?'

'No,' said Sam. 'I mean I don't know. I hope not. But all this stuff about the Dreamwalker's Child rising up against the Darkness. To be honest, I'm not sure I believe it. What could I do against someone like that?'

'I don't know,' said Skipper. 'But then things don't always turn out as we expect. You of all people should know that.'

'Yeah,' said Sam, 'I guess I should, shouldn't I?'

There was silence for a while, and when at last he spoke again his voice sounded careful and sad.

'You know the thing that really scares me? It isn't Odoursin or his marsh dogs, or anything like that.'

'What is it then?' asked Skipper.

'It's you, Skipper,' said Sam.

'Me?' said Skipper gently. 'Why me? I'm your friend, Sam, remember?'

'I know,' said Sam, 'and that's what scares me. These past few weeks . . . well, I've had some of the best times ever . . . some of the scariest too, but definitely some of the best.'

He swallowed hard and looked across at where she was turning a pebble over in her fingers.

'You're the best friend I ever had, Skipper. You taught me how to keep going when everything seemed lost. But now – now I've got this strange feeling that everything's going to change again. And the thing is, I don't want it to, Skipper. I don't want it to be over.'

In the darkness, Skipper reached for his hand. 'Nor do I,' she said simply.

At first, Sam wasn't sure if he had imagined the sound or dreamt it. He turned to check on Skipper, but could tell by her deep, regular breathing that she was fast asleep.

He rubbed his eyes, sat up and peered into the darkness.

There it was again: a rustling sound, as if something was moving through the undergrowth. There was definitely something out there.

'Who's there?' he called in a terrified whisper, hardly daring to speak. 'Who is it?' He felt the hairs standing up on the back of his neck and he shivered. *Don't let it end here,* he thought. *Not here. Not now.*

And then an odd thing happened. It was as though all the cold fear inside of him suddenly warmed, melted and dissolved into a liquid heat that coursed through his body and filled him with a strange happiness. He couldn't explain it. But all the dark worries and fears that had filled the depths of his sleep were at once swept away, and he felt the excitement of a small child once again, creeping down the stairs on Christmas morning to see what magic had been woven during the night.

Without another thought he rose from his bed and began to walk in the direction of the sound, pushing his way through cool green leaves until at last he found that he was standing on the beach in front of the lake.

The three coloured moons hung low in the sky. Their reflection shimmered brightly upon the surface of the water, bathing the whole landscape in a strange, eerie light.

For a long time there was only silence.

Then Sam realised that someone was standing beside him.

He turned and saw that it was a man dressed in a simple woollen robe. Sam felt sure that he must be quite old, but it was hard to know for certain. His long dark hair was interwoven with silken threads of red and gold and he wore a necklace of green stones. Set into his left earlobe was the tiniest of sapphires.

'Hello, Sam,' he said. 'I have been waiting for you.'

He put his hand on top of Sam's head and Sam felt as though a door inside him had been flung open after a long, dark winter. Every hidden corner was bathed in brilliant sunshine and all the dust, dirt and decay that had accumulated over the years was carried away on the heat of a summer wind. It was the most wonderful feeling.

'Come and walk beside me,' said the man.

'How do you know my name?' Sam said after they had gone a short distance.

'I have always known you,' replied the man, 'and I have always been with you, although you may not have recognised me.'

'Was it you on the marshes?' asked Sam as they continued along the shore. 'Was it you who changed me when I first arrived?'

'I may have altered the way others saw you for a while. But I could never change *you*, Sam. Real change can only come from the choices that you make.'

'Who are you?' whispered Sam.

'My name is Salus,' replied the man, adding with a smile, 'for now at least.'

It was the oddest thing, but although Sam was certain that he had never met him before, this man didn't feel in the least bit like a stranger. It was as though Sam had known him all his life.

'Are you part of the Olumnus?' Sam asked.

'Part of the Olumnus?' Salus repeated, and Sam noticed a twinkle in his eye. 'No, I am not part of the Olumnus.' He smiled and then added, 'The Olumnus are part of me, and so are you. But perhaps we will not speak of these matters just yet. There will come a time when you are ready to understand such things, but for now we must concern ourselves with the present.'

There was silence for a while as they walked along by the water's edge.

Then Salus spoke again. 'You have done well, Sam. You and your companion have borne your troubles with great courage, and she has a strong heart for one so small. But, you know, these are times of great danger and there is still much work to be done.'

Sam stopped and turned to look at him. 'Please tell me,' he said quietly. 'Will I ever go home?'

'Do you want to?' asked Salus.

'I think so. I mean yes. Yes, I do. Of course.'

'But?'

'But . . . if I go home it means I'll never see Skipper again.'

'Does it?'

'But she doesn't belong in the world that I come from.'

'And do you belong here, Sam?'

Sam shook his head. 'No, but that's because they made a mistake, isn't it? Commander Firebrand showed me how it all happened, how they missed the horsefly and everything.'

'Commander Firebrand is a good man, but there are many things beyond his knowledge. Sometimes the things that we may think of as mistakes are not really mistakes at all.'

Sam was quiet for a while as they walked. Then he asked: 'Am I dead?'

Salus looked at him with serious eyes. 'Do you feel dead?'

'No,' said Sam. 'In fact, I've never felt so alive. But I think that in my world I might be. And if I am, then I'll never be able to go home, will I?'

His mind was suddenly filled with memories of the people and the life that he had left behind. He tried in vain to fight back the sadness that swept through him, but he could not stop it and tears began to well up in his eyes.

'You know, Sam, sometimes we forget that rain must fall before the harvest can be gathered in.'

Salus laid his palm across Sam's chest and Sam could feel the beating of his heart beneath it.

'This ache that you feel inside, Sam. It means that you will always be looking, always searching, never giving up. Sometimes we find our loved ones in the most unexpected places. But for now, you must follow where it leads most strongly.'

He bent and kissed Sam gently on the forehead. 'It is calling you home,' he said.

The next morning as they prepared to set off back to the airbase, Skipper said, 'I had the weirdest dream last night.'

High above them, a bird circled the mountain peak before catching one of the warm air currents that rose unseen from the slopes and gliding silently away across the valley.

'So did I,' said Sam. 'I guess there must have been something in the air.'

Then they hoisted their packs up onto their shoulders and set off down the steep mountain track once more.

Neither of them spoke of it again.

Thirty

It was six in the morning. Hekken looked out of the window into the grey dawn and watched the long convoy of tankers rumble across the tarmac to the waiting lines of sleek, blood-sucking mosquitoes. There were five hundred of them in total and in less than twenty-four hours, five hundred pilots would take part in the most important mission of their lives.

Meanwhile the first tankers were beginning to pump the mosquitoes full of the glycogen-rich fuel which would power up their nervous systems and activate their muscles ready for tomorrow's operation.

Further down the airfield stood four long red tankers with a circle of armed guards around them. Although the tankers were stationary, their engines were running constantly in order to power the heating units that kept their precious cargo at a constant temperature of 37 degrees Celsius: the temperature of the human body.

Deep inside the tanks, teeming viruses swam blindly through the warm blood, driven by an unconscious need to search out the human cells which would enable them to spread and multiply in their billions. Soon there would be new blood for all of them.

Hekken allowed himself a brief moment of self-congratulation. None of this would have happened without his vision and persistence. Wasn't he the one who had encouraged the scientists to work that little bit harder? Of course. He and no one else. Without his guiding hand the viruses would never have been ready by now. Admittedly, he had threatened their families a bit, and one or two people had disappeared in the process, but you couldn't expect to make an omelette without breaking eggs.

As for that idiot Martock, he would certainly think twice in future before trying to put one over on Hekken. Now that Odoursin had seen the success of the virus programme there would be plenty of opportunities to reduce Martock's influence with the Council, Hekken would see to that. It shouldn't be too difficult to persuade Odoursin that he needed an efficient, proactive deputy who could get things done. Not a piggy-eyed has-been like Martock. Hekken could see it now. He would get great pleasure from personally taking Mr Piggy on a one-way trip to the slaughterhouse.

A knock at the door jolted him out of his reverie and he turned away from the window to see Warner, the section leader of the special forces, walk hurriedly into the room. Warner was a dark, muscular figure who was not given to shows of excitement and Hekken guessed that he must be in possession of some important news.

'What have you got?' asked Hekken.

Warner smiled, which in itself was unusual. 'We've found the boy,' he said.

Hekken's eyes glinted. *The fly in the ointment*. 'So I hear. Where is he?'

'Over at the western airbase. We've inserted a four-man team who've been laid up in the mountains for a few days watching the area. Latest information is they've trained him up as a pilot.'

'A pilot?' Hekken was surprised. 'That must mean they're planning to use him against us. They must have wind of our operation. What's security like there?'

'Pretty tight – the perimeter's well guarded.'

'Any chance of an attack from the air?'

'Not a hope, I'm afraid. Their air superiority in that area is total. We had to land our unit fifty miles away and then travel at night to avoid detection.'

'You're not being very helpful, Warner,' said Hekken irritably. 'You know the prophecy as well as I do. The boy is a major threat and needs to be removed. The whole success of our operation could depend upon this.'

'I'm sorry, General. I didn't mean to give the impression that it was impossible. But it's a high-risk mission.'

'Mr Warner, look out of the window. Everything we are doing is high risk. We are trying to influence the shape of the future here. If you're worried about a few soldiers falling over and hurting themselves, then perhaps you ought to retrain as a nurse. Now can you get the boy or can't you?'

Warner had stood to attention while Hekken was speaking and now he snapped up a sharp salute. 'Yes, sir, I believe we can,' he said crisply.

'Thank you,' said Hekken. 'In that case, do it, and do it now. Whatever it takes, get your team in there and deal with him once and for all.'

'Deal with him?' asked Warner uncertainly.

'Yes, deal with him,' repeated Hekken. 'You know . . .'

He pushed two fingers against his temple like a gun.

'Blow his worthless brains out.'

As Warner saluted and turned on his heel, Hekken walked calmly over to the window and looked out across the airbase. As the sun rose he could see that the months of planning had finally paid off. Down on the tarmac, his dreams were starting to come true.

Thirty-one

The auditorium was full of pilots in uniform and there was an excited buzz around the room. Sam sat in the front row with Skipper on one side and Mump on the other.

Zip, who was next to Mump, leant across and offered Sam a stick of chewing gum. 'I like to give Mump something to do with his mouth besides talking,' he said. 'Good bloke and all that, but he does tend to talk rubbish most of the time.'

'Hey!' said Mump, offended.

'Shh!' said Skipper. 'The briefing's about to start.'

A hush fell across the auditorium as Commander Firebrand strode to the centre of the stage and the houselights went down.

'Is he going to sing?' whispered Mump.

'Shut him up, someone,' said Zip.

'Good morning, everyone,' said Firebrand, 'and welcome to Operation Apocalypse.'

He nodded to someone off-stage and the screen

behind him lit up: a blue background with the words 'OPERATION APOCALYPSE: PHASE ONE' picked out in red.

'Nice graphics,' said Mump to no one in particular. 'Tasteful.'

'The information that you are about to see and hear is classified,' Firebrand went on, 'and for reasons of security the details of this operation have been kept from most of you until now. As you know, up to this point our mission has always been to preserve the balance of life on Earth.'

Sam thought about the squadrons of wasps controlling fly populations and the footage he had seen of the wasp attacking the horsefly in his garden. Now that he was a trained pilot, he was determined to put his newly learned skills into practice. He would do whatever he could to prevent Odoursin from carrying out his terrible threat to mankind.

'In recent months,' Firebrand continued, 'we have had to contend with Odoursin's forces trying to upset that balance in their efforts to make things harder for the people of Earth. You have been on the front line along with our land and sea forces, making sure that they do not succeed. And up until now you have been very successful. However, we have received some information which could change all that. Allow me to show you why.'

The image on the screen was replaced by an aerial photograph of Odoursin's airfields showing the huge squadrons of mosquitoes lined up in their hundreds, stretching as far as the eye could see.

'This photograph was taken from high altitude at 0800 hours yesterday morning. We know that Odoursin has been breeding mosquitoes for some time now, but this concentration of so many at one airfield is a very recent and worrying development. An even more worrying development, however, is this . . .'

A strange image appeared on the screen that looked to Sam like some kind of curious yellow jellyfish.

'This unusual-looking creature is a virus. Until recently, very little was known about it, but we have managed to access enough information from our spies in Odoursin's camp to know that it is deadly to all human life. Odoursin's scientists have discovered a method of transferring it to humans via mosquitoes, and once it gets into wild mosquitoes on Earth there will be no stopping it.'

A wave of excited chatter flowed around the audience and Firebrand held up his hands for silence so that he could continue.

'Even as we speak, this virus is being loaded onto mosquitoes ready to launch an all-out assault on Earth tomorrow. If the assault is successful, we will be powerless to halt the consequences. In less than a year, every single human will be wiped off the face of the Earth and everything that we have worked so hard to preserve will be lost.'

There was another surge of shocked conversation around the auditorium and Sam felt his resolve hardening into cold anger. He clenched his fists and stared at the virus on the screen, the virus that would kill the people he loved. He knew that from this moment on there was no turning back. Whatever it took to stop this, he would do it.

Once again Firebrand held up a hand to signal his wish to carry on.

'We now know that Odoursin has been planning for many years to destroy what he sees as the human plague and then use Earth's natural resources for his own ends. Once the humans are removed, the difference in scale will actually benefit him and his followers. Food and other resources will always be plentiful and no other species will have the intelligence or desire to challenge him.

'Once he has achieved domination of the Earth in this way he plans to close the fabric gaps we use for access, consolidate his power base and build his Vermian Empire into an unstoppable force. Then he will return and annihilate us too, preventing any future challenge to his leadership. Make no mistake: Odoursin has a singular, ruthless vision of a new world order and, as far as he is concerned, nothing is going to stand in the way of him achieving it.'

The image on the screen changed to a bird's-eye view of the enemy airbase. Sam recognised the shape of the large building where he had fallen into the tank of mosquito larvae. Along with some of the other buildings in the photograph, it was marked with a red arrow, indicating that it was a target.

'Your mission then is this,' said Firebrand, using a pointer to identify the relevant locations on the photograph as he spoke. 'One, to destroy the laboratories where the virus is manufactured. Two, to destroy the mosquito breeding tanks and the larvae in them. And three, to destroy the adult mosquitoes on the ground before they have a chance to take off. You will be working alongside a squadron of commandos from our land-based forces who will plant and detonate explosives and neutralise any opposition.

'Dragonfly Squadron will attempt to enforce a no-fly zone on Earth near the fabric gap where we believe the mosquitoes will enter and take out any who make it through. But the success of the mission really depends on getting to them before they reach that point. Once they get through to Earth it's likely to be dusk. The mosquitoes will have the advantage of better night-flight capability, which will make things a whole lot more difficult for us. So it's absolutely crucial that we destroy them on the ground.'

Firebrand's expression was grave as he looked around the room. 'Are there any questions before we move on to the detail?'

A pilot several rows back asked a question about air defences and Firebrand nodded.

'Yes, as you know, there are defensive batteries of nerve-gas dispensers stationed several miles outside the perimeter of the airbase. The gas is very similar to that which our pilots have occasionally encountered during flights on Earth.'

'What's he talking about?' whispered Sam.

'Think of fly spray,' Skipper whispered back. 'Whopping great canisters of the stuff. They put an invisible curtain of it up when they see you coming. Next thing you know, the aircraft's crashed and you're picking bits of cockpit out of your teeth.'

'Oh, right,' said Sam. 'Nasty.'

'In addition to the outer defences,' Firebrand went on, 'the airfield has a ring of ground-to-air missiles spread around the perimeter. Ten minutes before the main assault, special-forces raiding parties will disable the gas batteries and electronic jamming devices will be employed to confuse enemy radar.

'At the same time the recently acquired horsefly will be used to covertly land another raiding party inside the perimeter fence, where commandos will take out the remaining air defences. Then at 0300 hours the main assault group will hit the airbase and commence mopping-up operations.'

Firebrand paused. He looked out into the auditorium and his gaze swept across the faces of the pilots with such force that each felt as though they were being addressed individually.

'In a moment you will break up into groups to receive detailed plans of your part in this evening's operation. But before you do, there is one thing I want each and every one of you to be absolutely clear about: this operation cannot, must not, fail. You have one chance and one chance only to get it right. And get it right you must. For the future of millions – in this world and others – depends upon you. Do not fail them.'

There was silence for a moment as Firebrand gave each person the opportunity to feel the weight of responsibility that lay upon them. Then he added simply, 'Good luck, everyone.'

The groups dispersed to various planning rooms and the next few hours were spent laboriously going over the layout of the Vermian airbase and studying plans of the target buildings. Sam and Skipper's recent experience meant that the two of them were detailed to fly the newly repaired horsefly right into the heart of the enemy airbase with the first wave of commandos on board.

Sam knew that if they were captured they would almost certainly be killed. But despite his fears he said nothing, for he felt certain that this was the most important thing he had ever been asked to do in his life. Everyone was depending upon him. He was determined not to let them down.

They were informed that the horsefly had been refitted with dual controls 'in case any problems are encountered during the mission'. Sam saw Skipper blink a couple of times and guessed that she was thinking what he was thinking. The planners obviously thought there was a high probability that at least one of them would get injured or worse on the way into the base.

One way or another, he thought, it would be a night to remember.

When the briefing finished they were sent back to their quarters to try and get a few hours' sleep. As Sam walked into his room he discovered his bedcovers turned back, his pillows plumped up and a steaming mug of hot chocolate on the bedside table. Sanderson was in the process of drawing the curtains to shut out the afternoon sun.

'You know, Sanderson,' said Sam, 'you'll make someone a wonderful wife one of these days.'

'Indeed, sir?' replied Sanderson, smoothing out the last of the wrinkles from the curtains. 'Am I to interpret this as a proposal?'

Sam grinned. 'Sorry, darling, not this time. I've got a busy few days ahead of me. Maybe when I come back, eh?'

Sanderson smiled a rare smile. 'You take care, sir,' he said.

Then, after brushing a last speck of dust from Sam's uniform that only he could see, he was gone and Sam was left alone with his thoughts.

Crossing his hands behind his head and propping himself up on his pillows, Sam kicked off his boots and wondered what on earth he was going to do for the next few hours. It was all very well telling them to get some rest before the mission, but it was easier said than done. There was too much going on in his head.

He sipped his hot chocolate and rubbed his eyes. Come to think of it, it had been an exhausting couple of days what with the trek up the mountain and then the early start this morning. Maybe he'd just go through the plans a couple more times in his head. Or maybe he'd just . . . shut his eyes for a while.

Two minutes later, Sam was fast asleep.

The sun was beginning to sink behind the mountains when the first shadowy figure climbed through the hole cut in the fence and ran across open ground to the pilots' accommodation block. He was quickly joined by three other men, one of whom wore a small backpack. Each carried a pistol fitted with a silencer.

The first man pulled out a pencil-sized CRB and aimed it at the entrance door. There was a blue flash, but the door remained intact and the man swore.

'It's not working,' he hissed. 'They've used some kind of material that's resistant to the beam.'

He tapped the other man's backpack. 'We'll just have to resort to the old-fashioned methods. We'll go up onto his balcony and blow the windows. By then every man and his dog is going to know that we're here, so it's straight in, kill the kid and away again.'

The others nodded.

'OK, let's do it.'

They made their way to the corner of the block and edged along the outside wall, stopping every few seconds to check that they hadn't been seen. Although kitted out in dark clothing, their experience told them that the slightest movement – even at night – would increase their chances of discovery.

Once they reached the balcony, the second man took out a rope and grappling iron, the hooks of which were covered in foam padding to deaden the noise. He threw it up over the balcony and the hooks caught on the railings first time.

In less than a minute, the four men were crouching on the balcony outside the window. One of them pressed what looked like a lump of soft clay against the window and pushed a detonator into it. He attached the detonator to a length of wire and then gestured to the others to get down. They huddled at the edges of the balcony and turned away, covering their ears as he touched the wire to a battery.

There was a tremendous roar, a shattering of glass and a sheet of orange flame leapt out into the evening air. In an instant, the men were on their feet and running into the room through a pall of black smoke. They went into a crouch and, holding their weapons out in front of them, fired continuously into the sleeping form beneath the bedclothes until their clips were empty. The shape in the bed jumped and twitched as the bullets thudded into it, pieces of wood and material flying up into the air.

When the firing stopped, the first man lowered his gun, stepped forward and pulled the bedclothes back. Underneath was a row of shredded pillows and a whole mess of feathers. Nothing else.

There was a noise behind them and the man turned around in time to see the wardrobe door slide back and an immaculately dressed manservant step out into the room.

'I'm sorry to disappoint you, gentlemen,' said Sanderson, 'but I think the person you are looking for may already have left.'

He then narrowed his eyes, leapt into the air with a cry of 'Ooooooh-sah!' and scissor-kicked two of them neatly back through the broken window with such force that they crashed straight through the balcony rail and disappeared over the side. As the other men raised their guns to fire, Sanderson flipped over twice, landed at their feet howling 'Eeeeeeeeeee' and launched himself upwards with an explosive 'Yah!' He finished with a double punch of such ferocity that they both travelled horizontally through the air before smashing noisily into the bedroom furniture.

Sanderson bowed slightly, paused to remove a hair from his lapel and then bent down and picked up a small transmitter that had fallen onto the floor. He examined it briefly and then slipped it into his pocket. Intelligence would see to it that whoever sent these thugs received a message confirming a successful operation. That would buy Sam a bit more time.

'You do realise,' he said to the men who lay groaning on the floor, 'that all of this damage will have to be paid for.' He stepped forward and raised an eyebrow at the one who was lying among the splintered remains of the bedside table. 'Tell me,' he said, 'to whom should I send the bill?'

Thirty-two

The sun was setting behind the mountains and the few clouds gathered around the peaks were soaking up the last of the red and orange rays like blotting paper. As Sam pulled back on the stick and lifted the horsefly smoothly over the perimeter fence, he could see the rows and rows of wasp squadrons stretching out across the airfields below him, awaiting their final orders to attack. He thought back to his first flying lesson a few short weeks ago and smiled to himself, remembering how he'd panicked that first time and flipped the wasp upside down. Already it felt like a lifetime ago. Now flying had become second nature to him.

He pulled back a little harder on the stick, opened the throttle and felt a surge of power from the insect's wings as they climbed higher into the evening sky. After all the wasp training he had done, the horsefly felt slightly heavier on the turns but, despite the extra weight they were carrying in the back, it still had 'plenty of grunt', as Mump would have put it.

Sam found his thoughts returning to that summer morning long ago when he had found a horsefly in his bedroom, captured it under a glass and held it up to the window to look at. It was incredible to think of it now, but one of Odoursin's pilots must have been staring straight back at him, wondering whether Sam would destroy him or let him go. It was strange when you thought about it.

How many other things were hidden just below the surface, things that would never be seen or even imagined?

His thoughts were interrupted by Skipper, who was peering out of the side window and pointing downwards. 'Hey, did you see that?' she said.

'No,' said Sam. 'What was it?'

'A big orange flash,' said Skipper. 'Down by the accommodation blocks.'

Sam shrugged. 'Probably someone cooking one of Mump's special recipes,' he said. 'Too much chilli powder.'

Skipper nodded. 'Yeah, you're probably right.' But she stared back at the flames and guessed from their location that someone still wanted Sam dead. Things were getting a bit too close for comfort.

She turned her head to look into the rear compartment of the fly. The aircrew had stripped out most of the original fuel tanks, leaving only enough for a one-way trip. If they survived the initial assault, their orders were to hitch a ride back on one of the transporter moths that were due to land once the landing strip had been secured. In place of the fuel tanks, the rear compartment was now filled with sixteen heavily armed commandos. They huddled together in the darkness, their serious eyes staring into space from half-hidden faces that were smudged and smeared with camouflage paint.

'Are you all right back there?' asked Skipper.

'Yeah, no problem,' said the troop commander, a young man in his early twenties. 'The lads are looking forward to letting off some fireworks.'

There were a few smiles and nods of agreement, but Skipper could tell that behind the bravado most of them were feeling pretty nervous. They were all professional soldiers, highly trained and ready to do whatever it took to get the job done. But they were also young, with their lives ahead of them, and they knew better than most that the promise of tomorrow could be taken away in an instant. Tonight's rich, beautiful sunset might be the last they would ever see.

It was a sobering thought, but luckily Private Binton chose that moment to break wind with a volume and violence that are seldom heard outside of an elephant's enclosure.

'Sounds like the fireworks have already started,' said Skipper, and everyone laughed except for those nearest the epicentre, who, protesting loudly, held their noses and cuffed Binton around the head.

'Now then, lads,' he said defensively. 'I was only trying to get us there faster.'

Sam and Skipper took turns at the controls as they flew on through the night. The idea had been that they would each get some rest on the long flight, but in reality they were both too excited and nervous to sleep. Sam took over from Skipper again for the final approach as the clock on the instrument panel blinked on to 0240 and the cockpit radio crackled into life.

'Control to Trojan Horse, control to Trojan Horse. Come in, Trojan Horse, over.'

Sam leant forward and flicked the intercom switch. 'Control, this is Trojan Horse. Go ahead, over.'

'Trojan Horse, please confirm your position and estimated time of arrival, over.'

Sam scratched his head and peered at the array of dials glowing red in front of him, but Skipper was already a step ahead.

'Grid reference 247359,' she offered helpfully.

Sam put a thumb up to acknowledge her assistance and then spoke into the intercom again.

'Hello, control, our position is now 247359 and our ETA is 0250 as planned. No resistance encountered as yet, over.'

'Roger, Trojan Horse. Main assault force is airborne and ETA is 0300 hours. Reminder that neutralisation of enemy air-defence systems remains a priority, over.'

Sam gave Skipper a wry smile.

'Yes, thank you, control, we hadn't forgotten. Firework display will take place as discussed, over.'

'OK, Trojan Horse, understood. There'll be a bit of a

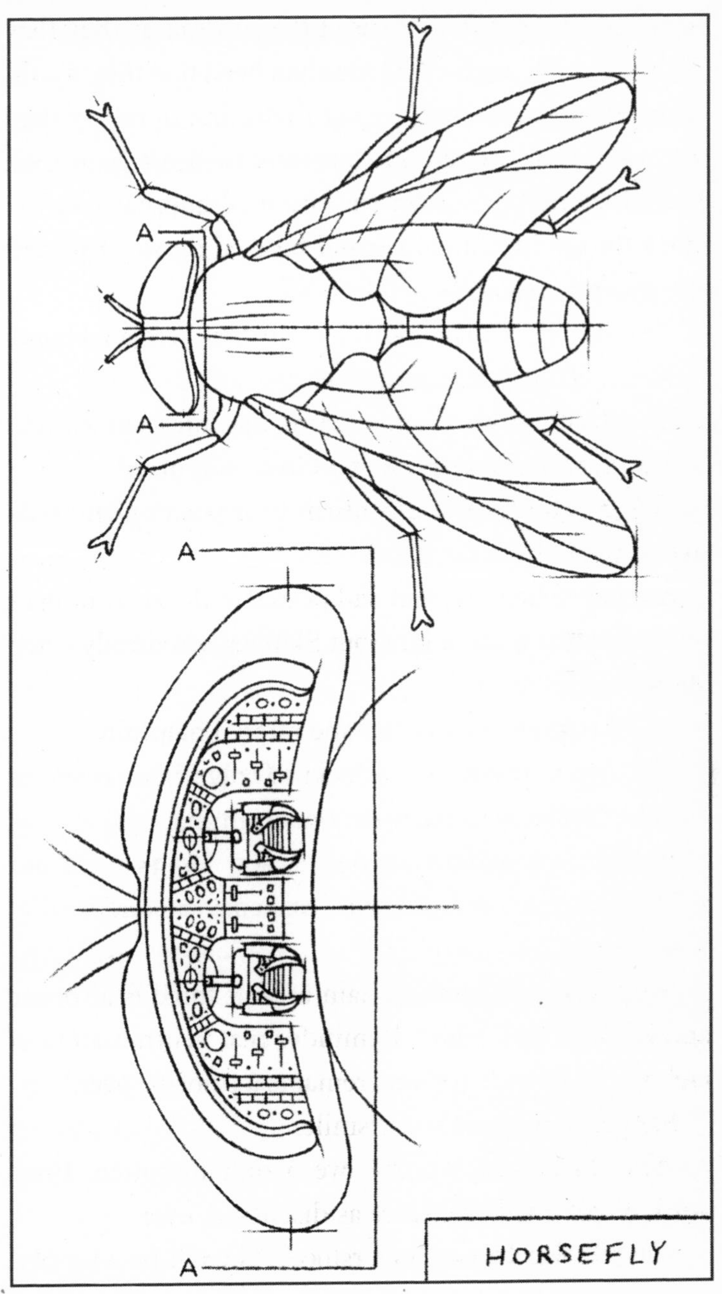
A
A
A
A
HORSEFLY

party waiting for you when you get back. Good luck, over.'

'Thank you, control. We look forward to it. Out.'

Sam flicked the intercom off and saw for the first time the lights of the enemy airbase up ahead in the distance.

'OK, everyone,' he said, taking the horsefly lower so that it skimmed just a few metres above the marshes, 'six minutes to landing.'

Hekken was enjoying himself immensely.

For once, the news was all good and the Council was listening to him without any annoying interruptions from Martock, who was pleasingly subdued after their last encounter. Hekken knew that he was on a winning streak and, more importantly, the Council knew it too.

'The last of the viruses have been loaded and the attack force will leave in the next half an hour,' he told them. 'As far as we can tell, our operation – under cover of darkness – will be virtually unopposed. Although intelligence sources have been warning us for some time that Vahlzian forces may be preparing to strike against us, we have had no new information to suggest that an attack is imminent.

'By tomorrow morning it is conservatively estimated that as many as five hundred humans will have been infected with the virus. Better still, it is the height of the mosquito season. At this very moment, tens of thousands of wild mosquitoes are hatching from puddles and ponds within a ten-mile radius of our target zone. In a matter of weeks – long before the first symptoms even appear – these wild mosquitoes will have infected thousands of humans. Their presence at all major airports will ensure a rapid global spread which will be impossible to prevent. The extinction of human life will have begun.'

It was all going rather well, thought Hekken. He was gratified to note that there were nods from several members of the Council and audible murmurs of approval from among their ranks.

It was time to give them the cherry on the cake.

'One more thing,' he said, looking pointedly at Martock, who was shifting uncomfortably in his seat. 'From now on you can forget all this talk about the Dreamwalker's Child.'

He drew himself up to his full height and looked straight at Odoursin, savouring this moment – the supreme moment – when he would finally receive the recognition he deserved.

'I have just received coded confirmation from our special forces that the target has been destroyed,' he said triumphantly. 'The Dreamwalker's Child is no more. Nothing can stop us now.'

He watched Odoursin's eyes light up and saw the bitter smile begin to form on those withered lips. It didn't get much sweeter than this. He was just allowing himself to imagine what he would do with the new-found power that would surely now be given to him when he saw something which chilled his blood and caused him to let out a small, involuntary cry.

Through the green glass of the tower he watched in horror as a dark shape flew silently past the window and then disappeared from view.

Hekken immediately registered three things: one, that it was a horsefly; two, that all non-mosquito flights had been cancelled; and three, it was headed straight for the airbase.

'If Your Excellency will excuse me now,' he said hurriedly, 'I had better return to my post for the final phase of operations.'

Odoursin raised a hand to signal his assent and Hekken walked as calmly as he could across the marble floor towards the lift. The moment he reached the ground floor, however, he ran from the lift doors like a man possessed.

There was a light bump as the horsefly touched down, then a blue flash from a CRB reflected in the cockpit canopy and Sam heard the troop commander shout, 'Go, go, go!' as the first team descended on ropes from the belly of the fly and hit the tarmac running. There was shouting, the crackle of automatic weapons and then night turned to day as a flare ignited in the dark sky, floating down on a tiny parachute and illuminating the whole scene in a bright and eerie light.

Sam caught a glimpse of the four-man commando team as they ran towards one of the missile batteries, stopping occasionally to fire sporadic bursts from their machine guns before zigzagging their way across the tarmac towards the target.

'They've seen us!' shouted the commander behind him as the light from the flare cast strange shadows across the cockpit. 'We've got to hit the other targets immediately!'

Sam pulled back on the throttle and once again the horsefly lifted up into the air. He knew there were three more missile batteries spread out around the airfield and, now that they had lost the element of surprise, speed was of the essence.

He was nearing the second when, from the corner of his eye, he saw one of Odoursin's soldiers sink down onto one knee, hoist a long metal tube onto his shoulder and aim it straight at them.

Recognising it from his training as a hand-held anti-insect missile which would home in on their wing vibrations, he banked violently left and, as Skipper shouted 'Missile!', hit the decoy button, which sent twenty miniature horseflies the size of footballs shrieking off in all directions behind them.

For a moment, everything seemed to happen in slow motion.

Sam watched the missile scorch out of the tube and streak across the airfield towards them, but just as he thought it must surely hit them it suddenly changed direction and began to pursue one of the decoys across the airfield instead. There was a loud explosion as it found its target and then erupted into an orange fireball which lit up the night sky before crashing down into the main control tower and setting it alight.

'Go, go, go!' shouted the troop commander as they touched down again, and the second team disappeared through the hatch.

'Two more left,' said Skipper. 'We can do this,' she

added urgently, as much to herself as to Sam. 'Come on! We can do this!'

They had dropped the third team of commandos off and were heading low across the field towards the last missile battery when there was another ear-splitting explosion and Sam watched in horror as the right wing of the horsefly disintegrated in a sheet of fire.

'We've been hit!' he shouted, and immediately felt the searing heat of the flames as they began to burn and crackle around his seat.

The horsefly listed sharply to the left and Sam saw to his dismay that they were flying fast and out of control straight for the doors of the larvae factory.

'Brace, brace, brace!' shouted Skipper.

Sam just had time to throw his arms up in front of his face before the world erupted into a deafening fury of flame and fire and they smashed through the factory doors, splintering them into a thousand pieces.

As the fly skidded to a halt between two large tanks, Sam released the buckle of his harness and frantically scrabbled in his breast pocket for the CRB. He had banged his head on the instrument panel during the initial impact and the metallic taste of blood flooded his mouth and nose.

'You won't need that,' said Skipper as he pulled the CRB from his pocket.

Sam noticed as she gestured towards the back of the fly that her clothes had been scorched by the flames and her face was blackened and bruised.

'You OK?' he asked her.

'Oh, never better!' She winced, pulling him from his seat. 'But I don't think we'd better hang around.'

Turning his head, Sam saw that the entire back section of the fly had been torn off and was now lying about fifty metres away next to the wrecked, smoking doors of the factory. Incredibly, the last members of the commando troop were already jumping out of it, guns blazing.

'OK,' he said. 'Let's go.'

Hekken stood alone at the shattered window of the smoke-filled control tower, his face white with anger. For a few seconds he was unable to believe what he was seeing. Below him, three out of the four anti-aircraft batteries had been blown up and reduced to useless, twisted metal. Flames leapt from a hole where the doors of the larvae factory used to be and from all around the airfield he could hear the rattle of small-arms fire being exchanged. Why the hell hadn't Intelligence seen this coming?

It was chaos, a mess, and someone would pay for these mistakes, he would make sure of that. He had come too far and worked too hard for everything to be ruined now. As for those animals out there who were trying to destroy the fruits of his labours; he would have his revenge on them too.

But that would come later. Now was the time for urgent action.

Angrily, he pulled the radio handset from the desk

and pressed the transmit button. 'Attention, all aircrew. This is General Hekken speaking. We are under attack. I say again, we are under attack. All units proceed to aircraft for immediate take-off. Repeat, all units proceed to aircraft for immediate take-off!'

As the sirens began to wail, Hekken replaced the handset and watched the steady streams of aircrew run from their barracks to the waiting mosquitoes.

So they had used the horsefly to slip past the air-defence systems and destroy the missile batteries. Very clever, he would grant them that. And the only reason he could see for them wanting to destroy the missile batteries would be that they were planning a major offensive against the airbase.

But they hadn't reckoned on his secret weapon, his pride and joy.

Several years ago, when the threat of western air raids had been strong, Hekken had insisted on the building of a ring of nerve-gas batteries, despite resistance from certain members of the Council. It had never been used and some people had argued that it was a waste of money and manpower. But Hekken had always argued its importance as their first line of defence against attack from the air. Now he would be proved right once again. No more aircraft would get through. If they were foolish enough to try a major assault from the air, then they would fall from the sky in their hundreds!

Quickly picking up the handset again, he flicked the channel frequency and pressed transmit.

'All units, come in, all units. This is General Hekken. Air attack is imminent. I repeat, air attack is imminent. This is not a drill. Prepare for immediate action, over.'

Hekken released the transmit button and waited for one of the battery commanders to reply.

But when the only sound was the crackle of static, the only reply a constant white noise hissing from the air-waves, Hekken realised with a sickening feeling that the last of his defences had been breached.

They were on their way and there was nothing he could do to stop them.

Ripping the handset from its socket with a frustrated cry, he threw it across the room, where it smashed into pieces against the far wall. Then he ran through the smoke, down the twisting stairs and out into the cool night air, where the first mosquitoes were already taking off.

'Where are the wasps?' shouted Skipper in desperation as she heard the unmistakable whine of mosquito wings starting up. 'They should be here by now!'

'I don't know,' said Sam, breathing hard as they ran out through the burning factory doors. 'But if they don't get here soon it will be too late. We have to *do* something!'

'Over there!' said Skipper, pointing towards a group of aircrew who were wheeling some portable steps over to a line of mosquitoes. Sam could see the bloated, dark red abdomens of the insects hanging heavily above the tarmac and knew they must be fully loaded with virus-filled blood.

Skipper unclipped a drill bomb from her belt and held it up in the darkness for Sam to see.

'Remember these?' she said.

Sam nodded.

'Then you'll remember what a big bang they make. I'm going to create a diversion, so keep your head down until you hear the blast. As soon as it blows, run like the clappers up those steps and don't stop until you're in that mosquito. I'll be with you as soon as I can, OK?'

With that she was off and running.

Sam gingerly edged as near to the steps as he dared, then lowered himself to the ground and buried his head in his hands. At the same moment there was a tremendous, deafening roar as the drill bomb exploded and ripped one of the mosquitoes apart. Sam felt the hot blast-wave race over his head and heard pieces of the mosquito splatter onto the tarmac, bursting like a thousand water balloons.

Instantly he was on his feet, barging the stunned aircrew aside and racing up the steps with all the speed he could muster, his arms and legs pumping like pistons. Gasping with exertion, he activated the CRB and, as it flashed blue, he jumped through the hole and landed in the co-pilot's seat.

It was hard to say who was the more surprised, Sam or the pilot, who was finishing his pre-flight checks. But before either of them could react, Skipper had leant in from above and used her CRB to create another large hole in the pilot's side of the mosquito.

'Nothing personal,' she said, then put her feet on his shoulders and shoved him through the hole. There was a brief cry of surprise, followed by a dull thud on the tarmac below.

Skipper slid down into the now empty seat and peered out of the hole. 'Byee!' she called as the man struggled to his feet. 'We'll send you a postcard.' She sealed the hole again and proceeded to activate the mosquito's wings.

'There's just no pleasing some people,' said Sam, ducking behind the instrument panel as the man began firing wildly at them with a pistol. Then the ground was falling away behind them and they followed a string of mosquitoes up into the strange and milky twilight which lay hidden beyond the clouds.

Thirty-three

It was like trying to fly through custard. The clouds had turned a thick, dirty yellow and the mosquito's wings were labouring at full throttle, paddling slowly through the dense atmosphere.

Skipper must have seen the look of concern on Sam's face because she said reassuringly, 'Don't worry. It's always like this.'

Sam's brow furrowed still further. 'What is?' he asked, confused.

'The crossover,' said Skipper. 'From our world to yours. Remember what I told you about the gaps in the fabric between our worlds?'

'Yes, sort of,' replied Sam uncertainly.

'Well we're flying through one now,' she explained. 'We should come out the other side in a minute.'

'How are we going to stop them when we get there?' asked Sam, catching a brief glimpse of a mosquito up ahead before it disappeared into the cloud again.

'Good question,' said Skipper, pulling back hard on the throttle in an effort to squeeze more power from it. 'I've no idea what's happened to the wasps. Hopefully there should be a bit of a reception party for the mosquitoes when they break through, but they should have been destroyed on the ground. Here, take the controls for a minute.'

Skipper swapped places with Sam and then climbed through a gap in the seats towards the rear section of the mosquito.

'Where are you going?' asked Sam, struggling to hold the lumbering insect on a steady course through the dense yellow fog.

'I'm going to ditch all the blood from the tanks,' said Skipper. 'That way we can fly faster than the fully loaded mosquitoes and make sure that at least this one can't be used to infect anyone.'

Sam peered ahead through the screen, but couldn't see a thing. He felt vulnerable, as though he was hurtling down a road into thick fog, unable to see the traffic ahead.

Suddenly the mosquito lurched forwards and upwards so rapidly that Sam's stomach seemed to be left behind; the throttle raced and he saw the air-speed indicator rise at an alarming rate.

'Skipper!' he yelled at the top of his voice. 'What are you doing back there?'

Skipper stuck her head between the seats. 'It's OK,' she said. 'I've ditched the blood tanks, so you can ease off the throttle a bit now.'

Sam closed the throttle slightly and the whine from the mosquito's wings became less frantic.

At that moment, the yellow cloud began to merge and spin in front of them, forming itself into a tunnel with walls which spiralled and narrowed towards a tiny black hole in the distance. It reminded Sam of bathwater disappearing down a plughole and up ahead he could clearly see the line of mosquitoes, flying steadily towards the dark point at the end of the tunnel.

'This is it,' said Skipper, sliding back into her seat and buckling up. 'As soon as we get through to the other side, I'll turn this thing on.'

She produced a small flat disc with a circle of coloured lights on it and placed it on her knees.

'What is it?' asked Sam.

'It's an identification beacon,' replied Skipper. 'It sends out a signal which lets our forces know that we're on the same side. After what happened when we flew home in the horsefly, I took the precaution of borrowing one from the stores before we left. I thought the –'

Skipper was interrupted by a peculiar low rumbling sound that seemed to be coming from somewhere behind them. The conversation stopped and they both listened intently. The noise quickly grew in strength and intensity until it sounded like a thousand powerful motorbikes screaming up behind them at full throttle.

Sam glanced up at his rear-view display screen and saw to his horror the deadly black and yellow painted faces of wasps approaching at an incredible speed.

'Turn it on, Skipper!' he screamed in panic. 'For God's sake, turn it on now!'

Skipper quickly pressed the centre of the disc and the circle of coloured lights sparkled into life with a series of musical bleeps. Sam held his breath as a wasp bore down on them, its face filling the screen before it vanished once more, veering off at the last second and scorching past them with a deafening roar. Moments later, twenty or thirty more wasps came streaking past them at such velocity that Sam had to wrestle with the controls to stop the mosquito being swept away in the backwash from their wings.

'Woohoo! Oh *yeah!* Ride 'em, cowboy!' cried Skipper as they gyrated and bucked through the turbulent air. She waved a hand around her head in a circle, as if twirling an invisible lassoo. 'C'mon, pardner. Let's go git 'em!'

Sam gave her a look. 'I worry about you,' he said.

The walls of cloud blurred around them as the mosquito gathered speed; seconds later they were sucked through the darkness and into the bright moonlight of a warm August night.

They were above an oval pond surrounded by a lawn. An enormous Victorian building stood at one end and the rest of the grounds were bordered by flowerbeds and a high wall which ran around the outside.

'Watch out!' shouted Skipper as a wasp suddenly shot past the cockpit in pursuit of a blood-laden mosquito. Sam turned hard in time to see another wasp ram a mosquito in front of them, bursting it open like a ripe tomato. A third wasp flew right up to the cockpit, hovered briefly as if to check them out, and then peeled off at speed across the pond on the tail of another mosquito. There was a loud roar as three more wasps criss-crossed in front of them and Sam automatically put a hand up to shield his face.

'This is crazy,' he yelled. 'We'll get killed if we stay here.'

He banked the mosquito hard to the left and then flew low across the lawn to a dark flowerbed, where he slotted the wings into reverse and landed neatly on a large green hosta leaf.

'What now?' said Sam. His heart was thudding in his chest and he was breathing heavily.

'Look,' said Skipper.

As he looked out from the shadows of the flowerbed, Sam saw the wasps make several high-speed passes over the lawn. They flew back and forth in a line formation and on each pass more wasps joined them, so that soon they resembled a huge black and yellow sheet stretching from one side of the grounds to another.

'Oh, wow!' said Skipper, nodding her head approvingly. 'They're doing a full-sweep manoeuvre. I've read about it, but I've never actually seen it done. This is brilliant!'

It certainly looked impressive, reminding Sam of some carefully choreographed dance. 'What's it for?' he asked.

'To make sure nothing escapes. They're using it to hunt down the last of the mosquitoes.'

Sam looked at Skipper nervously and pointed to the small disc on Skipper's lap. 'Are you sure that thing's still on?'

Skipper held it up so that Sam could see the coloured lights flashing. 'Relax.'

'Yeah, well I hope you brought some spare batteries. How come we never did this sweep thing in training then?'

'Too risky. Textbooks say it should only be used in the direst emergency.'

'Why?'

'Well, for a start, it's abnormal insect behaviour, which could draw the attention of humans. And secondly, there's very little room for pilot error. You can lose a lot of aircraft if it goes wrong.'

'What do you think they're doing now?' asked Sam.

The wasps had gathered into a churning black and yellow ball above the centre of the lawn. After a few moments they shot upwards at high speed, gaining height rapidly before bursting outwards like a firework across the night sky.

Skipper looked puzzled. 'I don't understand it. They've only completed a couple of sweeps. They can't possibly be sure at this stage.'

There was an eerie silence, followed by a low hum like the sound of a distant generator.

'Can you hear that?' said Skipper.

'Yes,' said Sam, puzzled. 'What is it?'

Skipper shrugged. 'I'm not sure. But I think we're about to find out.'

The hum grew louder and louder. It seemed to be coming from the far end of the garden.

Sam and Skipper looked at each other in amazement and then turned to look at the wall just as a glittering mass of dragonflies crested the top and poured over it like a shining waterfall. They flowed across the lawn in a solid wave, their powerful jaws snapping, crunching and destroying the last of the mosquitoes.

'Oh yes!' shouted Skipper triumphantly. 'It's Dragonfly Squadron! The cavalry have arrived! Way to go, fellas!' She jumped out of her seat, clapping and cheering, then threw her arms around Sam and kissed him, making him blush a deep crimson.

Over Skipper's shoulder, Sam suddenly became aware of a grey shape floating up from beneath the leaves in front of them.

'Hang on,' said Sam. 'Look over there. Is that what I think it is?'

Skipper turned round in time to see the unmistakable shape of a mosquito rising from the shadows and flying across the lawn towards the building at the far end.

'I don't get it,' she said. 'Why haven't they destroyed it?'

As he flew the mosquito out of the shadows, Hekken felt a cold, clinical pride. This was it: the moment he had waited for all his life. Soon the deed would be done and the future would be theirs. He smiled bitterly as he thought of tonight's surprise attack. He had to hand it to them, it was a brilliant operation. They had blown up the base, destroyed his mosquito squadron and now they believed they had won. What they didn't know, of course, was that Odoursin and the Council had long planned for such an eventuality. If this was war, then they had plenty of options up their sleeves. It would be a temporary setback, nothing more. And he, General Hekken, would keep the faith. The essence of the Dreamwalker's Child had been destroyed and now – the irony of it was beautiful – its earthly body would become the poisoned chalice from which the rest of mankind would be forced to drink.

He pulled back hard on the joystick and the mosquito climbed sharply towards the top of the building. As the ground dropped away below him he was buzzed several times by huge dragonflies which flew in to investigate, but after a brief inspection they disappeared off again.

'That's right,' he whispered as another one flew past. 'Keep checking. Keep him safe. Make sure nothing happens to your precious child.'

Hekken thought of the soldier he had discovered trying to steal his mosquito and how the man had tried desperately to hide the disc before Hekken had killed him. Now it lay on the seat where it had fallen and Hekken smiled to himself as its coloured lights twinkled in the darkness. Oh, they were clever all right. But not clever enough.

And now they were going to pay for it.

Pulling back gently on the joystick, he flew the mosquito quickly and quietly through the open window of the hospital.

'Maybe the mosquito is being flown by one of our pilots,' said Sam, pulling the stick back and trying desperately to ignore the dragonfly which hovered in front of them, grinding its jaws together in a threatening manner.

'No way,' said Skipper as, much to Sam's relief, the dragonfly flew off again. 'If it was one of ours he would have ditched it by now and the ant squadron would have picked him up.'

She suddenly became more animated. 'Look, Sam, he's going into the hospital! Come on – we have to stop him!'

Sam opened the throttle and the whine of the mosquito's wings filled the cockpit.

'Hospital?' said Sam in surprise. 'Why would he want to go in there?'

Before Skipper could answer, they flew through the window. The room was dark except for a small nightlight next to a bed in the centre of the room. As Sam scanned the shadows for the other mosquito he saw that the bed was occupied by a young boy. There was an oxygen mask over his face and a tube leading up from his arm to a drip suspended from a metal stand. The boy had some bruising around his face but, apart from that, he looked quite peaceful. So why did Sam feel so uneasy?

'There it is!' shouted Skipper. 'On his wrist!'

Sam looked across to where Skipper was pointing and saw that the mosquito had landed, settling on the boy's arm, with its swollen red abdomen raised diagonally into the air. There was something in the way it held itself, a terrible, graceful arrogance in its bearing, which suggested it somehow knew the awful significance of its evil cargo, and Sam felt a cold anger rise within his heart.

Hekken flicked the switch which activated the mosquito's feeding system and was rewarded by a quiet hum as the tubes of the proboscis slid out towards the boy's skin.

He leant forward and pressed another button, turning on the pump which would bring infected blood up to the salivary glands for transferral to the boy's bloodstream. That done, he flicked a switch and heard the sharp blades of the mouthparts begin to slide against one another, ready to slice the surface of the skin open.

He licked his lips in anticipation. Just a few more seconds and the mosquito's feeding tubes would probe the rivers of blood that lay hidden beneath the skin. And into those rivers would float the seeds of destruction.

Sam felt as though every nerve in his body was firing at once, bringing together every sensation and emotion – past, present and future – all telescoping down into this one moment of time, screaming at him that this awful thing, this terrible act that was about to take place, must be stopped, whatever the cost.

'No!' he shouted, his face twisting with anger and fury 'No, no no!' And, slamming the stick forward, he opened the throttle and sent the mosquito plummeting into a steep dive towards the deadly grey insect below.

Hekken paused. What the hell was that whining?

He looked up just in time to see the iridescent green of the mosquito's eyes as it raced towards him. He threw himself to the floor at the same moment that the attacking insect thrust its proboscis into the cockpit and punctured the seat where he had been sitting. There was a huge crash as part of the screen fell in and Hekken scrabbled frantically across bright green shards of shattered eye, cutting himself in his desperation to escape.

'Get away from me!' he screamed as the sharp proboscis plunged into the cockpit again and again, spearing the instrument panel and stabbing viciously through the air around him. 'What the hell are you doing, you fool? It's me, Hekken!'

At that moment, through the broken canopy, he caught a glimpse of the figures in the other cockpit and for a second he froze, unable to take his eyes from the faces he saw within.

'No,' he cried. 'No, it can't be – you're dead! It isn't possible!'

Then, as the sharp, scissor-like jaws cut through the top of the head and peeled it back like a tin can, he threw himself in a blind panic through the splintered screen, just as the broken mosquito slipped finally from its perch and tumbled uselessly to the hospital floor below.

Sam slumped in his seat, his head in his hands. For the first time, it all seemed too much and he felt lost, like a ship slipped from its moorings with nothing but grey sea stretching to every horizon. Skipper had taken over the controls and as he watched her guide the mosquito up into the air again he began to shake uncontrollably and his limbs felt like lead.

'I don't know what's wrong with me,' he said weakly. 'I just . . . I don't think I can do this any more. This place, this feeling I have.' He struggled to find the words to explain. 'I just feel so heavy and tired, like I'm being dragged under. Do you feel like that?'

'No,' said Skipper softly, 'but that's probably because I'm already in the place that I'm supposed to be.' She pulled back on the stick and the mosquito climbed higher.

'Shouldn't we be getting back now?' Sam asked.

There was a pause and then Skipper said gently, 'Not this time, Sam.'

'What do you mean?' Sam was taken aback by her reply. He noticed how unhappy she seemed, and pushed himself groggily up into a sitting position. 'What is it, Skipper? What's the matter?'

Skipper shook her head sadly. 'That night on the mountain,' she said, 'I made a promise.'

Sam was puzzled. 'What kind of promise?'

'I promised that I would take you back,' she said.

Sam shrugged. 'OK. Good. Let's go then.'

Skipper shook her head. 'No, Sam. Not back to Aurobon. Back *there*.'

Sam stared out of the cockpit window at the boy lying in the hospital bed and was suddenly hit by a terrible shock of recognition. He bit his lip and was silent for a while, unable to take his eyes off the figure below. He felt drawn to it, as though invisible forces were pulling him downward and reeling him in.

'Oh, Skipper,' he said at last, 'it's me, isn't it?' He leant his head wearily against the glass. 'It's me.'

Skipper nodded. 'Yes, Sam,' she said. 'It's you. You're going home.'

Sam looked into the sky-blue eyes that had always burned with such life and hope and was shocked to discover that they were full of tears.

'I don't want to go,' he said simply.

Skipper stared straight ahead through the screen and used the back of her hand to brush away the tears that were forming.

'Why does it have to be like this?' she whispered. 'Why does everything have to be so hard?' She leant forward to check the fuel gauge and, as she did so, a hand reached out from the darkness behind her and grabbed her by the throat.

'You think this is hard?' hissed the voice in her ear. 'Let me show you what hard really is.'

Skipper gasped for breath and smelt the leather of the black glove that held her by the throat. She knew immediately that it was Hekken, knew that he must have jumped clear of the falling mosquito and used his CRB to get into this one.

Sam reached across and tried to pull Hekken's hand away, but he was growing weaker by the second and

Hekken shook him off easily. 'Touch me again and I'll tear her throat out,' he hissed.

Sam slumped back into his seat and felt the last of his strength slipping away. He could only watch helplessly as Hekken tightened his grip on Skipper's neck.

'Thought you had it all worked out, didn't you?' Hekken sneered. 'Thought you'd get your little friend back to where he belonged, be a hero and save the world – was that it?'

With his other hand, Hekken held a glass bottle in front of Skipper's eyes and waved it around. It was full of red liquid.

'Guess what?' he said. 'Bet you can't.'

But Skipper didn't need to guess. She knew what was in it.

'No? Give up? Well, let me give you a clue. There's enough in here to kill your little friend and, ooh, let me see now, oh yes, everyone else on the planet. I'll just put it into the feeding tubes and let nature take its course. And here's the fun bit. Are you ready?'

Hekken took his hand away from her throat and grabbed her by the hair. 'You're the one who's going to deliver it. Personally.'

Skipper shook her head in an effort to break free, but Hekken's grip was too strong.

'Ow, let go. You're hurting me!'

'Oh please,' spat Hekken, 'I haven't even started yet. Now turn this thing around and let's get it over with.'

Skipper looked about frantically for a way out.

At that moment, through the screen, they saw the door of the room open and a man walk in. Hekken immediately became edgy. 'Quickly, fly under the bed,' he hissed. 'Fly somewhere dark until he's gone.'

Skipper hesitated.

'Do it now!' Hekken screamed in her ear and in that moment Skipper knew what she must do. Her heart felt curiously light as she turned the mosquito around and pulled the throttle back as far as it would go. Hekken would not win and that was enough. It would have to be enough.

'What are you doing?' shrieked Hekken as the mosquito continued its climb towards the man's face. Skipper could see into the man's eyes now. They were sad eyes, full of sorrow, but there was kindness in there too. That was good.

The man looked at them and lifted his hands.

Hekken screamed.

Then there was only blackness and a forgetting.

Sam's father walked across to the sink and washed the remains of the mosquito from his hands. That was the trouble with having the windows open on these hot summer nights, the bugs always found a way in. But it was nothing any more; just little fragments of inert material washed away with the rest of the day's dirt and dust.

He dried his hands on a faded green towel and as he did so a small sound behind him made him stop and listen. It seemed to be coming from the direction of the bed: a tiny sound, like a whimper or a cry.

Turning quickly around, he saw to his shock and amazement that his son was beginning to move. He watched in silent disbelief as Sam's arms rose softly from the bed and then, unable to contain himself any longer, he ran through the double doors and out into the long, echoing corridor.

'Sally,' he shouted, 'come quickly!'

Back in the silence of the room Sam's arms continued to rise, slowly stretching upwards and outwards as though reaching in vain for something precious that had been lost.

Thirty-four

As the weeks went by, Sam grew stronger. At first he was able to take only a few faltering steps, but every day that passed saw him walk a little further until, finally, he was allowed to go home.

Summer was almost over; already the green leaves on the trees were beginning to fade and the nights were drawing in. A cool wind blew in from the east, carrying drifts of dandelion seeds across the fields and hedgerows to the places where they would lie still and silent through the winter, waiting for the first whispers of spring to awaken them.

Sally Palmer lay in bed, listening to the wind in the eaves.

'Do you think he's all right?' she asked as Jack turned off the light. 'He seems so sad sometimes.'

'It's bound to take time, love,' said Jack. 'He's been through such a lot these past few weeks.'

'I know,' said Sally. 'I just want him to be happy, that's

all. Maybe when he starts school again he'll make some new friends.'

'Course he will,' said Jack. He reached across and patted the mound of her belly under the duvet. 'And when this little one arrives, he'll be able to play the big brother.'

'Yeah,' said Sally. 'We'll make sure he's involved, eh?'

'Definitely.' They were silent for a while, and then Jack said: 'You know, I thought he was lost for ever. I thought we'd never get him back.'

Sally stroked his cheek in the darkness. 'I know, love. But he found his way home, didn't he? He found his way home.'

That night she had the dream again.

She was running barefoot through the forest. Behind her, shouts and screams rose from the burning houses and she heard the harsh voices of soldiers calling to one another across the marshes. Heavy boots crashed through the undergrowth and she saw dark shapes moving through the trees. The fear caught in her throat and she ran faster, faster, hearing the sound of her own breathless sobs as the footsteps came closer.

Reaching the edge of the forest, she jumped across a ditch and stumbled exhausted into a field. In the distance, flames danced in the darkness above the village.

She heard the sound of voices, floating on the night air towards her. Raising her head, she saw the soldiers walk calmly across the field towards a young woman who had fallen to her knees.

Sally took a deep breath and felt the wet grass beneath her, and the cool breeze, and the lifeblood dancing around her veins.

A gunshot.

Voices fading to nothing.

When at last she opened her eyes again, she saw that the young woman was standing in front of her. A gentle breeze ruffled her blonde hair and Sally saw that she was beautiful. The woman reached out her hand and touched Sally's cheek.

'I knew that you would come back,' she said softly.

Sally took the woman's hand in hers and felt how cold it was.

'I promise that I will take care of her,' said Sally. 'I will love her as you have done.'

The woman squeezed Sally's hand for a moment before letting it go.

'Thank you,' she said.

Then she turned and walked away into the darkness.

From all around there came the beating of wings and Sally felt herself swept high above the fields and trees, up into the cool sweet air beyond. She saw the little mound of earth all covered in daisies and her heart ached, but then the world fell away beneath her and as she flew up to the stars she saw how small everything really was, and all the pain and fear in her heart subsided.

She was in a clearing in a forest. Above her the night sky was littered with stars.

Walking slowly towards the base of a tall tree, she knelt softly on a bed of pine needles and moved the branches aside. She smiled and reached into the basket.

Awake in the quiet darkness, Sally squeezed her husband's hand. 'Jack,' she whispered, 'I think the baby's coming.'

It was early afternoon when Sam walked with his father through the double doors and into the ward where his mother lay propped up on her pillows, holding a small white bundle in her arms.

'Hello, love,' she said. 'Come and say hello to your baby sister.'

Sam smiled. 'Can I hold her?'

'Of course, love. She belongs to you too, you know.'

Sam took the tiny bundle and cradled her in his arms, feeling an inexplicable wave of happiness wash over him.

He pushed back the little crocheted blanket and looked down at his new baby sister. She was so warm and tiny and alive, he thought.

She was beautiful.

For a moment she lay quite still, lost in milk-white dreams. Then, as Sam moved slightly, she stirred and the weak afternoon sunlight warmed her face. With a yawn, she opened her eyes and looked up at him.

She had quite the bluest eyes he had ever seen.

Acknowledgements

My grateful thanks to:

Norman and Betty Voake, Jon Voake and Kim 'Horsefly' Green for suggestions and help with early drafts; everyone at Faber and Faber, but especially Julia Wells for superb editing; Tim and Daisy Voake for laughs and inspiration; Phil Burner, Neil Sinclair, Rob Hawkins, Dave Hayward, Chris McFarlane, Dave Cahill, Marc Lebeau and all at Kilmersdon for friendship and enthusiasm; Sam North for film fun; Clare Conville for mugs of bubbly; Patrick Walsh for fridge expertise and Tory Voake for everything.

Special thanks to Ed Jaspers for advice, faith and alchemy . . .

Steve Voake